# Crossings

## THE LIGHTBEARERS SERIES
### BOOK TWO

## JEN LOWRY

*To Eli, for dreaming with me*
*To Solomon and Samuel, my loves forever*

CHAPTER 1

## Free Falling

There is a tricky thing about fainting, and not just the weak feeling where you stumble, hold on to a chair, regain your composure and keep at it. The fainting that was always so prone to attack me came with no warning and when it hit everything went black. When I would come out of it, I felt as if I was still in the black even though the brightness of the world would shine all around me. But not this time. When I came out of it, I swore I was in a dream. Things like this just can't be real.

I heard his voice. I took a minute just to feel Seth's huge hand caressing my face. He was so present even with the light touch of his fingers against me. His voice was rough with emotion, strained, as if he, too, might have had an attack.

"Baby, oh God. What did you do, Bree?"

Bree was my little angel, calling me home. I didn't have to open my eyes to see what she would look like right now. She was like a little love fairy and I couldn't help but feel the smile twitch at the corners of my lips.

I couldn't find my voice still but the words kept reverberating in my brain, hitting in my core. Because wherever my Tucker was, so was Alex. My eyes flew open.

1

Seth said, "Jazzline, you're alive. Oh, God. I thought..."

Bree's laughter was melodic. "Let her up for some air, for crying out loud."

I felt my body being moved from his chest but not too far away. He smelled so good. He positioned me on his leg and my head had nowhere to go but drop to stare at the dark blue jeans he was wearing. My favorites on him. Funny when you wake up from a dream you notice even the stitches.

Who fainted these days anyway? Oh, yeah, me. I knew that he had told me we were in Scotland. Bree was rambling. My hand trailed along his neck, and I buried my head in his long hair. Just give me one more minute to sit here like this before the world crashes.

I felt the touch of Bree's hand on my arm. She was always breaking up our little private moments. Somebody should have been paying closer attention to her and Tucker.

I felt her tiny hand on me and the strength that was tingling right below the surface was different. She had something coursing through her that felt like an electrical shock had just pulsed through my body.

"What was that?"

She smiled. "Well, you finally got your voice back. I think the first time I crossed, it felt like I had the flu for a week. It's the baby. She's trying to tell me something. She's excited that I'm talking about her daddy."

How could she know the sex of the baby? How could the baby tell her anything? I looked to Seth and he was frowning, too.

"You don't know if it's a girl yet. Just calm down. Let's take Jazzline to the house."

I put my hand around his neck and whispered, "Not yet, please. Just a minute. I need to get a grip on where I am."

Bree said, "You're in Scotland, at Loch Duich. You're home."

She took her hand off of my arm but I could still feel her power through me and I felt stronger. Somehow, just by her touch, she cleared my head of all thoughts of sickness. And all of the memories came back. And all of the pain, and the hope, and the doubt, and the planning.

"Seth, where are Tucker and Alex?"

He didn't answer me. His hands were now cold when they were once so warm. I knew the signs his body made when he was close to death. I recognized the change even if I didn't understand it all.

Bree released buckets of tears like rain. Brianna Rain. How appropriate. I never knew that names could mean so much until I met the MacKenzies.

"Bree, what's wrong? What is it? You better tell me."

Seth lifted me from the ground, and I planted my feet. Seth gave her a warning glance and I knew that they both were hiding it from me. Bree turned and walked in front of us. They were experts at keeping their identity, their powers, and their family from the world but I could see right through them.

They still thought Alex and Tucker were dead.

I didn't fall for it and focused on the hills and valleys around us. A crystal blue sky with dotted white clouds hung like a brilliant chandelier above us, and it was as if I were living right in a painting.

Seth might as well have carried me since his strides were so much broader than mine as we walked across the meadow. There was a cottage ahead. It was something from a fairy tale. I remembered as a child reading books where characters lived in stone cottages with little chimneys where smoke would puff out like billows of clouds. Wood was stacked along the sides of the small house. There was a horse tied along the wooden fence by the door. The horse whimpered and whined as Bree approached. She rubbed his mane and he snorted and rose on his hind legs.

Seth warned. "Stop touching, Bree. Now. You don't know what you're doing."

I tried to find the meaning behind his words but none of it made sense.

The door burst open and I saw Aunt Shea standing there with an apron on, flour on her cheeks, and her face rosy with anticipation as she stepped out onto the stone path. Then, it turned to confusion when she saw Seth. When she saw me, her lips formed a perfect round circle, and I wanted to laugh because she looked like something straight out of an old cartoon.

"What have ye gone an' done now, Brianna? Ah told ye tae stay in th' house. Seth, tell 'er tae listen tae me."

Seth scowled. "Good luck with that, Aunt Shea. You were the one that said you'd be responsible for her. So, I guess you're responsible for this."

"How am I supposed to stay in the house until the baby comes? I can't just sit inside. I'll lose my mind."

Aunt Shea frowned. "Ye should've thought a bit before ye went an' got pregnant."

Bree's head dropped.

Seth lowered his voice, "Bree, why?"

She didn't answer him, brushed by Aunt Shea, and went inside the small cottage. The warmth welcomed me right away, and since I was a beach girl, it felt way better inside the quaint cottage than outside. The fireplace roared and the smells of the cottage invaded my senses. Why was I so weak? I wanted Bree to touch me again for that energy boost but Seth was blocking her from me, maybe intentionally. Not because he didn't trust me. Because he didn't trust what none of us understood yet.

Bree went to sit on the leather couch and leaned back, propping her feet up and sighing. She rested her hands across her stomach in a natural pose, not like the first night I saw her do it. Aunt Shea went back to the tiny kitchen and stirred the pot on the gas stove. Seth and I just stood close together. He was squeezing my hand, and I wasn't sure if it was for his strength or to reassure me. It was as if he didn't want to step inside the cottage. Like it held a secret that he didn't want to share with me, and I was feeling more uncomfortable by the minute with my back on the red wooden door.

Aunt Shea turned to Bree. "Ye could have at least told me that ye were bringin' them over fur a visit. Ah could've been ready."

She stirred the pot and some of the beef stock sloshed out of the side, spilling onto the burner making it sizzle.

Bree said, "Don't you see? I've got to go back for them."

Seth exploded. "Are you out of your mind? You know you can't do that."

She shrugged, twisting a strand of her strawberry blond hair that fell in a beautiful wave around her face. "I don't know that. I brought her here, didn't I?"

I asked as I moved to sit beside Bree, "How did you do that?"

Seth gently pulled on my hand. "Stay with me, Jazzline."

Aunt Shea interjected and swatted a dish towel at Seth, "Okay, now. Don't scaur th' poor lass. It's not that extreme, yet."

Seth's eyes narrowed. "Yet? Aunt Shea, she brought Jazzline here. Without bridges. Without touching. Through a phone. Seriously. If you don't see the danger in this, then it's time that all of you wake up. Jazzline will now cross. She crossed because of you, and I could lose her." His voice cracked on the last word, and I understood how terrified he was.

Aunt Shea said, "I'm sorry. I told her tae stay in th' house. I think I have tae lock her up."

Bree crossed her arms across her chest, and her eyes became wild. "Lock me up, you wouldn't dare."

Seth bellowed, "If she doesn't lock you up, then I will."

Aunt Shea turned around, back to her work in the kitchen. I couldn't handle it anymore. I had to speak. "Seth MacKenzie. What's going on?"

"I don't know."

"Great. Just great!" I felt the words exaggerate off of my tongue, and I bit my lip.

Seth pulled me closer to him, and whispered, "Let's go somewhere."

He didn't wait for my response. Just escorted me out the door into the bright sunlight. Now I understood why the cottage needed a roaring fire. There was a brisk chill in the air, and I found the goosebumps rise in protest on my skin. He noticed them too and murmured,

"If I would have known we were coming here I would at least have made sure I dressed you for it."

I looked down at Bree's pajamas, and I blushed. "Seth, please let's go back so I can get some clothes."

His voice was soft but I could hear the warning behind it. "You stay here and let me go get you some. Don't go back in."

I leaned against the door and put my arms around my waist. The horse snickered at me as if he found me comical. My life was a tragedy, a comedy of errors. Seth carried out a bundle of jeans, a shirt, socks, even shoes that sat all together in the palm of his hand. He led me with the other around the side of the cottage to a stable. My nose crinkled at the smell.

He handed me the clothes and gently pushed me through the double doors to a caretaker shop. "I'll wait."

"You mean, you want me to change in here. The house has a bathroom, I'm sure."

But the door was already closed behind me and I readjusted my sight once more. The sunlight streamed into the window stalls. One sandy colored horse snorted. I would have laughed at myself, too, if I were him. I made it into the borrowed designer clothes.

What had happened here? Seth said he didn't understand. He was acting all strange around Bree, not wanting me near her. Like she could hurt me. It didn't hurt when she touched me. I felt strong. I needed to barge by him and burst through that door and throw my arms around her in a big hug like she often gave me back home. But I knew that I wouldn't be able to get past Seth, even if I tried.

Seth was leaning against the barn door, his eyes closed. We should have been taking senior pictures, not this. Anything but this. His face seemed peaceful now. Like he had needed this moment himself to recollect and gather his wits about him. I needed more than a moment because when he saw me my brain went to mush. He tried to smile at me but it didn't meet his eyes and I knew that he was confused or scared. I didn't know which. And I couldn't place it or read his thoughts. He was guarding himself as we went walking again. His hand was still cold. Making me chillier than I would have realized.

"What is it, a hundred degrees back home?"

"It's half of that here. Remember where you are."

How could I forget? But I didn't say that. I couldn't say anything. We walked in silence. His strides slowing so I could keep up. My mind was still in the place where I was juggling between the real and the impossible. Somewhere in the middle. The world I crossed into was breathtaking, and my heart thundered against my chest. No wonder

Seth loved it here. Once we made it to a small paved road, he stopped and waited.

I looked up at him, wondering what would be next. Was this a place where we'd jump back? Would this be over before it started, and I'd never get to look for them?

I didn't have time to ask him because the roar of the engine coming up the one lane road was in stark contrast to the sound of silence that had enveloped me only seconds before, and I cowered behind Seth again. My senses on alarm.

"It's okay, baby. It's just Colin."

"Colin? What is he doing here? I thought he was at MIT?"

Then, I got it. Secrets. Cover-ups. This family was so good at it. I believed it. But why shouldn't I have? What else had Seth told me was a lie? What about his plans for next year? They sounded so normal. Going off to college in Charleston or at Chapel Hill for Astronomy. If it was normal, then it wasn't Seth. He lied to me. When Colin came to a screeching halt in a tinted black Land Rover right in front of us, I refused to get in.

Seth was still holding on to my hand and tugged me a little. I shook my head, my eyes tearing. "Astronomy?"

He sighed. "It's not the time for that."

He was right. That was the truth. It was time to find Tucker and Alex. I'd deal with Seth MacKenzie later.

Colin smiled at us through the rearview mirror, his face turning a little red when his gaze met mine. "Hey, Seth. Hey, Jazzline. I thought your visit was planned for next month? Where's Momma and Daddy?"

"Bree brought us."

Colin's eyes narrowed. "Brought you? Through the bridge?"

Seth leaned forward and put his hand on his shoulder. "No."

Colin laughed. "I told Aunt Shea to lock her up."

Seth sat back. "Well, as you can see. She didn't. But I will."

I frowned. "Lock her up? Why?"

Colin shook his head and Seth closed his eyes as he leaned back against the leather seat. They didn't talk again until they pulled into a quaint town that only could still exist in a foreign place. Shops lined the streets, all different color patterns on brick fronts. A coffee house. A book store. Dry cleaning. A pub. Another pub. It seemed real enough. People were on the streets, walking and laughing. A kid was kicking a soccer ball down the hill and running before it went out in the street. It was a real place. I was not dreaming. I couldn't come up with these props and extras if I tried.

Colin turned on a side street and pulled into a tiny driveway of what looked like a painted row of dollhouses. His was the blue one, with marble statues of a hawk towering at the massive door. I heard a click and knew a recorder was hidden in the stone. Why did someone so young need security measures?

Colin's house was what I expected. It was just room after room of books, a mess of papers, computers, a tiny kitchen, and a bathroom. He was stepping over books and warning us not to touch anything.

Seth smiled. "He has a system."

"Was this place broken into while you were gone?"

It reminded me of those action movies where the criminals break in to steal a secret file. I bet he had a few of them tucked away in here, but I bet nobody could find them.

He didn't answer me. Just went into the kitchen and I heard him fiddling through cabinets and putting a kettle on. He was making tea at a time like this. Seth pulled me along and sat me on the couch but I was sitting around so many folders and papers that I felt my body sit rigid as stone as to not disturb his work.

"What is all of this?"

"Research."

"About what? I thought he was into computers?" But then again, I knew nothing.

"Research about our family."

Colin brought two mismatched mugs. I had one with a nose on it from some advertisement of allergy medicine. He sat at his swivel chair at his desk and switched off his computer before turning back around to us.

Colin leaned in, resting his hands on his knees. His voice became strong, and it surprised me, "Now, tell me everything."

# CHAPTER 2

# Here I Go Again

Seth replayed the details of what happened since their parents had supposedly escorted Colin to Massachusetts to attend his summer freshman program at MIT. I closed my eyes and tried to block out the sound of Seth's voice when he told about Tucker and Alex's accident. I tried to think of a song lyric, anything, that could distract me. But the only song I could hear was the Beatles, "Here comes the sun..." and I knew that it was the last song that I heard before...well...before they jumped.

I felt the tears threatening to come, and I hated it. If I cried then that would admit they were dead, and I couldn't do that just yet. The conversation turned to Bree.

"When she called, she was frantic, out of control. She said that she'd found Alex and Tucker. When Jazzline heard her screaming, she fainted in my arms. And then, the next second, she was gone. Jazzline just disappeared. I had to take the bridge and found her with Bree, right where she pulled her through, Loch Duich, in the meadow. Not near the bridge. Not near the bridge at all. Bree brought her here through the phone."

Colin started to pace. "But that's never been done before. To just bring somebody through like that, just by thinking it?"

"She's desperate, Colin. She's strong. Stronger even now. You haven't touched her, have you?"

He laughed. "Why, do I need to? Will I catch something?"

"This isn't funny, Colin. With the baby, she's unpredictable. She's dangerous." His voice was low and then it was becoming clear in my mind. Her father's words to her came back to me, "You will have to endure this on your own, with Aunt Shea."

I couldn't help myself. "What happened to Aunt Shea?"

Seth sighed, "Not now. Please, Jazzline."

Colin waved his hand to me. "She seemed to make it in one piece."

Did I now? "I need to know what is going on. I heard Bree say she found them."

"Listen to me, Jazzline. You don't want to know."

"You better tell me, Seth MacKenzie. Where is my baby?"

It wasn't just about Tucker. It wasn't just my best friend. It was Alex.

Colin got up and started out the front door. He looked back at me, and I could swear that I saw tears in his eyes.

"I'm going down to the corner to get us something to eat. I'll be back in a couple of hours."

How long would it take for him to get freaking bologna and cheese? Or was he going to travel to another country for it? Seth nodded at him, and then he was gone.

"Jazzline. I don't know how to explain this. The family doesn't understand how it could've happened."

So, the family knew. And I didn't. I should have been the first one to know.

"I can handle it."

"I don't know if you can. Because it's out of our hands. There's no turning back the hands of time."

I thought about the one gift that I would want and it would be a gigantic number two pencil with a huge pink eraser on the end to wipe this all away. It was going to be one of those conversations so I knew that my chances were not looking good, and my stomach dropped.

"I have to know. Please, Seth. Just tell me."

My hand reached out to him, and he was no longer cold. I knew that back at the cottage something was there with him. It had to be for his body to be so rigid and tense. His eyes were darker and narrow. His hands were warm again, and his eyes were a soft, liquid gold.

"They went back to 1746. They died at the Battle of Falkirk. I'm so sorry."

"1746. You mean like the year 1746? How could you possibly know this?" My voice was still surprisingly calm. This wasn't real.

"Because of this."

He handed me two manila folders looking like the thousands that were cluttering the apartment. Written in Colin's perfect script was the name, Tucker Lane MacKenzie. The next folder was for Alexander Dumas MacKenzie. Here was a description of my baby listed in a family tree of the MacKenzie clan. It showed where he was brought into the family in July of 1745.

I traced over my brother's name with my fingertips from the printed chart. Here he was. His name was there. I flipped through the pages, reading excerpts from family history explaining his tales of the New World. Or what an eight-year-old could recall of his life in America. It also detailed how the MacKenzie's were trying their best to send them back to the future? I saw another name that I recognized. Colin MacKenzie. Colin was there. Mr. MacKenzie sent his brother Colin back through to find them for me because he would've recognized them because he was there with them. He lived during their time. Colin, the MacKenzie who never grew old. Why didn't he say anything before?

The last page of this thrown together research held a photograph. A picture that was not as clear as I would have hoped but I held it up to the light to make it out as best as I could. It was a picture of two tombstones, side by side. I could read the names. Tucker Lane MacKenzie. Alexander Dumas Chicand MacKenzie. Tombstones. But I had to know that. And I couldn't help but laugh. They had to be dead. That was why Seth couldn't see them. That was why he could not see them afterward. They had been dead for over two hundred years.

"Jazzline. Please, baby, are you all right?"

I smiled at him. My body rocked back and forth with newfound excitement. "Don't you see. This is the best news. They can be found. We have a date. We have a time period."

"Do you hear what you're saying. There's no way we can go back in time. We can't go back, just in between."

"But you don't know that. You don't understand this just as much as me. They did it and survived. Well, for a little bit anyway. So, we have a chance. A chance, Seth. Don't you see it? That's all we need."

He could see nothing but the bottom line of the death certificate. I now knew anything was possible. He taught me that.

"My brother Colin has thought of all kinds of ways that we might get them back, but none of them will work. I need you to understand this, Jazzline. If there was a way that I could bring them back myself, I would. I would risk everything for you. Don't you know that? Not just for you, but for Bree. We need Tucker here to keep her baby alive or maybe even her."

His voice broke and his hands covered his face.

"Why? What is happening to Bree?"

"I know it sounds crazy but Aunt Shea is our only source of this knowledge. To make a long story short, she was young and pregnant. They snatched her soul mate from her in an untimely death and when she lost him, her light...her gift...it went out. It disappeared, taking her baby with it. Somehow the baby just didn't exist anymore, just like her soul gift. As if something connected the two. Bree could lose every-thing if we don't find Tucker. We don't know what will happen to Bree or the baby. That's why Colin has delved into this wholeheartedly."

I stuffed the papers back into the folders and started for the door. "Well, then I have to find them. What are you waiting for?"

"Jazzline. We can't find them. We don't know how."

"Well, we have to try something. We can't just sit here. Take me to the graves. I want to see them for myself."

I couldn't believe that I was asking this. To go to the grave of my brother. Speaking it aloud meant that I had accepted it on one level. Okay, they were dead to this time, but maybe, still alive in another. If I could flip now, I would snatch them right back. How would I ever explain this to anyone without being committed? That was why this family had lived in secrecy their entire lives. I might not have understood everything, but I got that loud and clear.

Colin pulled up into the driveway, and was carrying up two brown grocery bags filled with food. He looked at me puzzled and asked, "Did he tell you? Do I need to leave?"

"No. You need to take me somewhere." I walked past him as he juggled the bags.

"Let's get something to eat first." He turned and went into his house but I didn't follow.

Seth walked by Colin, grabbed the keys from his hand and apologized. "I'll be back later. Love ya, brother."

"But I bought food."

Seth knew me, and I wouldn't stop. At least he could accept that about me. "Jazzline. What are you planning to do?"

"I don't have a plan."

"Promise me that whatever you do or think or feel or even consider in that pretty little head of yours, you'll tell me. All of it. Swear it."

I crossed my big toe. "Promise. Now drive me to the cemetery."

"You don't know what you are asking me to do. But I told you that I'd do whatever I could for you. Just when we get there, don't be alarmed if I start running to the car."

At first, I was clueless to what he was referring to, but then I thought of Alice Flagg.

"What did Alice say to you?"

"She told me to marry you as soon as I could. She told me not to waste a second of my life. To always tell you I loved you. She was the one that made me ask you when I did. It was her warning that pushed me to ask you. Her words wouldn't leave me alone."

"So, you weren't going to ask me to marry you until a ghost turned up the heat?"

"I was going to ask you. I was just going to wait until your birthday. We already had a surprise planned, all of us were in on it. Even Alex."

He pulled off the road and parked along the gravel side. A car whizzed by and they honked the horn at us. He put the car in park, got out and flew around to my side to open the door.

"Jazzline, hurry. Get out of the car."

"Why?"

"Okay, rule time. If I ask you something weird, and it doesn't make logical sense understand that I have a good reason for asking and just trust me. Do you trust me?"

"Yes. With my life."

"Then, get out of the car."

I watched him open the back door of the SUV and slip inside. He turned his back to me but I could tell he was talking by the way he was carrying on. Someone had made it to our back seat.

"Alex. Is it Alex? Baby, is it you back there?"

I tried to open the door but Seth locked it from the inside. I knocked on the window. "Seth, open it."

"It's not Alex. It's something else. Just give me a minute."

He didn't say someone, he said something. I backed away from the car and edged myself to the trees.

After a few minutes, he opened the car door and motioned for me to get inside. "It's gone. Not all souls want what's best for us. Get behind me Satan was used by Jesus, and it can be used by us, too. When a demon shows up in your backseat, that's about all you can say to make it go away."

"Oh, my dear Jesus." I turned to look in the backseat. Empty. No trace of anything there.

"It's gone. We're almost there. You're taking this a lot better than I expected. You haven't flipped out like I thought you would."

I remembered Bree's touch. "It was your sister."

"Huh?"

"She did something to me when she touched me in the field when I first woke up after I fainted. She felt like electricity. She gave me strength somehow. I feel stronger. Like I'm ready for this. Ready to find a way."

It was true. I was focused and clear-headed, still clueless but hopeful.

"I have to keep you away from her. She's dangerous. I'm telling you."

I smiled at him. "You are the one overreacting now. Come on, Seth. You're talking about Bree."

"Aunt Shea, remember. There's more to that story."

He put on the turn signal and turned off onto a narrow, potholed dirt road. The cemetery was nestled between a long line of oaks on both sides that towered over us in their thousand-year-old stance, guarding the entryway to the MacKenzie family plots. I saw the visible change in Seth, and it was disturbing. His eyes grew like a shadow, his face paled, and his knuckles clenching the steering wheel. What had I asked him to do?

"Don't get out until I call to you. I can find the tombstones. Please, Jazzline. Just trust me."

"Okay."

I'd never walked in a cemetery before. But I was a fan of late night Friday horror flicks. Mainly vampires and serial killers, stalker cars and cats. Never supernatural Scottish ghosts. Would I feel them around me? I knew someone was here. He had never looked so sick, except on the night of the accident.

I saw the older tombstones near the back of the lot. I didn't want to go that far from Seth but I knew I had to. I hated this. Every second of it.

Even though I felt stronger than I'd ever felt in my life, no touch from Bree could prepare me to see my baby's name on a blue slate stone. Alexander Dumas Chicand MacKenzie. Born August 17th. Died January 17, 1746. Young Warrior Died Before His Time.

My hand traced over the Celtic knot carvings. He was killed in battle. The thought of my baby being out there on a battlefield. I remembered Alasdair at the Highland Games. His tiny frame attacked by brute, ugly men who had no mercy for him. I remembered how Seth stood with him, fighting, teaching, and blocking. Did Tucker do that for Alex? They died on the same day. In the battle just like Colin's research said. I knew the date of their death. That was more before. Now, I just had to figure out the rest.

I made it back to the car and Seth sounded like he was hyperventilating.

"Seth, are you okay?"

He started the car and spun the Land Rover until it rocked to its side and sped down the dirt road, rocks flying, wheels spinning. It wasn't like him. I held onto the door handle wondering if it was safer to jump out of the moving vehicle or ride it out.

When he hit the road, his reckless behavior didn't stop. He was out of control. Seth's eyes were wide, crazed and I knew that he might not even be seeing what was in front of him since he was swerving into the other lane.

"Seth, stop it!"

When the SUV skidded to a stop along a side road and out of traffic my heart was still beating one hundred and fifty miles an hour, the speed we were just going.

His voice was shaking, "I saw them. They were there."

"I know. I saw the date."

"What?" His voice rose. "You went to see a date?"

"Yeah, I couldn't see it in the picture and I wanted to know when they died."

He laughed, sounding manic. "I could've just told you that, Jazzline. The Battle of Falkirk was January 17, 1746. I know my Scottish history. You took me there for that?"

"I'm sorry. I didn't know. Really, Seth. I never thought..."

I forgot that Bree once told me he was a walking Scottish encyclopedia.

"They died in January. Five months is enough time for me to bring them back before Bree has her baby. She can't be too far along. She must've been able to sense the baby early because of her power."

Five months to flip back in time and bring them back. I could do that. Easy.

"I heard me in that conversation. Not us. Jazzline. I swear. If you do something stupid... I'll... I'll.."

I whispered, "Did you see them?"

His hands went to his face. That was all the answer I needed.

"Was it Alex? Tucker? Who?"

"They were both there. Hovering over you and pleading. I could not hear them but I didn't have to. I knew that they were warning you. I could see it on Tucker's face."

Tucker wanted to tell me something. To warn me. Even though I knew that it was wrong of me I wanted to beg Seth to turn that car around right now and go get Tucker for me, bring in Alex and keep them with me in the car. I'd always told him we could stuff Alex in the trunk with us and drive away in the sunset. Never thought it would be a two-hundred-year-old ghost.

My voice broke, "What did Alex look like?"

"Don't ask me that. Don't, Jazzline. I swear it."

"Please. Just tell me."

"He was touching your hair."

My hand flew to my hair and grabbed it as if I could fill him still lingering there.

"Was he hurt?"

He started the car and pulled out onto the highway again. "I will not tell you anything more."

"Yes, you will. Seth, I mean it. You better tell me. I can't live with you knowing, and I don't. This is my brother. My baby. Was he hurt?"

His voice sounded like steel. "What do you think, Jazzline? He's dead."

I shut down. I would not do this. I would not have a fight with him. I wouldn't tell him that if I wouldn't have met him, they would've never gone over the bridge. We'd never been in that blessed play and on our way to an after party. Alex would've never been alone with Tucker. We were always together. My silence hurt my ears. I'm sure he could sense the battle raging in me but he did not provoke me anymore. He was silent and the hurt sat between us. It made me so sad.

When we pulled back up to Colin's, he shut off the engine but didn't move. "Please accept my apology. I'm just feeling so emotional after that...that back there. After all of this. I can't even imagine how you must be feeling. I don't know what to do. I love them, too."

"I need Bree."

I had to talk to her. She brought me here. She could send me back in time. That was the only way that made sense.

"No. You're going home."

What did I have to go home to? My baby was buried here. I couldn't leave.

He hit speed dial as he dragged me up the steps with him.

He roared, "Colin."

He didn't even knock, just busted in, papers flying with the whooshing of the wind at the force that Seth was bringing with him.

Colin was tearing into a peanut butter and jelly sandwich, holding another manila folder in his hand, jelly dripping down it. "What is it?"

Seth ignored him and turned his attention to the phone call. "Momma, thank God. Call Jergen. Now. I'm taking her to the airport. She's coming home. Meet her there. I'll call you. Love you, too. She's fine...she's fine... I'll call you back."

My arms crossed over my chest, my feet in the six-year-old defiance stance. "I'm not going anywhere."

"Oh, yes, you are. Enough of this madness. You and I...we... Colin, you were so right. I swear if I could go back. If I could just take this all back. Colin, take her before I...before I..."

He couldn't finish. Just stomped past me and slammed the door to one of the back rooms. I heard it lock. He was actually the six-year-old.

Colin chuckled. "I've never seen him lose his temper once. Not even as a child."

I didn't answer. I wouldn't leave. I heard something break through the door. What in the world was Seth doing in there?

Colin frowned. "Let me get you out of here before he destroys my place. Come on."

I wouldn't move. "What is happening here?"

Colin shrugged. "I have no clue but I think we need to go to the airport."

"I'm not moving."

Colin saw this and called out to Seth. "I'm a little human out here. I can't pick her up. She won't come. What am I supposed to do?"

Seth flung open the door, made it two steps to me and picked me up by my waist and threw me over his shoulder.

"Like this, Colin."

He was beyond reason and had gone mad. And I couldn't speak. He threw me in the backseat and handed Colin the keys. Colin drove out of the driveway without a word. He didn't look at me through the glass but I could tell that he didn't enjoy being a part of this.

I saw the landscape around me and could not feel a thing. I looked for my billboards that I'd counted so many times on HWY 17 at Murrell's Inlet. Advertisements for Broadway at the Beach or the Aquarium, or some other beach attraction. Alex and I used to play a game trying to memorize the signs so the next trip down the strip he would get points if he got them in order. There were no billboards. Only sky. Wooly cows and lakes beyond lakes that seemed to melt into magnificent mountains. Nothing like home but all like home to me.

Alex ran through these fields. Maybe dove in the lake. Maybe this was the bridge that brought him here. I imagined him and Tucker, in their Phantom costumes, ending up here on their first night. Scared, confused, out of their element. What became of them? I knew the MacKenzie family took them in to be in their graveyard with their last names carved on their slate. But what else could've occurred in those months?

When we made it to a thrown together airport, my stomach did its first lurch and flip since I'd arrived by Bree's telepathic travel. I preferred her way of travel much better. Colin opened the door and watched my face. Would he be able to stop me if I ran? No. I knew that. But where would I run to? Seth didn't want me here anymore. I had no one.

Colin handed me two familiar manila folders as I stepped out of the car. He acted as if he were expecting Seth to pop up behind us. "Here. Take them. Don't you dare tell him I gave you these. Go back to South Carolina, and then figure out how to get back here. Think about it, Jazzline. You seem like a smart enough girl. Think about it."

"What do you know?"

He sighed, stepping closer, his glasses sliding down his nose. "I know that you'll have to go back and do this alone. Seth would only bring you back here to our present time because that's what he's connected to. You might just be special to come through the phone like that, so who knows where you could travel if you tried. He can't go back. None of the family can. They can just move back and forth from here to there. Time does not bend for them as it did for Tucker and

Alex. But for you? I don't know. There's a missing code here I haven't broken yet, but I will. If it happened for them, and they are connected to you... It makes me wonder. With time, I'll figure this out. All we know is they bent time. Maybe there's something you need to discover, too. Go back to the bridge where they crossed. Try it yourself. It's the only way of knowing."

"But could it work?"

"I don't know. I don't know how to tell you this when there are no absolutes."

"If it works, how can I make it back?"

"I don't know. But find my Uncle Colin when you go back and tell him this when you see him, luceo non uro. If you tell Seth that I said..."

"I won't say a thing to him. It looks like he just broke up with me anyway."

He'd sent me away. He did the one thing that he promised me that he would never do. He left me the minute he locked that door against me.

"He loves you, Jazzline. Don't forget, you are his soul mate. He cannot live long without you."

"You mean, he'll die. Like something that happened to Aunt Shea?"

"No. I didn't mean it like that just metaphorically. You really don't get us, do you?"

"Do you?"

"No, not really. But that's what I'm trying to do. That's what I've been working on for years."

He handed an airport attendant a pass and she smiled at him. A security guard stepped forward and grabbed me by my arm, firm enough so I wouldn't spring.

I began to panic. "You're not coming with me? I have to fly alone?"

"Get used to it, Jazzline. Jumping, flying, what's the difference? Keep your eyes closed the whole time. It won't seem to hit you as hard."

I couldn't tell if he meant flying in a jet or jumping off a bridge. I'd remember that and follow his advice. He seemed like the only one that cared enough to give me any.

# CHAPTER 3

## Jump

His mother was waiting for me at the terminal when I stepped off the plane in New York. I'd always wanted to go to Central Park, take a carriage ride, ice skate in the park under the Christmas trees lit with a thousand tiny twinkle lights. I pushed the sleeves up on Bree's grey flannel shirt and started to cry again. That was all I had done on the eternity of flight. I closed my eyes and cried the second that I hit the seat. It was a nonstop flight of drowning.

I took the pin out of my hand and slipped it to her when we boarded the next private jet heading home. This time she was beside me as I cried but she didn't speak. She didn't have to. And neither did I. She saw my story, and I heard her sob once. Then, she regained her composure when a stewardess leaned over to ask if we needed anything. I needed Seth. She needed Bree. We needed a plan.

She whispered, "I will not help you, dear. I cannot. Please understand that I will have no part in this." She slipped the comb back into my hair. "I cannot see anymore. It would be as if I were your accomplice and Seth..."

"Why did he do this? Why did he send me away? He's not coming back is he?"

Mrs. MacKenzie held on to my hand, "I don't know what's going on, dear. He hasn't returned my calls. I can only imagine he feels he's doing what's best to keep you safe."

"He promised me he would never abandon me. He pushed me away."

She hugged me fiercely. "He loves you so much, Jazzline. The thought of losing you. Of you being hurt or lost or separated from him pushed him to do this. I just know it."

"But he did it anyway. He's separated himself from me by an ocean. And for what? Because he tells me Bree is dangerous? He tells me we can't go back?"

"Shea killed our mother by accident, Lord rest her gentle soul. Seth was right by what he did. Just wait. Just wait for him. He'll try his best to do what he can for his sister. He loves Bree how you love Alex. He will do what he can."

Aunt Shea killed their mother?

"Take me home, please."

"Come home with me and Mr. MacKenzie. We already think of you as our daughter. I thought you couldn't go back to your house?"

"I know where they are. It's different now."

I couldn't tell her that I needed to be by myself to plan this out and go back. I couldn't tell her the truth because somehow, I knew if I did Seth would jump back tonight and try to stop me.

"Whatever you wish, dear. But you call me, whenever, whatever time. Here is my number." She slipped me a card from her purse. "Promise me you won't do anything without talking to the family first."

"I won't." I'd already hashed this out with Colin, so that counted.

Even though it was in the middle of the night, all of the lights were on in the house. I laid my head against the door and prayed for the strength I needed to do this. And then I opened the door.

Momma and Luke were on the couch. The TV was on but it was playing infomercials. She looked up at me, and I bit my lip. I could not tell her the truth. What could I say?

"You missed the funeral today."

My thoughts were that we'd all missed it, but I refrained. I kept walking, going down the hallway to my room. I didn't look Alex's way, just touched his door with my fingers, letting it drag across his Venom Poster.

I whispered, "I'm coming, baby. Just hold on."

Momma didn't follow me, and I was so thankful. I couldn't face it. I couldn't tell her what had happened anyway. All that happened but made no sense flashed in my mind. I'd gone to Scotland and back with a faint and a cell phone. I sat before the tombstones of times past where her child had been killed in a battle for Scottish independence. Seth kicked me out of the country without even a word to me.

I fell across the bed and stared at the ceiling for hours. Plans ping-ponged themselves across the table, and it was hard for me to keep my thoughts in the lines. When I went to Scotland how would I maneuver in that landscape? I had a difficult time as it was handling my home. My familiar surroundings.

Thinking about Tucker's initial grasp of the language gave me hope for them. He could at least ask for the MacKenzie's. I wouldn't even know how to do that. He was strong, with a towering presence about him. I was weak. I was a puking, fainting, little no talking woman. I would be considered a witch and burned at the stake. I was sure that was going on back then. Okay, what could I do?

I decided instead of looking at the ceiling, I'd hit the closet instead. What could I wear that would blend in? I had the dress from the night of the play, but that was at Seth's house. After the accident. I had only one thing that would work. Bree stuffed my highland costume in my bag that I'd worn to the festival. This would have to do. I couldn't show up in jeans and a t-shirt. Witch, for sure. But if I wore the MacKenzie plaid I wouldn't have to say a word. I could play mute girl so I wouldn't get in too much trouble for sticking my foot in my mouth. That could be my superpower name. Mute Girl...coming to the rescue. I could hear my theme song music, now.

I took a long, hot shower. I wasn't sure when it would happen again. I grabbed a picture of Alex, Bree, and Tucker that was taken at Medieval Times. I had no pictures of Seth, but I closed my eyes and felt the breath of him against my face as if he were standing right over me.

I love you, Seth MacKenzie. You will forgive me for doing this if I forgive you first.

What else could I take with me? I wasn't sure what could go. What would be valuable for me? Not money. That wouldn't help. Not a cell phone. I wouldn't think that towers could make it back in the day. The reception would be worse than it already was. I could leave a trail of notes. If Colin was as good a researcher as he appeared to be, he'd find them. They would know that I'd jumped. And Seth would know that if I didn't make it back that I loved him.

I grabbed one of my notebooks from my desk drawer and stuffed it in my bag with a pen, along with Colin's manila folders that he'd snuck to me. More proof. My eyes scanned my room once more and there was nothing here of importance. Everything was across the sea at this time or the next.

I opened my door to the dark hallway. They'd gone to bed. Nobody to stop me. Nobody to question my dress or motives. Just the way I wanted it. I grabbed a plastic zipper bag and stuffed all of my things inside. If I jumped and it didn't work and everything was ruined, it would destroy all the research. I thought for a second that I should leave Momma a note, but I just left the house, carrying one small shoulder bag draped around me like a tourist. I wanted to keep my proof close to my heart. Just in case, I couldn't find the words to explain. I had at least this to help me. Tucker and Alex had made it six months. I could do it, too.

I hated the thought of having to walk to the bridge at Pawley's Island. So, I took out my cell and called for a cab. Cell service and money before the jump were useful. The cab driver was a middle-aged man with a grandfatherly face. He frowned when I asked him to let me off at the bridge.

"Miss, are you sure? It's four o'clock in the morning. I don't know about this."

I handed him the fare and got out. He couldn't stop me. I wouldn't be swayed now. Before I could change my mind, I climbed on top of the concrete bridge and plummeted over, my arms dangling, my eyes shut, hearing the screams behind me grow fainter by the fall. The wind pressed against my face, taking my breath even before the water could.

My heart thumped in my chest, and I knew I was free of this. Until I hit the water and felt it crashing up against my face like a thousand stinging bees all at once overtaking me. My dress caught around my ankles and I kicked frantically to bring myself back to the surface.

I heard the cab driver screaming, "Are you crazy? Get out of there! I'm calling the cops!"

Oh, God. It didn't work. I didn't jump. Well, I'd jumped. But I didn't cross, and I was sure that if the cops came the only trip I'd be taking would be to a jail cell or a hospital for watch. But I couldn't do that. I wouldn't get caught. Time was slipping from me, not my mind. My body found the strength to swim to the other side of the inlet and make my way up against a private pier. As soon as I pulled myself up, I heard the sounds of the police sirens and knew I had to run. I adjusted the strap around my neck and sprinted as fast as I could up the deck and onto the small paved road that made the way to Pawley's Island elite homes. The MacKenzie home was just around the corner. It wasn't far now.

I tried to stop myself from running into the gate, but I was too fast down the hill and slammed against it, banging my wrists. The pain shot through my arm, and I cried out as I pushed the intercom button. I could still hear the sirens behind me and I prayed for them to be home. What if they had jumped, too?

But the gruff sound of a sleeping MacKenzie blasted through the guard system, "What is it?"

"Please. Mr. MacKenzie. It's Jazzline. I'm in trouble. Please let me in."

The door swung open, and I raced down and then up the hill of the driveway to their beachfront mansion.

Mrs. MacKenzie wrapped her robe around her. "What did you do, Jazzline?"

She knew what I'd done. What was the point in even telling her? Even with my pin in my soaked and tangled hair she could figure it all out on her own.

I fell into her arms sobbing. "It didn't work. I've got to make it work. It didn't work."

I spoke it over and over again. This was impossible. Why would I have thought that it would have worked when I didn't have a connection with Seth anymore? For all I knew, he hated me. He wished that he'd never met me.

She almost had to carry me into the family room, where Mr. MacKenzie was standing by the bar pouring a tall glass of whiskey. He frowned when he saw me and poured another glass. I was hoping it was for me, but he gulped them both down and came at me, just like I would have imagined Seth doing.

His voice was low but stern and with full effect, "You must not do that again. What were you thinking?"

"I have to find them."

Mrs. MacKenzie came back in with towels, a fresh robe, and the phone attached to her ear. Oh, God. She'd called Seth. The traitors. Mr. MacKenzie distracted me with his rising voice, "You could have drowned. You told no one of this? If you would have been successful, how do you think you could manage in 1745 Scotland? Jazzline, stop this madness now before you get yourself killed."

I couldn't lie any longer. I would jump again. And again. If it meant that I died trying then at least I tried. Maybe I was thinking of the wrong things when I jumped. Wonder what Tucker could have been thinking to take him back that far? Wonder what Bree was thinking when she brought me and Seth to her just by speaking to him? Was that the whole mystery behind the jump? It was a whole powerful mind over matter trick?

I tried to think back to the very second that I was jumping what had flashed through my mind. It was on that blessed cab driver and him thinking that I would commit suicide and call the police or jump in after me. I thought of that. I thought of drowning. Not of 1745. Not even of Tucker and Alex. It was all about connections to people and time and all about me. That had to be it.

Before I had much more time to ponder over all of the mistakes, I heard the door slam, rattling his mother's collector's pieces on her mantle. Seth. He stormed into the room, and his eyes were wild with fear. His face was red. He didn't speak to his parents. Nor to me. He just grabbed me and pulled me up to him and carried me out of the room and up the stairs.

When we were in his room he didn't dare cut on the light, pull back our ceiling for us to stare out at the stars. He just sat me on the bed and began to pace back and forth across the floor, cursing like a madman under his breath. I found myself just closing my eyes against his pillow to smell him, and I had a sudden urge to want to laugh in a moment of pain.

Instead, I said, "Why did you do that to me? I was closer to the truth there."

"I sent you back so you wouldn't do something ridiculous and you jump off anyway. You realize you hit the water traveling at high rates of speed that could have killed you." He stopped. His hands clenched tight against his side and he threw his head back and roared, "To you! Why did you do that to me? God, Jazzline. I just watched you die!"

He crumbled to the floor and put his head between his knees, his hair shielding him.

"I didn't die. What are you talking about?"

"I saw it. I saw you jump and hit the water. I saw you pulling under. I had almost made it to the bridge when Momma called me to tell me you were here. God, Jazzline. If you would have died... I... I..."

He flew to me then and grabbed me, pulling me up from his pillow to crush me against him. There was his smell. And it was so wonderful. His body was so warm, and I felt myself curling against him.

"Jazzline, do you even know how hard that was for me? To watch you drive away with Colin. To do that to you. To us. But I swear I thought it was the only way. I thought you would come home and just forget about me and move on with your life. And you darn well come home and bloody jump! Have you lost your mind?"

His breath was hot against my neck and I was shivering from the cold of the water still on my skin and the mix of his warmth. It was overwhelming. Maybe I had lost my mind. There went my heart to him, and I couldn't help myself so I kissed him. He didn't pull away.

"Never do this to me again. Don't jump, Jazzline. I'll lose you. I swear I know it. I can't lose you. If you jump, it changes."

"But, Seth. You can't ask that of me. You know what is at stake here. It's not about me or you. It's about Tucker, Alex, and Bree, and the baby. There has to be a way."

I had to try again. This time with the right mindset.

He laid down again and leaned against the headboard, pulling me up against his chest and covering my face with his hand. I closed my eyes against him and sighed.

"I didn't tell you what I saw at the cemetery. Jazzline. I saw you. You were there. The ghost of you with them. Don't ask me how, but it was you. Wearing this dress. Were you out there planning to jump when you were by their graves?"

He knew it before I answered him. "You know I was. I wanted the date so I could at least have a starting point, a reference. Something to go by."

"Well, you appeared. Tucker and Alex were there. I told you that. I told you that Alex was playing with the strand of your hair. But you were there. Baby, you were there. Wearing this blessed dress, bending over Alex and ruffling his curls like you always do. You had a smile on your face as if you were happy. And I went crazy."

He pulled me tighter against his chest. "If you go find them, you'll never come back. That's what I know. So, how can I unknow that? My mind circles it like a moth to flame. I can't deal with you crossing."

Could I live with the possibility of going back to save them and never returning? To never loving Seth and spending the rest of my life with him? I didn't know the answer to that.

"Do you love me?"

"You are my life." He pulled me towards him. His kiss was tender and slow.

"Then, let me go." But I couldn't go. Not yet. Somehow, I would. Seth saw it, so I knew it would be so.

"I can't. If I have to lock you up, too, I will."

"Bree? You locked her up?"

"Yes, but she's fine. She's mad at me but she'll get over it. She can't be around any of us. Where do you want me to lock you up?"

"Here. You think your momma could slip us food under the door?"

He chuckled, his deep laugh warming my soul. "Baby, I love you. Don't scare me like this ever again." His lips found mine again. I was tired of lying to him. It was better just to remain silent, especially when he was giving me his full attention.

He pulled away, his eyes sparkling. "What do you want for your birthday? It's..."

"Tucker and Alex for my birthday. They wouldn't have to be wrapped in a bow. Just both of them safe at home with me."

But I knew what Seth was referring to. He wondered if we were still to be married.

His finger found my ring and twirled it once more. A habit that I had grown so fond of. "Do you want to marry me, still? You didn't take this off."

"I would marry you tonight if I could." I pulled his hand up to my lips and kissed his fingers. "Let's go back together. I can't stay here. They are there, at least a part of them are. I want to go back to Scotland and be married there as we had planned."

"Jazzline, I don't think it's safe there, either but after what you just pulled, I don't know what's best anymore. I have to keep you alive long enough to marry you, I guess."

"Well, if I'm in Scotland. I can't jump anywhere. If I stay here the temptation is too strong for me. I'll try over and over again. I know it. I need to be far away from here." That would get him to take me back. It was Bree I needed, not the Pawley's Island bridge.

"Let's go talk to my parents."

I couldn't help but smile behind his back. Was I getting the hang of this battling with words thing or not? Maybe I could learn the art of conversation and getting what I wanted after all.

# CHAPTER 4

# Should I Stay or Should I Go

His father and mother were right where we left them, huddled together on the couch whispering. His mother had been crying, and my heart broke at the sight of her. Her perfect features were a little less perfect. Mr. MacKenzie tried his best to soothe his wife but it was to no avail.

Seth sighed. "I'm sorry, Momma. I had to do it."

"She did this to herself. That girl will be the end of us."

I knew they weren't talking about me. She must have known that Seth had locked Bree up. I wondered if they had even talked with her since she'd gone to Scotland with Aunt Shea. Then, I wondered how could Aunt Shea be around her if she were so dangerous.

Mrs. MacKenzie wiped the tears with the back of her hand. "How did she look? Was she showing yet? Was she sick?"

I smiled. "She looked beautiful."

"Oh," she whispered. "Munroe, we have to go over. I have to be with her."

He turned to Seth as if he were requesting backup. "It's not safe and you know it. You should know this more than any of us. I can't see your life come into danger."

Mrs. MacKenzie said, "What have you seen, Seth? I need to know. I know I've never once asked you, but now, I need this. Please, I'm begging you."

Mr. MacKenzie's eyes narrowed. "Seth, don't. She can't ask that of you. You can't be forced to reveal if you've seen something, and we can't know for sure anyway. Maura, you know what you ask of Seth is unreasonable."

She stood up and came to him, her delicate hand resting on his arm. Her eyes were pleading. She pulled on his chain necklace. "Please, Seth. Tell me what you see. I know you're wearing the shell and blocking me for a reason. I won't ask this of you again."

Seth released his mother and went to sit in his father's chair. I remembered doing the same when I faced my mother. It was the chair to feel strength.

"I feel this may be necessary for both of you to know, even for Jazzline. But I will not speak it unless you swear to me that you will reveal none of this to Bree. I don't know what it will do to her."

"Seth, I'm not sure this is the wise thing to do. I think that I need to speak to your grandfather first and draw wisdom from him."

Mrs. MacKenzie said, "You leave your father out of this. This is my baby we're talking about, and I have a right to know."

"Not this way you don't. And to ask Seth to do this? You know it could change. The course of life changes with every decision we make. Once you hear this it may not even be this way but you will dwell on it until it either drives you to tell it aloud or you go insane. I can't see this happen to our family."

Seth sighed. "He's right, Momma. You really don't want to know."

"I have to know, please. Don't you see? My momma died this way. I have never forgiven myself for not being able to stop Shea. If this happens...if this happens again how could I live knowing this time around we may have some kind of warning? Monroe, please."

"Seth. I leave this decision up to you, son. It's your gift. You are a grown man. You must decide how you will use it."

"Bree doesn't know her own strength. Her abilities are more powerful now. When she touched Jazzline, she transferred some of her strength to her. If she held on a little too long, if she did not release her or if she were farther along, the touch could have killed her. I know that. I've seen Jazzline die more than once the past few days. Not just by her decision to jump, which we know was unsuccessful. But I saw her with Tucker and Alex, and she dies with them. For that reason alone, she can't cross back."

"This isn't about me, Seth. What happens to Bree?"

"I hate to speak it aloud. I swear if one thing changes, one event, one decision, one thought, it changes the course of the future so I hate to speak it aloud. I hate to speak it for it to be out there in the universe."

"You can't change it. You tried with Alex by giving me the warning not to let him get in the car with Tucker. Just tell us what you see."

"Bree dies with the baby, Momma. That's what I see. I see Jazzline gone, and Bree, and the little one. I'm so sorry."

His momma cried out. "No, Seth. Not that. What do you see exactly? Tell me?"

"She's in labor and she loses her power. They both just fade away. They just go. They disappear. Just like your momma. Gone. I don't know where but it feels like death to me. It's a boy, but Bree swears it's a girl. Don't tell her because then she'll ask how I know, and she is relentless. She'll not give me any rest if she finds out I've seen anything. And we can tell her none of this."

I cried, "It can change. It can. It will. I don't believe that it's Bree's time. Why did she get pregnant? Why couldn't she have waited? Didn't she know about Shea? Didn't she understand the risks?"

Mrs. MacKenzie said, "Wait. If they fade away, what if they go back in time somehow. What if my mother isn't dead after all but bent time just like what we have witnessed with Alex and Tucker?"

Seth said, "We need to tell Colin all of this, I guess. That way he can look. We've never tried to trace our grandmother, never considering she moved through time."

"What happened to Aunt Shea?"

Mr. MacKenzie looked to his wife and she squeezed his leg, a silent approval. He began to speak, "Shea found her soul mate. God rest his soul, Connal. His name means strong wolf. He was wild. Free. Shea could not hold him during certain telling times. When we tried to search for him to let him know she was with child, we found him a little too late. They had caught him in a hunter's trap, gone before he could witness the birth of their child. Shea's grief couldn't withstand the struggle between the two and the light was gone. The baby was gone, and when her mother tried to save the baby, we thought she died from the force of the light. It was too much for any human to hold on to. Shea was broken when Connal died, and when the baby...well, took the life of her mother, Shea has not been the same. Now, with Bree pregnant and the uncertainty of it all, she'll do what she can to help her. We can't. No power that we know of can stop what may be with the birth of a child. That is why we did what we thought was best when we adopted Colin. We were too afraid to have a child of our own. A river and the star of the sea formed together...two waters colliding? What could that be? And look at the pain we've caused you Seth, and now Bree. Because of our choice to be your parents."

"Don't ever say that. No guilt or no regrets for me and Bree because of our powers. We are who we are because of both of you, happy, strong," he laughed. "Confused. A mess."

Mrs. MacKenzie said, "We don't regret having you both. We just regret that you had to have the gifts that you do, son. We love both of you more than ourselves."

"I know that, momma. My gift may feel like a curse to me but I know that it was what I was meant to be. I can't let it rule me in the dark any longer. It allows me to see to protect the ones I love. We have to find a way stop this from happening to Bree."

"I can do that. Maybe I'm the only one who can. If I can go back and find Tucker, bring him to Bree before the baby is born... Well, that will change what you've seen. Shea didn't have her Connal by her side. We get Tucker beside Bree and that changes the course again. You've only seen Tucker dead. You've not seen what will happen if he's alive. He may be the missing link here. Don't you see why I'm so convinced I have to cross?"

Mrs. MacKenzie said, "But you tried already, dear. You see that you can't jump. Why must you be so fixated on this? There's no way without powers. Has Colin thought of a way?"

"Not yet but he is interviewing the other clans and cross-referencing their research. He won't rest until he can find a way. We have five months left."

"Mrs. MacKenzie, would it be awful of me to ask to go back to Scotland? I know I didn't apply for the passport."

Mr. MacKenzie said, "What now? We just got you back?"

"She wants to still be married to me. Don't ask me why. She should run from us. That's what she should do if she knew what was best for her. Maybe this should never be, between the two of us."

Mr. MacKenzie said, "Don't hurt the girl like that. Look at her face, son. Do you love her?"

"Aye." He answered honestly to his father. There was no other way to be around him. "I love her more than my life."

"Well then, it's settled. We all know you only live this life once. Do not waste another minute of it trying to convince yourself that she's better off without you. Be married, live your life, have children if that is what you desire. Be happy, Seth. That's all we have ever wanted for you."

He looked at me and smiled. "When can we leave?"

Ask and ye shall receive. That would be my new mantra.

Mr. MacKenzie asked, "Will you take your comb out dear, for just one second?"

Oh, no. Plan backfired. How could I refuse? I slipped it and clenched it in my hands until the jewel was cutting into my palm. I couldn't speak in fear that my thoughts would betray me. His gift was mighty powerful, and now that I knew it, I was beyond intimidated.

He continued, "Thank you for trusting me. Now, what are your plans?"

"Don't do that to her, dad. I can't believe you. You're sitting here giving me the riot act about using my gifts, and you're trying to pull out secrets from Jazzline. She has no secrets from me."

He turned to me then and took the pin out of my hand and slipped it back into place. "Don't talk to him, Jazzline."

I pulled his hand down and gripped it. Thank God for his belief in me. Let me speak what truths I knew without breaking Colin's trust.

"Mr. MacKenzie, if I stay here, I'll jump again. I know I love your son and want to marry him. If I'm in Scotland, I'm safer there than here."

That was true. But that wasn't all that I was thinking and I was glad that I could choose my words, not have them willed out of me.

"If that's the case then, let's go. I need my sleep and what better place to get it than a cool bed in Scotland."

His mother asked, "If I'm there I won't be able to see Bree, will I?"

"No."

I said, "But she'll know you're close to her, and that might be enough."

Bree knew if I had one piece of the puzzle, the knowledge they were still alive, a folder from Colin, anything, it would be all of the motivation I needed to bring them back. Bree knew I wouldn't stop until we found them. She had more faith in me than Seth. He just didn't want me to die. I'd just have to figure out how not to.

His parents walked in front of us, holding hands, whispering as they went down the drive. We were going now. They granted my wish. The bridge was close to their house and we were there before I could talk myself out of it.

"If she doesn't make it through with us... I don't know if this is safe? I'm not sure. How about if we fly back? I'm sure the jet can be ready."

"Just hold on to her, son. Whatever you do, don't let her go."

He put his arms around me. "Don't worry about that. I'm not planning on it." And he leaped and I was flying and it was dark and it was light.

And I was standing with him, my feet on solid ground. Not pavement. Grass. Not darkness. Light. I didn't even have the effects of the jet lag with the change in the time zones. My breath came back to me, and I smiled and felt my exhilaration equally to Seth's relief.

"Thank God. You're safe. God, let me keep this girl safe."

It was a prayer I hoped for, too.

His father and mother trekked off down a path that stepped out onto a stone bridge. I looked around. This was a different place than where Bree brought me at the first cross. Mountains surrounded me by all sides and it was a stunning view. A landscape from a masterpiece.

"What time is it anyway?"

Seth looked at his watch. "That's odd. It's after nine in the morning. We're all messed up. We'll be sleeping all day today. How did the time change? Dad? Look at your watch."

"Well, I'll be. We are here earlier than expected. That's strange. First time this happened in a jump."

I said, "Something is happening with the bending of time. It hears me."

"What does?"

"Time. It's like it knows I want to go back. It's shifting like plates under the ocean."

"But doesn't that cause a volcano to erupt? Catastrophe."

"Or new land to appear, Seth. Can't you feel the charge? Something is happening to me I can't describe. It's like this energy."

Seth frowned. "I'm thinking it's Bree, Jazzline. Please be careful."

Mrs. MacKenzie turned around. "Wait until you see this, dear."

There was a castle waiting for us at the end of a mile-long stone bridge. A castle from a dream. It was as if I already stepped through time. I could only imagine the steps Alex and Tucker must've taken and their goofy excitement over it.

Maybe they walked this bridge. The connection to this place was overwhelming, and I could sense their presence here so strong. It was as if they were touching me. I turned to Seth to see if he was wearing the signs of them, too.

His hand was warm. They weren't here.

Mr. MacKenzie smiled at me as he let out a yawn. "What do you think of Eilean Castle?"

"It's beautiful. Really beyond words."

To be married in a place like this. To be here. A small-town beach girl from South Carolina. Amazing.

When we approached the massive studded doors, I saw Seth trace over a crest on the side of the stone entryway.

"What's that represent?"

"I shine not burn."

Mrs. MacKenzie said, "Okay, sleepy heads. Let's get off to bed. Seth, take her to the guest quarters on the second floor. Stay near here on the hall so you can keep a watchful eye in case we have a little dancing Bree on the loose."

When we were walking away, I heard her tell Mr. MacKenzie, "Like that really worked. He'll be there and you know it as well as I do."

Seth chuckled. "She knows me too well. I couldn't stand the thought of you being too far away."

He seemed as tired as I felt, and when we entered the sunlit bedroom, he went straight to the thick burgundy curtains and let them fall to the floor, blocking all signs that we were in the daylight hours. He pulled back the heavy quilts and pushed down on the pillows.

I yawned and stretched on the down-feathered bed. My heart rushed with an intense feeling of grief. Alex needed me somewhere...somehow...

Seth interrupted my thoughts. "I know you love me. I don't doubt that. I doubt your true intentions today. You'll still jump, won't you?"

He walked to the door, and I knew it was another day for a walk out. Would he break us with silence and separation?

"Seth. You can't run every time we face something difficult. You can't run from me."

He closed the door and leaned up against it. "I'm afraid I'm losing you every second."

"I'm here. Seth, I'm right here. Turn around and look at me."

"Will you stay?"

"I can't promise you that. It's Alex. Tucker. I have to try."

"Then, I'll lose you."

"You'll never lose me, even if I jump. I'm yours."

"Not if you jump."

"What have you seen? Tell me."

"I won't, so don't keep begging me. Get some rest. I'm right down the hall." He leaned over and kissed my cheek before leaving.

It wasn't long before I drifted off. I dreamed I was in a fog, an endless night of searching. I cried out to in the dark. I saw a man in the distance. He called to me and I ran. I ran, the fog blocking him from me again, and I knew I had to find him before he disappeared. Then I felt him pulling me out, and I was safe with him.

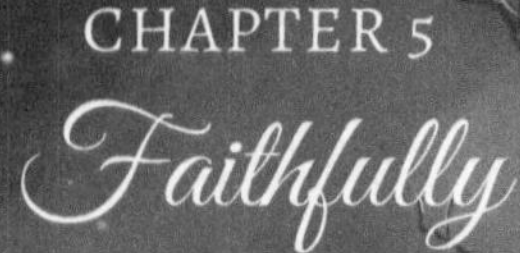

# CHAPTER 5
## *Faithfully*

"Jazzline, wake up. Wake up, baby."

My body lay still. I was sweating under all the blankets, and I felt like I might suffocate. "You were having a dream. It's okay. Is tú mo ghrá"

"What was that?"

"I love you."

"Mo anam cara."

"What was your dream?"

"I was in a fog and someone was there."

He didn't say anymore but I could see it behind his eyes. He'd seen me there, too. Had he seen who I was running to?

"Are you hungry?"

He already knew the answer by the sound of my stomach rumbling.

When we made it downstairs, I could hear we were fast approaching a blowout of mass proportions. What I didn't expect to see was a hot-faced Gillivary MacKenzie, the leader of the pack, with soft grey eyes now a raging thunderstorm. He was head to head with his son.

Seth blocked my view as if I were hit by imaginary daggers and I leaned into him like I could try to decipher their words from a glass against a door. No use.

Mrs. MacKenzie said, "Bree is my responsibility. I take responsibility for her actions. I will care for her."

Gillivary yelled, "Bringin' in Sassenachs tae this clan has not been good for us. An' Seth has done it now, too. Ye will not go near that cottage. Ye are not responsible fur her poor decisions. No, she must do this alone."

Mr. MacKenize said, "Finally, we agree on something. Maura will not step foot in that cottage. Shea will take care of her in her own way."

"What's going on?"

"Aunt Shea has run off in the forest and now Bree is locked in the cottage with no one to care for her."

"Momma, I locked her up. I'll take care of our little prisoner. Don't worry."

"But what about Jazzline? Who will take care of her?"

"I think I can manage."

"Jazzline will be safe here. I know she'll be protected in these walls. Can we please be hospitable and allow my guest some comfort of food and a change of clothing?"

Gillivary sighed and put his arm around his son. Mr. MacKenzie clasped him back. Amazing how one minute they looked as if they were about to tear each other's heads off and the next minute they were smiling and forgiving. This family was odd. I'd probably spend the rest of my life trying to figure them all out. At least I had that plan in place.

Mrs. MacKenzie had a new mission. "How rude of us. Come on, dear. Let's get you out of those clothes and into something more comfortable. I'll take you on a tour of the house after we fill you up."

"What did Seth mean by me being safe as long as I stayed inside these walls?"

She said, "You miss nothing, do you, dear?"

"No. I'm a good listener. Years of shutting my mouth, I guess."

Yet, she didn't answer. She must have been good at avoiding the

MacKenzie secrets line of questioning for years because she side-tracked me with a hot plate of breakfast food.

"What time is it?"

She grinned. "It's tomorrow, dear. You slept through yesterday."

Great, a riddle. Not with my head still fighting out of a fog. "You mean, I slept over 24 hours?"

She winked at me. "It seems like we all did. Strange, but it's true."

"I need to see Bree. I have wedding plans to make and she was the one that was to help me with all of that."

To be honest, I wouldn't know where to begin.

Seth entered and said, "You can forget that, Jazzline. Our wedding can be just as simple or grand as you want it to be and planned without Bree's help."

"But this would mean so much to Bree. I think that she was more excited about all of the plans than I was. The dresses, and the arrangements. She knows what I need. How could I even begin to plan a Scottish wedding?"

He took the eggs right out of the frying pan. "You'll figure it out. Our pastor can meet us here at the house with our immediate family. We can have a dinner and dance. Oh, and it comes with papers. We can't forget about those."

"You're being unreasonable. Bree can work from the cottage. This can be a distraction she needs to not be so...so..."

His eyebrows raised. "So...what?"

"So mad at you for locking her up. She may forget about her own timeline if she can have a part in this. Seth, I want this day to be special for both of us and for your family."

That was it. I did it again. Bree would be my wedding planner. I could see the lines in his face melt away.

"Aye, you get your Bree. But behind a locked door. Don't even think about breaking and entering. Do you know how to pick a lock?" He sighed and started to walk off again. "Never mind. I'll just dead-bolt it. Let me call the locksmith."

"Don't go to all that trouble. Bree won't cause me any harm. I don't have any powers for her to take. Remember?"

Mr. MacKenzie looked to his wife. "You told her everything?"

"No, she's a good listener."

So, Aunt Shea took her mother's powers. I wondered what Mrs. MacKenzie's mother was named for her to take her soul right out of her, then lose her own. And why did Shea go running off into the forest. I heard that but hadn't found the link yet. Seth couldn't physically be around Bree for the chance of her taking his death powers. Okay, I get it. This is kinda making sense in this round-about way.

My mind went straight to the thought that with me powerless, joined with Seth, what would our children possess? We would have no competing powers to contend with like his parents before us. Like Shea with her wolf love. Why then, was Tucker needed for Bree to carry this baby full term without complications? That still remained a mystery to me.

Seth broke into my thoughts with a squeeze of my hand. "Jazzline, are you listening? Look, Momma. You give her a compliment, and she goes off in la-la land."

"I'm sorry. Did you say something? I was just thinking about what kind of gifts our children might have."

My hand went to my mouth and then to my hair. I would've never spoken it unless my clip wasn't in place. Monroe was here and at it again.

Seth smiled. "Jazzline, where's your pin?"

"I don't know. It must have fallen out when we were asleep."

Mr. MacKenzie roared, "We? Did you say we? Didn't your mother warn you not to sleep in the same bed with her? Under my father's roof? She's talking about babies, too? What in the world has got my family so hot to jump with the first person they meet?"

"It's not like that, Mr. MacKenzie. Seth won't cross that line before we're married."

My hand covered my mouth again. MacKenzie was embarrassed for me, and she turned away. Was she about to laugh or cry?

Seth roared, "Jazzline, leave the room. Go find that pin now, before you curse us all."

I ran up the stairs but was confounded with doors all looking the same in every direction. I was too tired the day before to notice where we'd gone and my sense of direction was always a little clouded even on a clear day. I found myself in another bedroom.

Similar to mine, but different. It was occupied by a man. The smell of cologne was lingering as if he'd not been gone long. I froze when I looked up to see a portrait on the wall in need of a little restoration from the yellowing of the colors. But it wasn't the age of the portrait that shocked me. I'd seen many portraits of MacKenzie family framing these walls as I found my way up the staircase.

It was who it was that took my breath away. Before me was a life-sized Jazzline in a simple mahogany frame, wearing a Scottish plaid, similar to the one that Mrs. MacKenzie had sent to be washed and pressed for me.

I closed the door in fear. Whoever occupied that room knew me. Knew me from the past. Knew me enough to have me painted. Why would he have me hanging there in his room like some romantic reminder?

Seth laughed. "I knew you'd get lost. What are you doing by Uncle Colin's room? Ours is just down the hall, the other way."

Colin's room. Mr. MacKenzie's brother. The one that never grows old. The one that must not be his brother at all. I didn't move.

"Explain this one to me. How come Colin is your father's brother when he has lived all these years young?"

"Long story, baby. Not time for that one today. I've got to pick up a food delivery for our hungry prisoner. Do you want to come? I don't trust you with Dad trying to pull out thoughts from you, and Mom went into town to speak with the florists and caterers. So, you're stuck with me and Bree for the day."

I was glad he didn't enter his room. The storm that would follow would be destructive.

"Is your Uncle Colin and Aunt Sarah here?"

"You mean, Aunt Shea? I told you she ran off and left Bree. Are you okay?"

"No. I meant, Aunt Sarah with the twins, Devon and Donnell?"

He stood by the door, puzzled. "Who is Sarah? We have no twins in the family. Jazzline, are you okay?"

What was he talking about? I was sure they were there with the family at the Highland Games. I remembered how Sarah was found for Colin by Aunt Shea and she was another young one. I remembered the way he popped her on the butt as they ran off after Colin congratulated us on our engagement. I remembered the boys just as if they were sitting right here next to me, pointing out pretty girls at the dance and getting up the nerve to go and ask them for a slow dance with my encouragement on how handsome they both looked. But when I told Seth all of that his laughter turned to disbelief.

"Jazzline, what did you dream last night? How can you make up such a vivid story like that? Are you sure that crossing didn't cause you to lose a part of your brain?"

"I'm serious, Seth. I swear they're in your family. I met them. I'm not making this up."

"Listen, let's go find Bree before she starves."

He held out his hand to me, and I relented. He was clearly set on his belief that Uncle Colin's family didn't exist.

When we made it back down the stairs and out into the courtyard, I saw him. He was standing on a balcony. I lifted my hand to wave. "Look Seth, there's your Uncle Colin now."

Seth turned. He was one of Seth's favorites. I could understand why. I remembered how he'd embraced me and welcomed me into the family before all of the others. I remembered how I could've sworn he had tears in his eyes when our engagement was officially announced because his godson was getting married. There was more to this, and as I watched his hand raise in recognition of us, I wondered what he had been hiding all of these years. Apparently, it had been me.

# CHAPTER 6

# Right Here Waiting for You

I could hear Bree before I could see her. She was screaming like a banshee.

"Let me out of here, Seth MacKenzie. I know you're coming. You better let me out before I blow this whole place up."

I frowned. "Could she do that?"

He shrugged. "In theory, yes. Who knows what our little dancing queen can do? Did you know her name means strong one?"

"Well, how did she get her true love sensor from that? Shouldn't her name be Aphrodite or Cupid?"

I smiled at the thought of her running around shooting an arrow at Seth.

"No. Our parents had gifts remember. The first from two clans to have children. That's why we both have two gifts. My name means the appointed one, and I can also see, well, things. We think it formed to death because of Abhainn passing through me. Well, you know about me. Brianna means strong one, and there's nothing stronger than love, Jazzline." He pulled me closer to him and kissed me sweet and slow. "I shine not burn."

He opened the door to the cottage to a blast of heat. The fire was still roaring. Aunt Shea couldn't have been gone long. He stopped and turned to me then. His eyes narrowing. His hands awkward at his side.

"Jazzline, something just hit me?"

I pushed up the sleeve of the navy coat that Mrs. MacKenzie let me borrow. "What, that your hot? That it's hot in here."

"No. It's not that. You should be singing. I haven't heard you sing...since...well, since the accident."

But he was right, and I hadn't even noticed. Maybe I would never get it back. How my brain worked on a jukebox machine before was actually replaced with live words. My own. Strange. I couldn't tell him that I had nothing to sing for, because I swear, I had him, and I loved him.

I called out, "Bree. It's me, Jazzline."

I heard her anger turn to excitement, "Oh, Jazzline. Have you found them yet? Is he here?"

Seth added, "I'm here, too."

"Seth, leave her to jump. You know I have to have her to jump. I can make her, you know. I've done it before. I'll just do it again. Tell me the blessed date. I swear, Seth. I'll tear it down."

She needed to know the date. She needed the one valuable piece of information that I had branded into my brain. She was speaking to me but my mind was racing back and forth between now and then. Was she already controlling me? I could feel time moving yet stopping. I held up my watch to my ear and heard the ticking slowing to a lost heartbeat, almost to the point of stopping.

Her voice dragged. "Jazzline, I know you can hear me. Please go find them."

"Do you want to help Jazzline with her wedding plans or not, Bree? You're pushing it."

She clapped. "You're still going to marry him, even after you know he's locked his poor sister away like some crazed lunatic?"

He sighed, his hands going to his face again. "You know why I did it. You can't be sure you won't take any of us away, think of Momma and what she's reliving through this, and you could hurt the baby. We just don't know. It's safer for everyone this way."

"Even though I don't like it, and I still think he's exaggerating. He might be right, Bree. Do this for the baby. Do this for Tucker. You can't jeopardize the baby's health in any way. Tucker deserves to know his baby is coming so he can find his way back to you. Just hold on a couple of months."

There. Was that enough for her to know that I would jump for her? That I would go, but just let me marry her brother first. Let me do that one thing for me before I risked it all and maybe never made it back to live my life with him. I could at least have my time with him here, in Scotland, as Jazzline MacKenzie, before I died.

Seth put out the flames before they overtook the cottage and started warming up the food. He was farther enough away that I would try to slip to the door just to whisper the wedding date. Or a date. Any date.

He whispered, "Don't even think about telling her. You can't expect her to be able to control her emotions to send you back. Don't tell her anything."

"How is she going to be my maid of honor locked up in this room?"

"She can't be around the family. You know that."

Bree sighed, "A small price to pay for my little girl. Jazzline, I'm so sorry. Can you guys wait to be married until after Tucker comes home?"

"No. I'm ready to be married right now. This week. Can you at least help with the planning?" Because Seth says he loses me when I cross...maybe marrying him will seal that and change the course of whatever it was he saw.

"I've already sent off the dress designs. Seth, can I please have my laptop?"

"No."

"But, how am I supposed to get all of this out?"

"I'll link you with Colin. He'll fix your laptop all nice and child proof for you. On that condition, you can have it."

"Well, I guess I'll have to accept it. Has Colin figured anything out yet, you know, about the baby?"

He began walking to her door but stopped to look at me, puzzled as to how he would proceed. I would make it easy for him. I opened the door and stepped outside of the cottage, needing to get out and catch my breath anyway. The sound of Colin's name now stirred something unsettling in me. Even though I knew that he was discussing his brother's computer techie brain with Bree, and he did not attach the Uncle that he used to distinguish the two, the name was still the same.

Why did Colin have a portrait of me in his room, and what happened to his wife and children? Seth opened the door and pulled me back in, his eyes darting around as if he were scoping the place out before closing it behind him. Sometimes I wondered if he was super paranoid.

I asked, "What happened to Aunt Shea?"

Bree's sing-song voice was back. She wasn't mad anymore and must have known that I'd do what I could. "She had a message from Connal's family. It had something to do with the hunter."

Seth's voice rose in agitation, "Not that again. Why can't she just let the past die?"

I whispered, "I must be a lot like her."

He turned toward the door. "Now, I've got to go out there and stop her from killing somebody else. You women in the family, and soon to be in the family, are going to be the death of me, before my time."

Bree laughed. "At least you could warn yourself and know it was for real!"

He motioned for me to come with him but I wanted to stay a little while longer. Maybe I would have another chance to whisper 1745. I couldn't tell her that my shoe size was a 17 and there would be a wedding in 45 days. That would be too obvious to Seth and then he would probably never speak to me again.

If I could just marry this man maybe that's what I needed to pull me back.

Seth pulled me towards the door. "I've got to deal with Aunt Shea first. We have the engagement party at the end of the week. I'll see if Colin can get you a webcam so you can at least be there in spirit."

"Okay, whatever. Seth, you know I'm spitting mad at you but I love you to pieces."

"I know that. I love you, too."

I called out to her, "Please help me with the wedding, Bree. I'm depending on you."

Her voice was soft, just enough for me to hear since Seth had already walked outside, one step ahead of me with the hunt on his mind. "I'm depending on you, too, Jazzline."

I knew that. And I wouldn't let her down.

I said, "I told you she'd get over it. Maybe the wedding will help things after all."

He grabbed my hand as we walked down the path. "It will help me."

I kissed him on the cheek and held him close. My hands rested in his hair, and my lips found his in the tenderest kiss I could give him.

He whispered, "Please let me go. I've got to find Aunt Shea before she commits murder."

I didn't want to be the reason for Aunt Shea going to jail. I already had too much on my conscience now.

# CHAPTER 7

# Say You Say Me

Seth's eyes gleamed with boyish excitement. "Are you up for the hunt?"

His father grinned from ear to ear. "Aunt Shea again? Well, let me get my rifle."

Mrs. MacKenzie said, "Shea will lose her life over this. Why can't she just let the creature go?"

"Are you going to be okay? Is there something I'm missing? Seth, this isn't a battle, is it?"

"Don't worry about a thing, Jazzline. It's just deer hunting, baby. I'll be back before sundown."

Mrs. MacKenzie wrung her hands. "Bring Shea to me since I can't go near her or Bree at the cottage. If you find her, I need to speak with her."

Mr. MacKenzie replied, "If I find her? Don't worry. She'll be coming home with us, dear. And this time, talk some sense in her. Maybe I need to call Aileanna to come over and just lay on top of her or something. Couldn't we tie her up and force the light?"

Mrs. MacKenzie sighed. "If it were only that easy."

When they were out on their little hunting expedition, I asked,

"Please tell me the story of Aunt Shea. But first, tell me this. Where is Aunt Sarah and the twins, Donell and Devon?"

She frowned. "Who, dear? I don't know them? Do you need to call home? Is that someone you need to speak to you in your family?"

"Never mind. Don't worry about that. Please, tell me about Aunt Shea."

She sat down by the fireplace and pulled a quilt over her legs. This seemed as if it would take a while. She patted the leather couch and held out her arm for me to sit beside her. Her hands went up to smooth out my hair.

"Shea was a fairy spirit, given to my mother. She was always the brightest light of our family. No other members of my family had gifts, and her force was so powerful that she gave me my storytelling gift. We don't know how she transferred it. She just did. Maybe she didn't want to be alone with her powers and wanted to share them with me. She willed it all the same. It was already a quality that God had already blessed me with, the gift of story. I've been spinning them since I was knee-high, but more enhanced by her light. She was a love spirit. All of us, even those that shouldn't have. Like Connal. He was a wolf spirit and wouldn't let her alone. He was too aggressive, she was too forgiving. Well, she was pregnant and now alone. When my father and brothers went looking for him to force a marriage between them, they found him lying helpless in a hunter's trap. They tried to save him and when they took him to Shea, well, she could not handle it. Her light bursts within her and my mother was just gone, wiped away like a tear, the baby with her, the second that Connal died. Now, she's lived with the regret of her choices her whole life. If she would've never met Connal, or been able to control her emotions, our mother would still be alive. My mother would be here to meet you. She would've loved you. She was such a soft and lovely woman."

"I'm so sorry to hear that. I'm really sorry."

"That's in the past now, dear. I don't need Aileanna to bring me peace about it, Jesus healed it. It was an accident so there was nothing to forgive Shea for. She loved my mother dearly. I do wish Shea would leave the red stags alone. They were only trying to protect their clan from the wolves who hunted them."

"So, you mean there are deer and wolf people running through the forest?"

"Of course, dear. There are shapeshifters, just like there are apparently time travelers, and jumpers. Didn't you know that already?"

She said it so nonchalantly, but I should have figured since she'd lived a life of fantasy. This was all news to me.

"Come on and let's go shopping in town. I need a break away from these walls. They're weighing heavy on me. I need to pick up some things for Bree, too."

I grinned when I walked out behind her, running my hand along the wall. Momma loved watching an HGTV show called, If Walls Could Talk. I wondered what these walls were saying to Maura.

Shopping with Mrs. MacKenzie was a new experience. She was slow and deliberate, talking aloud at her choices as I listened to learn from her. We were at a high-end boutique and she was requesting a plaid design of a traditional engagement dress that would be appropriate for the Ceilidh at the conclusion of the meal. Lovely. Another dance. My favorite part of the Highland Games.

The shopping was a wonderful distraction for Mrs. MacKenzie, and her glow seemed to return once the grey of the castle was behind us. My mind was too clouded with talking animal lovers, the thoughts of Seth actually out there hunting one, and my portrait hanging in the bedroom of Colin MacKenzie.

As we were heading back to the car after a long day of shopping and dining, and shopping some more, picking out china patterns and choosing a registry, all of the things that Bree could not coordinate behind lock and key, my mind was still preoccupied at the face of the girl staring back at me from that oil painting looming over a fireplace.

As we turned into the drive, I asked, "Does Colin live at the castle with your family?"

"No. He wanted his own apartment in town."

I meant the fair-haired, bright blue-eyed like the Bahama waters, handsome, silk-talking Uncle Colin. "How about Mr. MacKenzie's family? Who lives here?"

It was possible that all of them lived under this roof as magnificent that it was.

She walked in with all of the bags, to be greeted at the door by more servants to grab and put away. She gave quick directions on what bags went to my room, hers, and Bree's for Seth or Shea to take later, then took me back to the study to await our men from the hunt.

"Mr. MacKenzie has two sets of children in his family."

She went by the mantle and held up the pictures again, as if I would ever forget their lovely faces. The MacKenzies made a striking group of men and women.

She continued, "Aileanna and Monroe are kin by Gillivary's first wife, Isabella. When she passed with sickness, he remarried with Rachel and had the second set of children, taking on Colin and having Abhainn. That is why the gifts are so similar to Monroe and his brother, Abhainn. The river runs through both of them. Plain spoken, Monroe takes the truth from you, Abhainn gave his truth back. Poor Abhainn, and Maggie, not to even think of the baby. When it is time for Alasdair to face his power, he'll need such a strong leader to protect him. That is why Seth, our appointed one, will take him in one day. You knew that don't you? After Abhainn's passing through Seth, Gillivary named Seth a guardian to stand watch over Alasdair."

I shook my head as if I knew exactly what she was referring to and I made a mental note to ask questions to Seth later. I needed more about someone else in particular, and he was far from ten years old.

"Well, then, what about Colin? You said that Gillivary took on Colin? What did that mean?"

"You really don't miss anything, do you? Well, do you remember his gift?"

"Yes, he said he was a young creature and something about him never growing old."

She laughed. "Aye, that's our Colin. He's such a sweet man, filled with the Spirit of the Lord like no other. So gentle and loving. So alone and tortured. We never understood why he punishes himself by not taking a wife. Not all of us are lucky to find our true soul mates, I guess. Imagine the millions of people out there in the world passing each other by without the knowledge like us. If we wouldn't have had Shea for me and Monroe, or Bree to bring Tucker to her light and then to see you and Seth... Every clan is not as lucky as us to have a love light. Even so, not every person is lucky in love."

"But what about Uncle Colin? Where is his family?"

"He's never found a soul mate and since he knows that such a concept exists in the world, he roams hoping that one day she will appear. He claims he refuses to settle. He wants the one woman that was made for him. But I'm sure that he's had many women, but not the one woman that is in his dreams, haunting him. Monroe worries more about Colin than all of his kin put together. He and Colin have always shared a special connection."

"So, what are they then, if they are not brothers?"

My mind was trying to organize this information as much as I could but I kept hearing the words soul mate and haunting. He was in my dream. It was Colin through the fog. It had to be him.

"Colin is a youngling. He can never grow old, dear. He has lived hundreds of years. His story is really his to tell, why don't you ask him?"

A smile broke out on her face as she took strides across the room. I turned in anticipation to see if Seth had managed a hunt without a trap set for him, but my smile soon faded when I connected with the eyes of the same man that had stolen all of my thoughts the whole day.

He smiled at me. His eyes were brighter than I remembered. "Ah, Jazzline. Welcome tae our home."

He took steps forward to me and put his arms around me as if he had known me all of his life. Not just an encounter at the Highland Games, but he'd hugged me there, too, so maybe it was just his way to be friendly. Maybe not. Because I could swear that when he hugged me, I felt the trace of his lips across my neck with a sigh in my ear. I froze as I felt my heart crash inside of me. A clanging of symbols.

Mrs. MacKenzie came behind him and grabbed him next, pulling him away from me, and I swore I felt the connection between us like a binding and twisting of rope right inside me.

"What have you been up to these days, Colin?"

His voice had a tone of regret. "Huntin', an' apparently, am not good at it today. I've been a little distracted as of late. Seth an' Munroe are comin' up now."

If Seth knew something was there between the two of us, he didn't show any signs of recognition, only beamed when he looked at Colin as if he were a best friend. They were close in age, by physical appearance, that is. Seth had told me that it was always wonderful to have his 21-year-old Uncle to hang out with his whole life. Especially with Seth being such a history fanatic.

Colin grabbed Seth and lifted him up off the floor, rocking him backward. "Ye think you've come here tae be married, huh?"

"That seems like the plan. Jazzline seems to be filled with her own ideas, but I guess I can manage to marry her before she figures any of them out."

Colin joked, but I knew it was meant just for me. "Well, if she gets tired ay ye, changers er' mind, I'll be waitin'. I've bin waitin' a long time fur a Sassenach."

I bit my lip. "I've decided. Seth will just have to put up with me."

Seth came over and put his arms around me, blocking me from Colin's stare. He was sweating, with his layers of clothing on, but I found myself just melting into him for not just a shield but a complete hiding place.

He whispered, "Are you okay? You're shaking."

I was now learning to speak openly but had a new problem. I would work on masking my emotions more.

Mrs. MacKenzie laughed. "Take the poor girl shopping and she's just exhausted, and I've been filling her head with stories all day. Sorry, sweetheart. I know it must overwhelm you."

Mr. MacKenzie tried to put his arm around her but she squinted her nose in disgust of his odor from the hunt.

He said, "You know it's deer pee, for the scent."

Shea came in and her nervous laughter quieted the room.

Mrs. MacKenzie flew across the room, her strawberry-blonde hair swishing perfectly with her fluid movement. "Shea, quit this nonsense now. Let's go talk. Tell me all about Bree. Is she eating? How is her mood? I've got tons of things for you to carry back to her."

Their voices trailed off down the hallway. Colin stepped forward, his eyes light. I could see the plan working right behind them. His voice was steady but the muscles were working overtime in his jaw.

"Why don't ye both go use some soap an' I'll entertain th' lass while ye clean up. Gets me a chance to know her the more."

Seth grinned, his face showing no signs of knowing. "Jazzline, you don't mind?"

I couldn't speak. I wanted to tell him not to leave me alone with this man, whoever he was to me, but then again, I needed this time with him to discover what was going on. I didn't know how but I was sure that Colin MacKenzie had the answers that I needed to save Alex and Tucker.

Mr. MacKenzie pulled Seth along, discussing how they could have let the stag get away, yet again. It was as if they were putting on the show for Aunt Shea's sake not meaning to kill the stag at all. I was sure that if those men wanted something that they could figure out a way to get it.

As soon as we were alone, I felt his hand find mine in a familiar way. He was so different from Seth. His touch not warm and covering me. But his fingers were comfortable in mine and he didn't speak as he led me through the door that took us out onto the courtyard. Was he taking me to Bree? Could he know how much I needed to be alone with her? My heart was flying towards heaven at each step.

The half-moon was above us, a starless night. Dark. One that was too still for its own good, because in the quiet of it I could hear every sound that my breath made, every heartbeat was closer to bursting. He took me to a corner of the courtyard away from view from the windows above on the second floor. I saw the lights flicker on. Our room. Colin was in the shadows but it could not hide the look that crossed his face. It seemed like the same look that Seth would give me after our feelings had run too close to the surface. It looked like conflict and pain and longing all in the smoothness of his face.

His sweet breath found its way close to my lips, drawing me into him for a secret that he would tell. "I've waited tae see ye fur so long an' I can't believe 'at it is real. Ye are real. I love ye, my Sassenach."

His velvet words fell against me and sent me back a few steps from him. I needed the distance from him. "Don't be afraid ay me, Jazzline. Ye don't ken, do ye? Ye don't know who I am?"

"Uncle Colin."

"Aye, Uncle Colin. I knew when I found ye I could ne'er have ye. But I love torturin' myself an' have held on to th' hope 'at I could steal ye away from him somehow."

His hand came out to touch me but I backed away another step. Better to be out in the open with him. Not hiding in the shadows like he was my love.

Why couldn't I find words to challenge him? To confront him with what he knew about me and what was this between us? But no words would come and I just stared at his lovely features. His strong jaw twitching, hair the perfect shade of honey brown with streaks of gold at just the right places. He was more than just a man, too beautiful to be real.

"Why am I hanging in your room?"

That shouldn't have been the first question I asked him. I should've gone straight to the point, like take me to Tucker and Alex. Why did you say you loved me when you don't even know who I am?

His leaned against the stone wall, crossing his arms against his body as if he had to do that to stop himself from reaching out and grabbing me. I found myself stepping back once more.

He chuckled. "Ye saw 'at, hmm? Oh well, I painted it of ye when ye left me. Just tae remin' me of whit I had lost. You've been wi' me ever since. Don't question that. Ever."

"Since the Highland Games? But that was just a few weeks ago. Where are your wife Sarah and the twins?"

"Huh? What are ye talkin' about now? If I only loved ye a couple of weeks, I could play it off as a crush. Say I gave ye to th' better child. Seth is so much better than me. Nae. I have loved ye fur over two hundred an' sixty years. Ye're my soul mate, lass. An' now 'at I've found ye again I don't think 'at I can ever let ye go."

I heard Seth's voice calling out to me, "Jazzline, where did you go?"

It was a panicking voice. One that spoke that he knew I was about to disappear, maybe even forever. I left Colin standing in the shadows ran towards the door and flung it open. I caught my breath, my cheeks burning higher than the flame that was now blazing in the fireplace.

I found my way back to the den. "I'm here."

He pulled me into his arms. His hair was still damp from the shower and his smell was so intoxicating. I wanted to forget every word Colin whispered to me in the dark but I didn't know if I could.

"When I called you and you didn't answer, I thought... I..."

"I'm here."

I couldn't think of any other words to say. Colin had gone or shrunk back into the shadows to hide his face from his nephew. From me. I couldn't stand the thought of him looking at me again with Seth beside me. How could I keep this from Seth?

"What is it? Where's Colin?" He turned to look out at the door that led to the courtyard.

I prayed for him to be gone. My voice came out too loud, "I don't know."

"Well come on. Are you hungry? My grandfather isn't back yet from town. We can eat in our rooms this evening. Aunt Shea has already gone back to take care of Bree."

He closed the door behind him. He told me he would be right back and left me there alone, too scared to move. Would Colin burst through the door and take me in his arms? Would Seth come in, and see the knowledge I was trying my hardest to mask.

When Seth came back, his eyes narrowed but he didn't speak. I couldn't either. When we made it to the top of the stairs, I hesitated. I could reveal this now. I could take Seth to Colin's room, show him the portrait, and it would be out there for him to deal with. He would probably want to hurt him, but then he could blame me for jumping and meeting Colin in the past. I was the reason for all of this confusion.

"What? Are you lost again?"

"Is it that obvious?"

"Here, baby. Always remember, two doors down."

My jukebox returned. It hit play to an old Dolly Parton song, Two Doors Down. We were two doors down, but so was he, just in the opposite direction.

"There. You're back. God, I missed that singing of yours. I was worried that I'd never...you'd somehow lost it."

"I've got to tell you something, and I don't know how to do it."

His voice became serious again as he shut the door behind us. "What's wrong?

I turned from him but his hands found my shoulders, and I couldn't help but lean into him. "Colin...he said... Colin said..."

He sighed and lowered his arms to circle my waist and pulled me around to him, staring at my face, trying his best to search me out. "I don't blame him one bit, Jazzline. I understand. How could he help himself? How could any man who sees you not fall completely, madly in love with you?"

"You know? Did you see something? A vision?"

He kissed me. "I didn't have to see anything only the way he looked at you, then looked at me. It was tearing him apart. He looked like I feel."

"Seth, what's all of this about? He said that I was his soul mate. I thought... I thought you said Bree said..."

He sat on the bed, pulling me down with him. "Don't you see, Jazzline. You jump through time. I swear if I knew how you did it, I could stop you. If you're back home or at this one, I'm still in danger of losing you. You jump and must meet Colin and well, I'm not born yet so it's not like he was stealing you away from me. He must know you're his soul mate from that time. I don't know, either. All I know from this whole story is that you still jump."

"But how?"

His fingers found my face and turned me to him. "If I knew, do you think I'd tell you? I'd be sending you to your death. I swear it, Jazzline. You don't see what I see?"

"I see that you love me. I swear I feel like I'm slipping away, being pulled away from you and I'm sitting right here. I feel my soul just drifting. Just love me, Seth. Before it's too late and I'm gone."

His kiss fell on me heavy and sweet.

Then, a loud intrusive knock banged us back to reality. "Sir, your dinner is ready."

Seth sat up, put his head down in his hands and let out a long sigh. "Aye, thank you. Just leave it there. I've gone and locked Bree up and we still have somebody bloody interrupting us at the worst times."

I smiled. "Or at the best of times."

He threw open the door and pulled the trays in, juggling them like a pro. It reminded me of Chica's. My past seemed like such a faraway memory. What would my mother think had happened to me? To wake up and find me gone without a note must have been devastating to her. Should I have called her to tell her that I was safe? Why lie? I knew that I was falling further and further away. It was better this way. To break away all ties of this time to take me back to get them.

I couldn't eat, and pushed his food around with his fork, never meeting my eyes.

"I hate I have to do this. I hate this between us. But I swear, Seth, you have to understand my need to go."

"Aye, I guess. It's more like an obsession with you now. I see that. Is that all you think about now? Is that all that fills your thoughts?"

"Not when you kiss me."

His hands were gentle in my hair, and those liquid eyes of his searched mine, as if he were trying to memorize everything about me. "I can't stand this anymore. Just bloody jump. Let me take you to the bridge myself. I'd rather throw you in and if you start to drown, if it doesn't work, I'll try to save you if I can. If I jump with you, we'll just go back to South Carolina. If you go off again alone and hit your head on a rock or drown or... I can't live with that."

If I didn't see his mouth moving, I would have sworn that those words came not from him but they did because he took my hand and started to lead me through the door.

My thoughts were frantic. I swear I wanted to scream no to him. A part of me wanted to stop him from this madness and tell him that I wasn't ready to jump yet. I needed to somehow prepare myself. I needed to talk to Colin, to Bree. I needed something more than this. Something was different. Before I jumped without hesitation, with no fear about what was to become of me. I was not thinking of what might happen to Seth.

"Stop. Wait."

My voice was strained and the stress was rising through my veins, the signs of an obvious panic attack about to wreck me full force.

"Seth, please."

We were in the dimly lit hallway but I needed to bring him back inside the room to stop this madness that had erupted so quick in him. His stance was an immovable force. If he wanted to have this conversation right here then that was fine with me. I pushed him in the chest, but he did not move.

"Get back in that room now, if you love me."

"I'm throwing you off that blessed bridge because I do love you. Come on before I change my mind."

He turned from me but his expression was not as stoic as he would have wanted. Pain, fear, death. It all crossed him at once and my heart was ripping away.

My hand reached out to him and touched his back. "No."

I found myself putting my arms around him. I knew that he would break at any minute. I whispered, barely able to get the words out. "What will happen to you when I go?"

"You don't care about that."

"Something isn't right. It was all about Tucker and Alex before. But I swear I'm missing something. What is it? Tell me."

I heard another voice then, one that had invaded my thoughts and plans all day. "She knows something, Seth. Don't lie tae 'er any longer.

Seth's eyes narrowed but he didn't turn to face Colin. "It's best if you leave, please."

Colin stepped back from the force of his words but didn't go. I found myself watching them both, my head going back and forth between their silent tennis match where no sound was heard except the hitting of the racket against my head.

"S... S... S..."

I could not do it. I sounded like kindergarten repeating a phonics lesson. I closed my eyes then and found my hands form the shape of prayer as if I was a child, repeating the Lord's prayer in my brain like I'd done kneeling beside my mother beside my bed. This would not work. My brain was reverting to memories of a child, and I was going back.

I was going back before I knew Seth. Tucker, me, and Alex. The three musketeers with no plans for summer except playing sniper and silent warfare against enemy armies with a controller glued to my hand or a tray to the other at Chica's. I was boring. I had a wasted existence of breathing in and out and moving through life wearing silence as a shroud. Even before that. As a child. I was just as boring and forgetful. Having no power and no voice. Here I was without breath and heart and soul and a choice that I would make would alter so many lives that everything was stripped from me all at once.

I could hear Colin's voice. He could not hide his emotions to a fault. The love was laced all in his words, and it cut at me. "There is a better way, Jazzline. I know a way."

My eyes stayed fixed on him but I couldn't speak.

Seth held his hand out and growled. "Leave us alone, Colin. I swear I'll... I'll..."

He sighed, "What? Kill me? Try it. It's about time."

"If I go back, do Alex and Tucker return or die along with me? What have you seen? What has changed?"

They both answered me at the same time, "No."

"You're both hiding something from me. It's more than me that dies. Who? What's changed?" I was torn apart by the knowledge that no matter what choice was made, death would be certain. Then, I knew. "If I cross, you die? Why?"

"I don't know. Maybe you kill me with your stubbornness." He chuckled at this.

"I'm serious, Seth. What do you mean you don't know?"

I heard a soft, female slur, "Can I say something?"

Colin said, "Shea, maybe now isn't th' time."

She ignored him. "So, ye gonna cross even though ye knew it brings death? Is it truly worth th' risk?"

"I have to try. Things can change. I've seen that. Seth, look how things changed so fast with Colin. There's no Aunt Sarah or twins. I can make this work. I know it."

Colin's eyes reminded me of a Tarheel blue. The only thing that normal seniors should be talking about? UNC Chapel Hill or Charleston? Not this.

Seth said, "Don't Colin. I can't bear it. Don't say it."

Colin ignored Seth's pleas. "The light is about hope. Hope in Jesus. Hope springs eternal."

My eyes were clear for the first time. Was it his voice that soothed away my fears or the knowledge that I could have a way?

"So, it's about hope. Hope to find. Hope to live." My mind finished, "Cross my heart and hope to live..." but I couldn't say those words. "Hope keeps the light going?"

He smiled. His velvet words affecting me in the center of my being. "Aye, love. I shine not burn. Th' hope burns within us. It causes us tae shine. Shea lost 'er hope when she saw Connall die. Are ye strong enough spiritually, that when ye see them your hope can bring them home?"

Shea said, "It can't be 'at simple. I had a bairn growin' inside ay me. Hope fur a new life. It would've been enough. Don't tell me I dinna' have enough. Tell this to Bree. See what she says."

My voice was growing more assured connecting the pieces to this million-piece puzzle. "No. Bree is different."

Shea asked, "How so?"

"Bree's name means strong. She has hope Tucker and Alex will be brought back. That's how she brought me here without the bridge. Somehow when we traveled again, we bent time. We moved a day. A day is not a century, but it was still the act of bending time. She can control this. It's up to Bree."

"Bree's unstable. Don't even think about going to her, Jazzline. She could kill you or send you way farther back than you could ever be found. Not even for Colin here."

"I'd fin' ye again. Just like I've found her now. Ah will ne'er let her go, Seth. I could bring her back if I wanted tae."

Seth roared, pushing me off of him and standing to face Colin. "Is that a challenge?"

Aunt Shea yelled, "Whit am Ah missin' here?"

I said, "Seth, stop it. Both of you."

Colin backed away, his voice laced with steel, "Aye, my father is home. We shall let him decide."

And with that, he strode off down the stairs.

"Whit was 'at all about?"

"Let's go face the judge. I pray for a swift verdict. Can you please watch her for me while I get my parents?"

He needed trial lawyers and supportive members to dab their eyes with a delicate handkerchief at the appropriate times. Who were my witness? Who sat on the jury? Where was my MacKenzie manual when I needed it the most?

CHAPTER 8

## *Keep on Loving You*

Gillivary said, "Whit have ye gone off an' done now, Colin? What are you saying about Jazzline? This is nonsense."

I couldn't speak under the glare of the formidable man with the gray eyes stared at me. I removed the comb and stared back at him. He'd see innocent, I'd hoped. Then, I realized that I must have made some mistake by doing my impulsive hairstyle change because I would have never imagined Gillivary MacKenzie to step back a couple of steps and hold his stomach in as if he'd taken a blow.

Seth seemed to be defeated in the corner huddled with his parents as I stood in the middle of the ring with the referee. Colin had Shea with him and by the looks of their corner the heated exchange between them was less than cordial and supportive.

"Who is yer father, child?"

"What?"

"Yer father. What's his name?"

"Doran Chicand. What does my father have to do with this?"

"Do you not know yer father?"

"We aren't close. Can we change the line of questioning here? What is going on?"

"I guess we save that fur another day."

Gillivary MacKenzie turned from me and slowly made his way to the massive dining room table. He sat at the head, of course. Like any leader or judge would do. A decision was being made and I hadn't heard the argument yet. He motioned for everyone and the room became dead silent as the family milled around him. There was only one set of hopeful eyes at this table, and they were the lightest of blues. Gillivary seemed older now than I'd ever seen him look. Before his presence was larger than life. Here, as his role in the family, he just seemed tired. He sighed and crossed his arms, leaning against the ornately carved, high back chair.

"In all ay my many years ay knowin' ye Colin, ye have ne'er requested a judgment. Why now?"

"Lives depend on it, father."

Seth was beside me, yet he wasn't. His hands were clenched together, his head down so his hair covered his expression. I reached up to touch his hair and pull it back so I could see and I wished that I hadn't. Tears were coursing down his cheek.

Colin was sitting on a great secret and he shifted his weight in the chair as if it were just too much to cover. His eyes turned to me then, and I couldn't allow myself to stare back at him.

He spoke soft, "Father, I ask yer permission tae take Jazzline as my wife."

My mind was screaming. Wife? Wife? Have you bloody lost your mind? What? I thought this was another way for me to cross over.

Seth spoke, his voice laced with poison. "I challenge that request, Grandfather."

Gillivary sat back. "I figured ye would. Colin, speak it now an' all of it. State yer case."

Mr. and Mrs. MacKenzie just held firmly to each other's hands, crossed together on their laps. They would not look at me, either. Shea was staring out the window as if she were expecting the hunter to sprint by to catch him. Her mind was elsewhere, it seemed. Gillivary's eyes were closed but right before they shut, I saw the lightning flash in them for only a second. It had begun.

Colin's voice was like liquid fire. I reached out and find Seth's hand. Seth's warm hand firmly grasped mine with immense pressure, but I didn't pull back because I needed the strength from him. Where was Bree when I needed her to touch me?

"Father, I love Jazzline Chicand. She is my soul mate."

He sat back with his arms crossed against his muscular chest. Was that it? Was that his case? The prosecution had to have more information than that.

"How can this be, Colin? Ye are mistaken. Clearly, Seth is soul matched wi' Jazzline. Ye are too late."

"Nae, father. It is Seth 'at is too late. I have been matched wi' 'er since 1745. I have first claim over 'er an' I have loved 'er fur over two hundred years."

Did I hear him correctly? I swore my brain didn't work around this heavy accent but I could stake my life on it that he said he had first claim over me like I was some piece of property to be bought, sold, or traded. My mind had an image of Seth and Colin, early American settlers, holding little white flags and racing to pummel them into the ground to stake their claim on the land. But they were driving their white flags deep into my chest and twisting at my heart.

"If I can prevent Jazzline from crossing she'll never meet you, Colin. You don't have a claim to her yet. She's sitting right here."

Me not cross? No. I would cross but what were my options:

1. Marry Seth, cross, and he die. Scratch it.

2. Not cross and have Tucker, Alex, and possibly Bree and the baby die. Scratch it.

3. Marry Colin, cross, and bring them back. Nobody dies. Possibly.

That hadn't been done yet. A new thing. A new direction. This could be the change that could make it all work.

"May I speak, please?"

Colin's eyes twinkled. That devil had already known he won. Gillivary nodded. I swore Seth was holding his breath.

"Answer me this, please. If I cross married to Colin, Seth lives? Seth doesn't die in this scenario? Do the circumstances switch and the outcome could be favorable for everyone?"

Colin grinned. "Aye. An' since we all know 'at I cannot die, we will both love ye an' be alive to tell about it."

"Then, I accept. I will marry you, Colin, on the condition that it is for the cross only. When I get back, we are going to be a statistic. A divorce. Then, I will marry Seth, pure as the day I'm sitting here, and I will be as pure as I am today, if you understand what I mean. And I swear, if you touch me, I'll find a way to kill you myself."

He chuckled. "Nae likely."

I didn't know if he was referring to him not touching me or killing him.

Gillivary stood then. Court was over. The verdict was in. I was to be married just to the wrong MacKenzie. He bent his fingers over the table, fists supporting him as he leaned in closer to us. Where was his gavel?

"Ah see th' course in yer min', Jazzline. Ye are makin' a right decision for now. We shall have a MacKenzie weddin' after all and this Sassenach might save the clan. Seth is to be a chieftain and be the protector of Alasdair. We can't lose that, and we don't want to lose Bree, either. You would sacrifice all of this for us?"

"For me as well. It's my brother and best friend that I'm going to bring back, remember. I'm doing this for them and for Bree."

"Well, I guess congratulations are in order, Colin. Seth, ye got yer'-self a good lass to love ye this much to save yer life."

Seth didn't answer his Grandfather, but stood from the table, knocking the chair back as he went over to stand by his parents.

His father held him back. From Colin or from me, I was not sure but the pain in his eyes tore at my heart and ripped it away. Colin could marry me and help me to cross. That was the plan. Nothing more. Nothing less. I just prayed I had the strength to stick to it.

# CHAPTER 9

# Don't Know What You Got

M r. MacKenzie held Seth back with all of his might. I saw the emotions playing out on Seth's face. Anger. Confusion. Fear. Did I seem as if I were happy about this decision? I couldn't lie. The pin was out and Mr. MacKenzie was very much present in the room. I was at peace knowing I'd protected Seth and saved our future.

A wave of nausea washed over me and I couldn't stop the weak feelings any longer.

Gillivary said, "Why don't ye go take care of yer fiancé. She needs som' time."

I turned to Seth, pleading with him to take me out of here but he wouldn't move.

"Seth..."

When I called his name. he flew from his father's grasp and ran out of the room. He was gone. Colin stepped beside me. I couldn't face him but my eyes reverted down to his hands, and I saw them coming up to steady my arm. I was against the table and had nowhere to go.

His voice was soft and invaded my senses again. "He was talkin' about me, Jazzline. Ye are mine, love."

"No."

No, I was not his. No, this was not happening. No, Seth was not out of that door. His fingers touched me like a feather, gently pulling me toward the entryway. What would Mrs. MacKenzie feel towards me? She would have to know that I was doing this for Seth and Bree. She would have to forgive me somehow.

She read my thoughts. "There's nothing to forgive, dear. As much as I hate to see Seth this way, you're right. This must be done. As selfish as I am, I can't stand the thought of losing Bree, and knowing that the cross somehow takes Seth's life. He needs to stay near medical attention of this time. You do what you must and when this is all settled, we'll figure out a way to make it right. We can rewrite the ending."

"I love Seth MacKenzie. When I cross, I'll bring Tucker and Alex back with me. After this is all over, I swear it, I'll have Seth MacKenzie as my husband. Don't go thinking this marriage is for real, Colin. Don't get your hopes up. Our divorce is inevitable."

Those were the words I'd remembered Momma speaking to my father at the end. It must have been the right choice because Colin's eyes narrowed. My heart was already promised to someone else.

Mr. MacKenzie said, "Jazzline, go on and get cleaned up. I'll find Seth. I'll go talk to him."

"Tell him...please...tell him I love him...tell him."

"Aye," was all he said as he strode out of the room.

I feared the worst as I let Colin lead me from the courtroom. Seth would not listen to reason. He called me stubborn. He was living in absolutes and said death made him see things in a different light. He would take this as an end for us, and I saw it as the only way for us to be. How could I live knowing that I'd killed my brother and best friend, Seth, and his sister and nephew?

Colin led me up the stairs and with each step I took the panic seized my chest. He turned to the left and stopped at his door. Two doors down in the opposite direction. I could not move. I would not enter his room. He sensed it in me and started walking again, this time to the third white door, directly beside his room.

A woman's room. Soft reds and pinks billowed around me. Thank

God. But the wing on the opposite side of the hall was too far from Seth.

"I'll go and get yer things."

As soon as he left the room my knees buckled and I fell to the chair. I found it harder to contain my soul within me from bursting out. Was my light about to go out? Was this what death felt like? Something was slipping in me, and I felt this shift. I needed Tucker and Alex. Now.

He stood by the door watching me, as if he were unsure of what to do next. I heard the bags fall and crinkle loudly. I saw the contents in them so plainly, a blue cashmere sweater, new jeans, a soft engagement dress.

"Oh, God." I breathed it out. "God, help me."

"I'm here fer ye, love. I'm nae going anywhere. It'll be okay, Ah swear it."

I wanted to ask him a million questions. The simple ones. How did we meet? The complicated ones. What could have ever made you fall in love with me? How will I ever be free of you? When can I have Seth again?

"I need to go to the bathroom."

He laughed a rich deep one that sounded as close to the word joy as I heard. "Nothing has changed, aye. Ye've been given tae me again, an' I'll treasure ye forever."

I went to the bags and grabbed my things and closed the bathroom door behind me. I needed space from him. I needed time. The thought of him just right outside my door as I undressed and threw the soiled clothes down a laundry chute made me want to shimmy my body through there as well. But my luck would have me ending up in a laundromat in Egypt somewhere, so I just stepped weakly into the shower and prayed for God to see me through this.

I'd always heard the older people speak in prayer requests how God would not give one person more than they could handle. Did He really think I was this strong?

Colin hadn't moved from the chair. I expected him to be gone when I came out of the bathroom wearing my pajamas. I ran a towel through my tangled hair.

He stood up and crossed over to me, pulling me into his arms. The towel fell on the floor at my feet, and he bent in as if he were going to kiss me. I pushed him back.

He grinned at me. "Ye won't be able tae stay away from me fer lang."

"Watch me." I pushed him again.

"I think I will." He seemed as happy as a schoolboy with high marks.

My frustration was boiling over. "What do you see? Tell me? I swear, what is wrong with you?"

He went over to the fireplace and struck a match to the kindling, and I watched the small embers begin to dance. I wanted to push him headfirst in the flames.

He turned to me then, his eyes remembering the past. "Do ye remember how ye felt when ye first found, Seth? Picture 'at same thing happenin' wi' me, and carrying ye around wi' me fur two hundred an' seventy-four years. 'At is what I live with. I see my very soul in front ay me. I see my life as it could be in this time. My heart."

"Am I really your soul mate? We don't have Bree to confirm it because they locked away her. How convenient for you, right? Is this a trick? Just to get what you want?"

It was time for the inquisition now. The trial was over but I felt like his had just begun.

"Each family has their own special gifts. I've seen 'bout all of 'em in my time. I've had a love sensor wi' th' MacKenzie's, just like ye have Bree now. I knew 'at my soul mate was comin'. So, I waited. Aye, waitin'. I guess it's what the Lord knows I do best. An' 'en, ye came up, and my Spirit cried joy. I'd seen it happen tae family after family, tae everybody but me. So, I felt it when I first pulled ye out. I knew it in my soul even before I've had tae see th' look 'at ye gave me."

I was intently listening, hanging on to every mesmerizing syllable. "Pulled me out? From where?"

"From th' loch. Ye cross but ye know 'is already true or we wouldn't be having this conversation."

"Do you know how?"

"Ye must figure it out. I only know what happened in th' past, love. I can't read th' future."

I knew someone who could, and I wondered now if it was different. Surely a different course had been set. What had changed for me? For him? Was he now alive?

"What's your gift?"

"Ye know 'at already. I can ne'er grow old."

Seth had two, Bree two. I didn't know if he was born to a set of parents who both had gifts. If he had another gift, I needed to know it now.

"Do you have any more gifts?"

"Th' only gifts I'm sure of beside me livin' fur eternity, is that I was born tae love you right and right I will."

"Stop with all of this love talk to me, Colin. You're wasting your time."

His laughter filled the room and I swore if Seth could hear us, he'd think I was in here having a grand ol' time three doors down.

"I've got all th' time in th' world, Jazzline. I'm a patient person. Just wait an' see."

"Well, I'm not patient and I think it's time I figure out this time travel thing. I need to know everything. Where are Tucker and Alex?"

He squeezed my hand. "I know 'at is why ye agreed tae marry me, tae get them back. I know 'at an' I don't care. I get ye this time around. Ye get them. Ye get what ye want in the end."

"But where are they exactly, like right now?"

"Ye think I can remember every minute detail from 'at long ago?"

I searched his eyes for the truth. I saw love. I saw hope. I saw an undying commitment to me.

"You seem to not have forgotten me."

He traced my palm with his fingers now, and it stirred something in me that was violently wrong. That feeling was only for Seth. "I know every single thing about ye. Ye are branded in my memory like ye were wi' me yesterday. Yer laugh. Yer voice. The way ye looked at me as if I mattered. God help me."

He pulled his hand away from me and rubbed his face.

"And I am to marry you, just like that." It sounded so simple. So quickly decided. "And just think, you never even proposed."

"That's where ye are wrong, Sassenach."

"How do you expect me to really marry you when I love Seth?"

His eyes were the crystal blue of the sky back home above the ocean roar. "Th' beauty of all of this is 'at ye do love Seth. 'At love fur him brought ye tae this family and gave ye tae me. I'm forever grateful tae my godson fur 'at. Ye love him enough tae keep him alive. Ye will love me, too. I know it. Our time is coming. Even in this time, it will be."

"I thought you said you couldn't tell the future."

"No, but soul mates can't help themselves. Ye will be my wife before too long. I believe that with everything in me."

"Get out. Just get out, now. I can't stand this anymore. You are making me sick with all of this."

At the thought of being in any man's bed, other than Seth's brought fear and dread washing over me layer upon layer.

"Get out. I mean it."

He stood up and seemed so sure of himself, gloating even. He didn't take the door that led out to the hallway, another door opened inside my room I thought was a closet. Through it, I could see my portrait hanging over his fireplace. We had adjacent rooms. How convenient.

His voice was low. "I'll be waitin' fur ye if ye need me. If ye want me."

There was no mistaking what he wanted.

When he walked through the door, I picked up my hairbrush and slung it at the door right as he was about to close it, missing him but flying into his room instead. Great. He laughed loudly again.

"Ye have tae come an' get it."

The lock was gone, and my stomach tightened. Whether the house had always been that way or Colin arranged it, I didn't know. Either way, I pushed a chair beneath the handle and prayed Seth would find me before I had to find out.

When I laid down to sleep, I couldn't find the words to give God a proper prayer. All I could whisper over and over again was, "Please God, somehow bring Seth back to me.

CHAPTER 10

## *Careless Whisper*

The fog surrounded me. A voice was there with me in my panic.

Bree was calling me. She was in labor, her breathing frantic and her screams were piercing the night. Her pain became mine, and I fell to the ground, feeling my insides being ripped away. Cries strangled me, and I knew that I was close to death. The fog covered me and the darkness was closing in. I felt a metallic taste on my tongue.

His hand found mine, tracing my palm, whispering through the haze of my brain. And then I heard his voice. It was not the one that I wanted to hear but I turned my head to it anyway. His hand was now on my cheek. His voice growing clearer through the fog and my pain was gone. Replaced by something different. A need. A need that started to overcome all thoughts of Bree and the fog and the darkness. He whispered again, and I reached for him. My eyes flew open when I touched the chest of the man of my dreams.

My throat was sore and I cried from the pain that still gripped my stomach. "Colin? Please, Colin."

Was I begging him to leave or to stay? He just sat there, holding my hand against his bare chest. When I realized that he didn't have on a shirt and I was touching his skin the embarrassment of the situation brought me wide awake. I looked down at my condition and thank God I was clothed under a stack of blankets. My hands brought the blankets up to my chin in some weird attempt to cover myself.

"Another dream? What was this one about?"

"Another? But I don't have dreams like this. Except one other."

The other dream of Colin in the fog pulling me out. Now, Bree was with us. That would be just like a dream to be disorienting.

"When yer wi' me all ye did was dream. What was this one?"

"It was you."

"It's strange how when ye were wi' me before all ye did was dream about Seth. An' now, 'at I am here wi' ye now, ye dream about me."

"Where is he?"

He grimaced, "Ye don't want tae know."

He stood up then and pulled his grey shirt over his head. I looked to the corner of the room at the chair by the fireplace and saw his shoes and his coat across the arm. He had stayed in here. How dare he?

The light of the sun streamed through the windows. I'd had a bad habit of forgetting to put on my watch, and I wondered what time it was.

He smiled at me. "Ye skipped another day, lass. One day closer tae marryin' me. Haven't figured ye out just yet with yer time difference. My brother told me it was the second time it happened, and it must be the strain of the cross fur you."

"Where's Seth?"

He pulled the chair closer to the bed. "Seth's gone."

Then, panic seized my whole body. "Where?"

He asked a stupid question. "Are ye hungry?"

"No."

But I lied. I was starving. And I wanted Seth. I pulled the covers back and stretched, my hair falling all around me in a mess.

"Let me take care of ye, love. I'll be a good husband tae ye, Ah swear it."

Husband. I'd come to Scotland to marry Seth. And now this. Colin. A means to an end. Didn't he know that? Had he no idea what was going on here or did he care? As long as he got me in the bargain. I stood before the dresser and stared at myself in the mirror and I couldn't believe that there were people in the world that wanted me. The MacKenzies were sure a messed-up clan of people. More than just with gifts but with their sight. That brought me back full circle to Seth again. What had Seth learned that drove him away? What had he seen?

"Have you seen Seth?"

I pulled my hands through my hair because my brush was still in his room. No, there it was placed right where I had picked it up and hurled it at him. He'd returned it. Even though it would appear a nice gesture it was an excuse to be back in here again.

"Aye, I've seen him."

"Where did he go?"

He was behind me now and I saw how we looked together for the first time. This is what people would see if they were looking at us, man and wife. One of the most handsome men on the planet next to the plainest girl in the universe.

"He's out huntin'."

But Colin's voice betrayed him. I could see the worry shadow his face.

"Do you love Seth?"

"Aye, He's my nephew an' I care fur him. He has always been one of my favorites."

"Then, why are you doing this to him? To us?"

He had challenged him for me, and if it would have been in the OK Corral, I was sure that we would've had an all-out gunfight.

"I'm not only doin' this fur ye. Ye seem to have forgotten th' part about Tucker an' Alexander?"

His voice was so smooth across their names, and I saw the flicker of humor there, too. He remembered them. Alex would have loved to hear how Colin spoke his name.

"Do ye want them back?"

"How dare you ask me a question like that?"

"I'm sorry, love. I know ye want them back. And I'm th' only one 'at can help ye without hurtin' anyone else."

"Is that what you think you're doing? Helping? Like you didn't hurt Seth when you told his family we were soul mates if that is even true? You could have just helped me cross since you seem like you know secrets you aren't revealing."

"Don't ye see 'at is th' only way?"

But as soon as he said it, I could feel the doubt rising even higher. There was always another way. Look at Bree and what she did to me and Seth. I was counting on Bree to help me find an alternative.

"Tell me the truth, please."

I let out a sigh, and before I could pull my thoughts together, Colin stepped closer. His hand brushed mine, and for one second, the world titled. He kissed me with enough longing that I forgot how to breathe.

Then, I remembered Seth.

"Stop it, please. We can't."

Colin released me at once, his face full of regret. "Forgive me, Jazzline. I should not have done that."

My hands trembled because my heart was being pulled through the eye of a needle of a mystery I didn't understand.

His lip twitched into a small smile as he wiped away my tears with his finger. "Never question if I'm yer soul mate again or I just might have tae show ye one more time. Then again, ask me now am I yer soul mate? I need to kiss ye again."

My hands pushed him back a little but just touching him again was too much for me. My fingers tingled. What was this?

He brought so many emotions out of me at once I didn't know who I was with him. "So, all a soul mate is, is it just this need?"

"So, ye felt 'at in yer soul, did ye now?"

I couldn't lie. "Aye. I felt it. And I hate that I felt it. Colin, I love Seth."

"Soul mates ur th' missin' piece. Th' other half made by God. It is more than just a feelin'. It's a peaceful knowing, and I doubted it even existed until I met ye. Now, I know the power of it. I can ne'er let ye go."

"But you will have to let me go. I jump."

"But ye cross tae me. So, I get ye again."

"You are impossible. Don't you know that?" Impossible to be the way he was. Immortal. Impossible to look that good forever.

"I've heard ye say 'at before."

"What else have I said to you?"

"'At' I'm handsome an' smart an' valiant an' brave an'..."

"Okay, that's enough. Did I ever say you were vain and way too sure of yourself and too confident for your own good?"

"Aye, 'at, too. Please let us go an' get somethin' tae eat. If ye aren't gettin' hungry, then I'm starving."

"I don't love you, Colin. I love Seth."

"Ye may not understand it yet, Jazzline, but one day ye will remember what we were. Until then, I'll wait."

# CHAPTER 11

# Waiting for a Girl Like You

**M**rs. MacKenzie was in the kitchen speaking with the staff about an upcoming dinner, a grand one by the sound of it. I reached for my pin and found it there, secure. I'd even put a couple of bobby pins to hold it down just in case it would slip out again. I couldn't stand the thought of Mr. or Mrs. MacKenzie pulling out my story anymore.

There were no signs of Seth and I looked through every open door as we made our way down and through the corridors. He was not in the kitchen, either. Colin nodded to Mrs. MacKenzie but did not speak to her.

"Mrs. MacKenzie, can I speak with you?"

"Aye, dear. One moment, please."

Colin said, "Maybe ye should wait until later. She seems preoccupied."

He shifted uncomfortably at the small table in the corner of the kitchen, and he picked at the napkin ring. Exaggerating it as if it were his wedding ring. He knew something. Colin was too easy for me to read which was so unlike Seth who was used to guarding everything so close.

"What is it? You know where Seth is, don't you?"

"What was it you would like to discuss, dear?" Her voice was polite as ever, but I felt the distance there.

"Where is Seth?"

She turned to Colin, her eyes narrowing. "I thought you would've told her?"

"I did tell 'er. I told 'er he went huntin'."

He got up from the table and went over to the counter. Before I knew it, we had plates in front of us. With the food there, with Mrs. MacKenzie's eyes drilling into my soul, Colin's presence with his leg touching my knee, I could not eat.

"Did Mr. MacKenzie go with him?"

"No, dear. He went alone."

Colin pushed my plate closer to me. "Please eat somethin', Jazzline. Ye will need yer strength."

"For what?"

"For your engagement party, dear. It will begin soon."

"What? We don't need a party. Just sign me up right now in the kitchen to marry this man and get it over with. No elaborate parties. What would that do to Seth?"

Colin said, "Seth's gone. He won't know it."

Mrs. MacKenzie said, "Keeping secrets will not help this situation."

"This situation? It's a catastrophe. Where is Seth? Take me to Bree. Colin, take me to her now."

Mr. MacKenzie walked in. "What's going on in here? I could hear you clear across the hall." He stopped when he saw us around the table. When he saw me, he took a step back. "You will do no such thing. You will not see Bree."

I turned to Colin, my eyes filling with tears. "Please take me to Bree."

"Nae. 'At is one thing I can't do fur ye."

Mr. MacKenzie stood beside his wife now. I went between all of them, studying their faces. I was ashamed because I could see the way that they were all looking at me. Even Colin. I was nothing to them but a situation. I was the cause for all of this pain in their family. If Tucker and I had never met them...

Before, when I first fell in love with Seth, I used to think what my life would have been like if Tucker would not have found Bree. And I was so thankful for that. For him finding her. I even told him that. And now, sitting here with the look in Mrs. MacKenzie's eyes betrayal. Mr. MacKenzie - liar. Colin - cheater. I saw it all so plainly.

If I could just go back...

My head started to swirl but I kept my bearings about me. Focus on Bree. I needed Bree.

It was like Colin read my thoughts. "Bree isn't stable. Trust me on this. I have seen enough of this tae know ye can't be around 'er. I can't risk it."

I didn't care that Mr. and Mrs. MacKenzie were there to witness this conversation.

"You've been around long enough to know another way for me to go through time. Tell me what the trick is. Tell me the way that I can cross."

A bell was ringing, sounding like chimes of a church. Mrs. MacKenzie put her hand out between us. "Don't worry your head over this now, Jazzline. We have guests arriving."

"Guests?"

She spoke through clenched teeth. "For the engagement party. Invitations were sent and Bree has invited practically the whole country."

"Oh," I breathed, "You didn't tell Bree."

Mr. MacKenzie said, "No, and don't tell her anything. In fact, don't talk to her. I forbid you to see her. Do you understand the danger? I promised Seth that I'd look after you."

"You make it sound like Seth isn't coming back. Colin? You said that he was out hunting?"

Mr. MacKenzie said, "Put yourself in his shoes, Jazzline. Do you think he could be here to witness this? The party? The wedding, for God's sake? He's gone off researching with Colin and he won't be back...until...until..."

I closed my eyes, "Until I bring Tucker and Alex home?"

"Aye, love. Until we get the job done."

"I won't embarrass you or Mr. MacKenzie in front of the guests you've invited but how can I hide my worry? Please know I'm doing all of this to save everyone, even if I still don't know how."

Mrs. MacKenzie pushed the plate towards me now. Sooner or later it was just going to land in my lap.

Mrs. MacKenzie reassured me. "We don't need to speak of this again. We know the intentions and the plan well enough. Go ahead and eat and then I'll help you get ready."

Colin smiled tenderly at me. Mr. and Mrs. MacKenzie saw it and a look of sadness passed between them. For me, Colin, or Seth, I didn't know.

"Brother, I've been waitin' my whole life fur my engagement Ceilidh, been to many of them, but now it's my turn. My weddin' to ye will be worth all the wait. Please give me this one indulgence before ye cross. Stand by my side and act as you love me."

"I can't do it. I can't stand here and pretend that I want to marry you. Is this really necessary?"

Mr. MacKenzie's eyebrows raised. "But you do want to marry him, and you just said you wouldn't embarrass us. We have dignitaries coming, dear. You don't understand the power in the room. Stay by Colin, and don't leave his side. Leave in your pin or suffer conse-quences we will never be able to save you from."

I turned to Mr. MacKenzie. "Ask him something for me, please?"

"Ah wood ne'er lie tae ye, Jazzline. Trust me. Ye can ask me anythin'. Monroe doesn't need to be here. She doesn't know the depth of my faith. She doesn't know I'm beyond lying."

I had a built-in lie detector man right beside me. No wonder the judge had a son with this gift. He would need to know the true inten-tions of those he was judging.

"Do you know I love Seth and that when all of this is finished, you'll have to let me go? Do you understand this situation?"

I loved the way the word situation did not do it justice. Yet, I was still using it.

His eyes twinkled. He was a lunatic. "I hear what ye say now, love."

"I didn't ask you did you hear me. I asked you did you understand. Mr. MacKenzie, ask him. Ask him does he know that I'll divorce him.

He'll have to give me a divorce. I don't want this to come back on me and have problems later."

Colin caressed my hand. "Ah will give ye what ye want when the time comes. Ask me an' I will give it tae ye."

This was ridiculous. Colin actually believed he had a chance with me. Where did his hope come from? That was it. The word I needed. Hope.

"It's hope isn't it?"

His eyes narrowed. "What do ye mean?"

"The absolute hope in the truth is what pushes you through. Yes, you have gifts. I don't. I get that part. But it is more than the gift that pulls your family through and pushes you back and forth between time and space. The light and hope."

Mr. MacKenzie looked at Colin. "Hope?"

"Hope. Aye. Jazzline has it. Do ye know Romans 8:25?"

Mr. MacKenzie recited as if he were an online Bible passage reference. "But if we hope for what we do not yet have, we wait for it patiently."

"Bree is waitin' patiently fur Jazzline tae bring Tucker back. She hopes it. Many block th' hope 'an it stops them from crossing or they lose faith and fall away from the truth. Bree is strong enough tae hope fur us all. Even Seth. She was strong fur Seth, so I'm sure she can take this little sprite through."

My voice sounded far away like I was in a tunnel. "What did Seth do?"

Mr. MacKenzie pushed on the chair, rocking Colin slightly. "You might as well tell her the truth now. When would there be a right time?"

"Where is Seth MacKenzie."

Just as if I were an officer interrogating a guilty suspect. I watched every movement, flutter of his eyelids, the clench of his jaw.

"Seth's gone huntin'. I told ye. But he's huntin' fur ye. He's gone back tae find ye. Told Monroe he will get to ye first before I ever set eyes on your face."

"But I'm here. I haven't tried to cross yet. I'm trying to wait until after the ceremony to be sure."

"Listen tae me, love. He crossed back. Bree took him back. He told 'er th' date an' 'at was all she needed. He's gone but we don't know where or when or even if it worked."

Then, it all came back to me. Bree screaming at us to tell her the date the first day in the cottage. She'd seen those same pictures of their brother Colin. The blurred ones. Purposefully blurred so that Bree could not know the date.

Mrs. MacKenzie cried, "Yes. He's gone. Now, come on and let's get you ready. The faster I can get you married, the faster you can bring my son back and fix my family."

"I'm so sorry. It's all my fault."

Mr. Gillivary MacKenzie entered the room and stood by the door. Gillivary put his arm around his adopted son and Colin's eyes lessened in fear and agitation. He stood right before me with his presence looming. All of them staring down at me was so intimidating.

Gillivary's voice was sure, "Don't ye dare blame yerself fur any of this. None of this is yer fault. You didn't cause that accident. Or Bree. Seth is strong. Smart. He will be braw. It is ye we are worried about crossin'. Ye will get yerself killed."

"I know that. Seth has seen it."

Colin exploded. "I wouldn't let 'at happen. I swear I'll protect ye and keep ye safe."

Mrs. MacKenzie was crying. "How can you be sure you'll find her? How can you know? If she crosses, it might even be the wrong time...the wrong century. She may not cross at all and we can't just jump in and save her, we will just flip to our other home."

Colin's voice broke. "I find 'er. I'm still standin' here lovin' 'er so it works, and I get to her before Seth. He jumped for nothing. She's mine. Th' pain is real 'at I feel fur losin' her when she comes back tae this time. I still feel 'at pain even as I look at 'er right now."

"Take her upstairs and get her ready, Maura. They're all coming up now. We don't want it to be this way but we will endure this night and get this blessed situation handled."

Gillivary spoke, "Do the night fur Colin. Can't ye see ye have caused him enough pain? Colin has never asked us one time for anything. We can give him this night."

His voice was the deciding factor. If they wanted a party, then I guess I would have to give them one. I just stood on stage as Christy and didn't skip a beat with a line or a song. I could do this and imagine myself under the lights. I was going to cross. It seemed like I owed him one for ruining then saving my life.

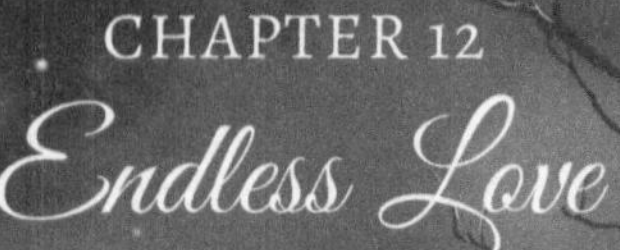



Mrs. MacKenzie smiled at me. I knew that she was thinking of Bree when she was pinning up my hair. I was thinking of her, too. How I would get through this evening without crying was beyond me.

I whispered, "Why did he do it?"

She frowned. "Colin seems to love you, dear. Don't blame him for this. He's a good man."

"No, I wasn't talking about Colin. I meant, Seth. Why did he go back?"

Tears were not stopping, and she handed me a tissue.

"He loves you, too. Now stop this because it'll make your mascara run and they'll think I've tortured you up here."

"How can this be? How could anybody love me enough to risk everything?"

I wanted to cross and now I'd have to find Seth, too. Didn't he know that it would be hard enough for me to go through to find Alex and Tucker? But now, to worry about him? How would I even survive? I understood why the family was worried about my crossing. I was feeling the fear settle myself.

"You're a beautiful girl, Jazzline. But it's more than that with you. You have your own light, and you just don't even know it. It shines sometimes so bright it's hard to look directly at you. All of us can see it. We've talked of your light and know with confidence it's your love of Jesus. I know I see it. Even now when your heart is torn, there is something that all of us MacKenzie's see. Seth and Colin, stronger because they are your soul mates, but we all see it."

She finished twisting my hair in place and I could breathe again.

"I have a light?"

"Every soul is light. God's spirit is a light that shines within us. Those like us, we just know our gifts. They are unique to us, special to us. But we are all born with gifts, natural abilities, talents. Gillivary seems to be questioning a lot about your father lately, and there may be more he knows and he's withholding. Your light is your voice."

"My voice? But that's not true. You know my story. You know I was silent for years. Years until...well... Seth."

"Seth is your soul mate in this time. When you connected, you found your voice. You can use the power that God has given you, to love others, to help others, to save others. Just like I know you will do."

There was a light tap on the door. "He's waiting for you. It's time. Before I leave, I want you to know that I love you like you were my own daughter. And I thank you for trying to save Bree, and now to save my stubborn Seth. My hearts are out there suffering, dying... Just bring them all back. Bring Seth back to me."

I grabbed her hand. "I promise I'll try. I just hope I can."

"Yes, you can and you will. And you will smile, and you will be what Colin needs you to be, for his sake. At least for tonight. If the clans here knew that Seth had disappeared, there would be trouble. Trust me."

"Why does everyone always skirt behind these words of trouble and protection and... What is it that I should know?"

"In due time, you'll know all you need to know." There was a tap again. "We're almost ready. Marry him, Jazzline. Then, cross."

"I know what I have to do, but I want to marry Seth."

"He knows that. I think he understands why you're doing this. He just wanted to get to you first. Who knows what he was thinking? So, let Colin live out his fantasy with you. And let's not keep him waiting, because I know Colin. He'll burst through this door in a minute if I don't open it for him."

She went to the door and swung it wide. His hand was in midair about to knock again and he lunged forward.

He laughed as he fell into Mrs. MacKenzie. "Sorry, sis. Is Jazzline..."

He didn't move. The longer he stood staring at me, the more nervous I became.

I whispered, "Colin?"

I always sounded as if I were asking him a question when I spoke his name.

His voice was strained and his jaw moved again. He was just as nervous as I was.

"Aye, love?"

"Are you ready for this?"

He frowned, disappointment now spread across his perfectly smooth and sculptured cheeks. "I'm not ready, yet. I wanted a minute wi' ye. Tae do this." He whispered to Mrs. MacKenzie, and she left the two of us alone.

I whispered, "Why do I have feelings for you? How can I with Seth in my time, and I haven't met you yet, not really."

He traced my cheek with his finger. "It's stronger now because he's gone. I don't have a competin' force tae drift ye from me. Ye are mine alone."

I closed my eyes to imagine myself at Chica's, waiting on eager customers. Not standing here, in this overly warm room in a plaid engagement dress.

When I opened my eyes to him, he was not there anymore. But kneeling down in front of me and I felt my body sway off balance.

Colin's smile spread across his face and lit his eyes like a sapphire dancing in candlelight. "Ah have loved ye since the moment I laid my eyes on you. Please marry me, Jazzline Chicand. Not 'cause ye have tae, but because ye want tae. Because ye love me. Count this as my proposal to ye."

I remembered my proposal on the beach by Seth. The choice was easy. It only took me seconds to know that the commitment that I was making with him was right. This new situation was the same. Seconds to know the answer. I had already agreed to it anyway. Nothing had changed. Except finding another soul mate and my man jumping through time. But that made this even more urgent.

I reached out and touched his face, then drew back my shaky hand. He caught it and with his kiss on my palm, I said, "I'll marry you."

Then, I felt the ring slide off my finger and my eyes flew open in a panic. My ring. I swore I'd never take it off, and here it was. Gone.

Colin said, "Please honor me by wearing what I have left of my mother. Promise me ye'll wear it."

He took off his necklace, a thin gold chain with an odd symbol dangling on it. He slid my ring from Seth on the chain and fastened it around my neck. His fingers lingered on my neck.

I closed my eyes and the image of Alice Flagg appeared. She wore the ring around her neck until she died. She never had the chance to be with her true love. And even now, she can't let go. Would I be that girl? When Seth said he saw me in the cemetery, which ring was I wearing on my finger?

I could feel him in front of me again, waiting. I opened my eyes to him, then down to the ring he slid on my finger. It was a beautiful ruby stone encrusted by a circle of diamonds. It was dainty and precious and very old.

"It's lovely. It's the most beautiful ring I think I've ever seen."

He stepped in closer. This time I knew that he would kiss me, for real. He whispered against my cheek, "Ye are so bonnie, Sassenach. May I hold ye?"

He was asking permission? Now he would turn out to be the gentleman. Why couldn't he have done it sooner?

"Please, don't. Not now."

"Just one?"

"One."

Colin's lips found mine the second that I'd given in. His arms were around my waist. He pulled me closer to him.

He finally pulled back. "We better stop now or I'm never gonna ask ye tae dance with me tonight.an' we have guests waitin'."

He stepped back and held out his hand to me. I found it so easy to hold his hand, even in this terrible situation.

When we made it to the landing, there were awkward stares, disapproving eyes, whispers caroling up the staircase that I was a Sassenach. I leaned into him and held tighter to his hand.

"And you wanted this?"

He grinned. "Aye, love. They have all just learned th' truth of it. My name wasn't exactly th' one printed on th' invitations."

My Seth. I just took a deep breath and tried my best to walk down the stairs with Colin supporting me so I wouldn't fall flat on my face. The family rushed us. The congratulations came with eyebrows furrowed, speculative glances, but the words were still laced with excitement. This family loved Colin, and they seemed surprised to see him so happy. And he appeared to be because his face radiated with light. He didn't have to fake the night away. I could put on a show for them, imagining myself back in the theater would be a life saver.

As we made our way around the room together, he whispered, "Will ye promise me ye will not leave me alone tonight? Stay by my side?"

"I will never leave your side. But now if I have to go to the bathroom, that's an exception."

He frowned. "No. I will not let ye alone even fur that around this crew. I'll turn my back."

"Stop it!"

He whispered, "We traveled all th' mountains together, Jazzline. Where do ye think ye peed at? Th' privy?"

My eyes widened. "Mountains? Huh?"

More people were coming around us but we got free seconds in to continue an actual conversation.

"Aye, th' mountains. You'll see. I don't want tae spoil it fur ye."

He was the perfect gentleman, and he was good to his word. He never left my side. Throughout dinner, he talked enough for the both of us. No one was interested in me than the story that Colin could weave about finding me again. They had brought his family up to speed on the situation. They believed it all, as outrageous as it seemed. But then again, this was the life that they rolled in.

After dinner, I found myself amid another dance. This time, it was harder to keep his promise to me with all of the twirling and switching partners. At the next song change, he stole me away and stepped out into the courtyard. The chill of the evening, mixed with the heat of my skin from being beside him all night was refreshing.

I giggled, and he smiled.

"What? What is it? What's funny?"

He still held me in his arms and twirled me around to the music. No one would bother us for the rest of the evening. I knew that it would be an all-nighter for the MacKenzie clan, and the party wasn't about us anymore. It was who could arm wrestle and be the champion.

"I was just wondering if I could take a case of Mountain Dew's with me to 1745?"

He laughed. "No, baby. Just ye, I'm afraid."

His words were no longer foreign to me. They were clear, yet thick like honey. We were dancing slower, swaying and he would swirl me every so often to make me feel even more lightheaded, even though they were playing a fast one through the doors.

"I'm afraid."

He brought me in closer to him and wrapped his arms around me. "Of what?"

I whispered against his shoulder. "Of you. Of crossing. A lot of things. What if you don't find me, and I'm lost with everyone speaking Gaelic?"

Colin's eyes glistened. "Don't ever be afraid of me, Jazzline."

"Seth is out there, and I'm here dancing with you. He's searching for me, for them, and I feel this way...this...with you. It's not right."

"It's how it is. An' Ah love how it is right now. May I hold ye?"

His eyes were already closed as if he were expecting a yes.

"Why do you keep asking me that? Why are you doing this to me?"

He opened his eyes at the last second, right as I was leaning in. "I don't want tae hurt ye."

"Hurt me? Don't you know how hurt I am right now? He's gone and I can't follow him until I...until we...hurt me? I'm beyond hurt? I'm numb. So, go ahead. Do your best. Kiss me. I'm already feeling like I'm falling in love with you, what else harm could it do?"

My voice was heavy, thick with pain and remorse, hate and love, fear and frustration. They came in pairs, bouncing off of one another as if they were playing it out on a pinball machine.

"Ye said ye loved me."

I wouldn't answer.

He grabbed my hand and started to walk down the path. "Say it again, love."

"Wh...wh...where are you taking me?"

He grinned as he found another entrance away from the family. "Tae somewhere we can speak plainly. Somewhere ye can breathe."

We were standing in front of my room before I could protest. He opened the door but stayed in the doorway, one hand braced against the frame as if he had to hold himself there.

"I won't cross this line unless ye ask me to," he said softly. "I only want ye to know the truth."

I shuddered. The truth. That was all I needed. "Tell me, honestly, Colin. Is there another way to cross without...without compromising the situation?"

"Let me tell ye the truth. Technically, I was yer first love."

My voice found the lyrics to *Endless Love* by Lionel Richie, and the music flowed out of me just as easy as before. Before Seth left. Before the accident.

He whispered back the next line in the verse, not singing, but his voice touching my heart so it was as if it were in perfect melody with mine.

"You know my music?"

He chuckled against my neck. "Aye, love. I was around in th' 80s, ye remember. I memorized every line. Your music was th' closest 'at I could get myself tae ye. Until now."

Then it hit me full force. "But you've been with this family. Does that mean you knew all along about me and Seth? And he was always so fond of you, loved you like a big brother. He talked so much of his favorite uncle, and to know that you held me inside all that time? Were you using him to get closer to me?"

"Nae, love, I wanted tae be there fur Seth tae teach him th' right way tae live, th' best way tae focus his light fur good so 'at when he did fin' ye he would be deservin' of ye. Everybody has a choice wi' their light. Seth's light is different. When death attaches, it can brin' th' darkness. I couldn't let 'at part of him take over. So, I became a mentor tae him tae make sure he was worthy ay ye. Seems like I did my job since he's risked his life tae save ye. I've taught him th' true nature of love like Christ loved the church."

Guilt washed over me again. Then, recognition of our impossible situation flooded my brain, making my body shiver with it.

"You can't love me, Colin."

He brushed his knuckles across the length of my arm. "Ye should have convinced me ay 'at a long time ago. It's tae late now."

"You could never really have me. I can't run with you forever and would grow old without you. Your soul mate is not me. It's Sarah."

It was hard to speak her name. I felt like I was betraying her. A woman that he'd never met. Her soft eyes, her long dark hair swinging down her back. I remembered the way he looked at her. The way he was looking at me now. Always wanting more.

He stepped closer. "Who is Sarah? Please, Jazzline. Ye are just tryin' tae talk yerself out of wantin' me."

I stepped back again as her image clouded my brain. His two boys were running after girls in the park. If they were going to be anything like their father, I pitied the poor girls that found them. They would not have a chance of survival. But maybe I did. Maybe I could find a way to survive this. My heart was drumming against my chest just at being so close to him and every inch of me wanted to close the gap but I focused on Sarah's face instead of Colin's.

"I won't live forever. What are you going to do? Wheel me around when I'm eighty, checking me into a nursing home? Playing the part of a doting grandson instead of a husband? Have you thought this through, Colin, really? Not just going with your emotions, but listening to reason."

"I don't care about any of 'at. I will love ye when I have ye, young or old. I will love ye when ye are gone."

His eyes betrayed his words. He knew I spoke the truth.

"You were supposed to find Sarah before Aunt Shea lost her light, because she was the one that found you a match that would live forever with you. She's just like you. You have twin boys. Handsome little ones, too. I met them. I met you. You came to the Highland Games with your family. You were so happy. Colin, please believe me. You find your soul mate and it's not me."

His eyes narrowed and I knew he didn't believe me. These people were insane. They could divulge all kinds of outlandish and bizarre secrets to me, but when I tried to throw in something I knew, it was like I had three heads or something.

He stepped into me again. We seemed to be dancing now more than we were down at the Ceilidh, which was still going on based on all of the loud noise that was below us.

"I know what ye are doing. Ye are scared tae kiss me. Ye are trying tae fill my brain wi' all sorts of nonsense. Toyin' wi' my emotions by throwin' in th' word family and children because ye know 'at is all I've ever wanted in my life. My own family. One wit' ye."

"I'm trying to tell you the truth. I'm not lying to you. I promise you I'm not saying this to hurt you, but you are right about one thing. I'm very scared to kiss you."

He leaned in closer still, his face near mine, his voice low and tender. "Didn't I tell ye tae never be afraid of me?"

I was breathless and confused and my voice was a wreck. "Please, Colin. Please, I'm sorry. I can't."

His head fell back against the wood. "What? Ye already told me ye loved me. Ye can't take words back like 'at. It doesn't work."

"Can you teach me to cross?"

His face was flushed, and his eyes were like a fog. I could never forget as long as I lived the way that he looked at me. It was like no other. Not even Seth.

"Don't ye know already?"

"I don't think Bree is unstable. She's too strong for her own good. If Seth is back in time now, I'm still in here with you so I think something must have went wrong. Do you still love me?"

"With all my heart, love."

"Then, he would've pulled me out by now, right? He's walking around bridges or moors? What? To hunt for me, and we're still here with you knowing me. His plan didn't work."

"I'm afraid not. But I would've done th' same thing if I was him. He wants first claim tae ye. He doesn't want me tae fin' ye th' way 'at I do. He wants tae be th' one waitin' fur ye when ye cross." He leaned back again and stared at the ceiling.

"But you still are here. Nothing has changed. So, I must still find you."

My stomach hurled an old sensation through me, and I knew that I would be sick. I ran to the bathroom and closed the door just in time. When I had the strength to walk out and face him again to tell him that something just wasn't right about this. I was still with Colin. Colin still loved me. But how many hours had Seth gone? Enough to find me and make it change back.

This was my chance. I opened the closet door, remembering what Seth had told me about the rooms at the castle being like the one in Bree's bedroom. Sure enough, behind the racks of clothes held the secret passageway. I slipped through it and found my way through the door to door, room to room, stumbling through in the dark. I knew that if I kept moving, I would find my way out sometime or another. And I was right and found a staircase that led to the courtyard. I bolted across the stones that led down to the cottage at the edge of the property.

The cottage held a very special young lady who could help me. I felt like a thief sneaking around the windows peering in. I still heard the words of Seth, the threatening tone that let me know to stay away from Bree. If he were here with me, then I would've listened. But he was gone and I had no other choice. Well, I did. But I couldn't live with myself if I did that choice back there at the castle. I prayed for Colin to forgive me. Please God, take care of Colin. I felt my fingers tremble when I placed my hand on the doorknob. I whispered, "Please, God. Take care of me." And I crept into the very silent room.

# CHAPTER 13

# I Just Died in Your Arms Tonight

There was an emptiness here now that was not before. This had Seth's hands all over it. He would know I would come and see her, and he hid her from me. I heard the words of Mr. MacKenzie. He'd promised Seth that he would take care of me. They had hidden Bree away. And Seth was pushing me to do the other choice back at the castle. Why would he have done that?

I ran through the rooms switching lights on and off as fast as I could to remain inconspicuous from a pair of two blue eyes that I was sure were looking for me now. I found Bree's room and began searching for something, anything. I found a jacket, that would help for starters because I was freezing. A red Bible was sitting by the bed and I saw a slip of paper sticking out of the end. I knew she had left me a note.

There, scribbled on angel stationery was an address. I tucked it into the jacket pocket and flew out of the house. I had to find Bree.

The crazy thing about this whole night was that I had no money or cell phone. I lost them both in the inlet when I tried to jump the first time. I would somehow convince Colin to take me to the address. He would do what I asked.

I ran back to the castle. I saw two cars beginning to pull out down the bridge.

I yelled, "Wait!"

Someone else heard. It was Seth's cousin, Douglas. I remembered him standing next to Tucker talking football, or soccer.

"What are you doing out here in the cold? I think Colin is looking for you."

I smiled. "I know. I've already seen him."

I'd seen him too much this evening, so much so that even if I closed my eyes, he was there with me. "I've got to go here. To take something to Bree."

I handed him the slip of paper with the address on it. He frowned at me, his handsome dark features questioning me but he just shrugged and began walking towards the line of cars.

Thank God for blocker pins and acting lessons under Mrs. Dot's care. I could do this. I tried to remember his gift but he was one of the few that didn't reveal it to me that night in the circle. I would buy me a book of baby names before traveling to Scotland again. I slid into his little red two-seater BMW convertible. Just big enough for two little devils to go skirting off into the night.

I frowned at myself and was ashamed. No judgments. Just drive. He didn't talk to me on the way there, wherever there was, and that made me more uncomfortable. He just stared ahead. When we arrived at the town it shocked me to see we were right where I was before, driving down the quiet street where Colin lived. If they were trying to hide Bree, they should have tried a little bit harder.

He didn't cut off the engine so that gave me the impression that he wasn't coming in. "Tell Colin hello for me. I'll see him another time."

It worked. I was far from Eilean and the other Colin. The dangerous one. The one that would steal everything away from me and give me everything in return.

"I won't forget this Douglas. Thank you so much for the ride."

"I won't forget either, lass. Trust me on that."

And then he left speeding and swerving around the corner.

I stared up at the brick duplex that concealed all of the madness of a MacKenzie who was obsessed with research and computers. I rang the doorbell and squared my shoulders.

"Who is it?"

"It's me. It's Jazzline. Please, Colin. Let me in."

He swung open the door and frowned at me. He was wearing plaid pajama bottoms and a white t-shirt. His hair was all disheveled and he looked like I woke him from a bad dream.

"What are you doing here?"

"I need to see Bree."

I was sure now that if he was hiding Bree his father would have given him strict orders to keep her away from me. Lovely. Why didn't I think of that before and sneak in through the backdoor, or break a window? It wouldn't be breaking an entering at a future brother-inlaw's house, would it? Probably.

He answered as expected. "Bree is not here."

Short. Sweet. That meant he was hiding something.

"Well, I'm freezing to death out here. Could you please let me in for few minutes before I have to go back?" Back in time, not to the castle. Uncle Colin would not be pleased with me if I had to go back there.

He sighed and opened the door further. Seth and Colin would probably both want to kill him for just letting me in. I'd be one step closer to Bree.

"Can I get you anything?"

Papers were still scattered, but more than before. He was a busy little boy.

I could be short, too. "Bree."

He sat down in his chair. "I told you, Bree's not here."

"Well, then. How about a bathroom?"

I would take my chances at spying. Colin wouldn't be here to be in the same room with me to pee. But as soon as the thought entered my brain, I heard a hard knocking on the door, a constant banging that let me know who was on the other side of it.

Colin glowered at me. "You're in it now, Jazzline."

As he moved through the house to go to answer the door, I looked in the rooms. There was no sign of Bree. Well then, why did she send me here? This was crazy. I felt like I was on some juvenile scavenger hunt that I'd played once at a pirate birthday party. At least the bathroom door had a lock. I remembered what Mrs. MacKenzie said about Colin breaking through the bedroom door. He could tear this one down.

The walls were paper thin. I heard his voice as clear as if he were standing in front of me. But I'd never heard him use such vivid language before. My feet came up at least two inches off the floor when I heard the first pounding of the door.

"I'm so sorry."

"It's okay, Jazzline. Just open th' door."

"No."

I held on to the side of the sink and wanted to just stick my head inside and turn on the water to let it run over me. Maybe it would wake me up from this nightmare.

"Jazzline, open th' door now."

"Give me a minute."

When I opened the door, he was waiting. "Ye are eager tae go tonight? Ye would fake sickness an' 'en run off?"

"I did get sick. I figured this would be my only chance to come and find Bree. See what good it did me?"

"Do ye know what 'at was like fur me back there. Tae go back tae brin' ye drink tae fin' ye gone. Tae see 'at red car fly off in th' night wi' ye inside it. Ah swear, Jazzline. Ye don't know th' trouble ye step into. Never ask anything of Douglas, ye hear me?"

But when I looked up to tell him that he was the most trouble I'd ever stepped into in my life, I stopped. Tears framed his eyes. and my words caught.

"How am I going to be able tae keep ye safe if I don't know where ye are?"

"Who's going to keep me safe from you?"

He laughed, the tension and stress leaving his body. "Aye, love. Good point. Nobody."

Colin said, "I hate to break this up, but we need to discuss something very important. Funny that you should come tonight, Jazzline. I found out a piece of information that you need to know for my brother's safety."

"What do you know about Seth?"

He pulled out a piece of paper that he'd printed off the internet. The website had been one that showed ancestry information. He could start his own, this guy, with all of his manila folders. I saw a high-lighted name, and it was one I loved.

My fingers danced across the musical sounding name of Alexander Dumas Chicand MacKenzie. Beside his name was written three words: Scottish trader and writer. He grew old. He didn't die.

But then, there was another, and my dancing heart stop. My heart stopped. Seth MacKenzie, deceased 1745.

Colin said, "But if Seth dies in 1745, he doesn't find Jazzline in the future. So, how do Alex and Tucker still flip back in time?"

It wasn't hard to figure out. "Even without me in the picture, Tucker and Bree are soulmates. This would have happened without me and Seth. Tucker and Alex would have been traveling to see Bree after the play. They would have crashed anyway."

Colin said, "But why would Seth die? Why would he travel back if not to find you?"

"To find Tucker for Bree. He would do anything for his family. You know this."

"Aye, I'd believe it, tae know Seth's character is to know he would sacrifice it all fur th' ones he loves."

A painful cry escaped my lips. "Bree, if you can hear me. I have faith in you, Bree. I have hope. Oh, Jesus take me to Seth right now. Jesus, take me to 1745 before it's too late!"

The paper crumbled in my hand and Colin touched me. I hit the floor with a crack of my knees and everything went black. HIS VOICE POURED OUT over my soul, washing me with warmth and peaceful-ness. I knew that I hadn't fainted. It wasn't that kind of feeling. It was just close your eyes and wake up in a dream feeling. Like when Bree called to me before on Seth's cell phone. Yet, I knew that I was in a dream when my eyes fluttered open to see the face of an angel.

"Seth, you're alive? You were here the whole time?"

I felt the laughter rise in me and flow like a maniac. What foolish trick was being played on me now?

He stared down at me. His face was ashen, and the pain was so raw on him. He seemed unsure of himself, of me, but I felt his arms come around me and smother me against his chest. My heart was home. Seth held me, and he wasn't mad.

My eyes adjusted to the dark. It was a dark place. He seemed as if he could not find his voice and bent down and kissed my lips. I sighed and flung my arms around his neck, holding him closer than I ever had before.

"Where are we? What happened?"

"I don't know how I'm going to get us out of this. Oh, Jazzline. What have I done?"

"What is it, Seth? Where are we anyway? I was at your brother's one second and now I'm in this place? What is this?"

"Bree did this. I was stupid, desperate. I knew that she was unstable but I felt like I had no choice. And now, you are here, too? Oh God, I don't know how we will survive it?"

He stopped speaking but his lips were still moving and I was sure that he was praying.

"You're scaring me, Seth. Please tell me what's going on, and why is it so dank in here? What's that noise?"

Rats scurried as if on command from under the bench, and my legs shot up. They were huge and sniffing, scampering through straw scattered on the stone floor.

I heard movement through the walls of the room and the door jingled open with the sound of heavy iron keys hitting the doorknob. Where were we? Why were we locked up? Was this Bree's joke? I would get her for this, and I started to giggle.

He hissed at me, his eyes narrowing as he ground his teeth. "Don't you dare say a word. No matter what happens. Don't open your mouth, swear it."

I nodded.

"Get behind me now."

I balled myself up behind him. He was large enough to hide my small frame, but I had to peek.

He was a large man, taking up the expanse of the doorway. His head was close to hitting the top of the frame, and he hunched over holding a tray in one hand and a lantern in the other. By the way he swung it, I could tell he was drunk. Working at the restaurant had given me the rare opportunity to see college guys on Spring Break that had been out on the Marshwalk bar too late stopping in by Chica's to see if they could find a Latin nightclub only to find a fancy dining room and a phone call to the cops. This guy was like that. Seth could just push him over if he wanted to.

The man slurred, "Here's yer scraps, ye trash dog."

The tray hit the floor and some bones and a piece of bread skidded close to Seth's feet. From my vantage point, I could only see the legs of the man now, and I cowered further into a ball praying that he wouldn't see me. Seth's body was still as stone, his shoulders held wide with his legs drawn in. He was still wearing his blue jeans and his dark green sweater, with his brown loafers. The same outfit as our court date so that placed him crossing as soon as the verdict was in. The man was in full Scottish dress. I knew that from the socks, hairy legs, and the way the hem of his kilt swayed as he turned from us and banged the door closed, locking it back.

Seth pulled me back in his arms. He kissed my eyes first, then my nose, then my cheeks, holding me as if he could keep the whole world from taking me away. I shivered underneath him and I wanted to ask him what was going on but it all started to make sense to me the more I grew accustomed to the dark. He found my lips and the kiss was urgent and painful.

"I can't believe this is happening. If I get back to Bree, I will kill her."

It wasn't when it was but if he got back.

"Bree? Where is she? She left me a note. An address. But when I went there, Colin said she was gone."

He sighed, rubbing his hands across my face, and in my hair. The touches that he gave me were rough and different. Almost like he knew he would be touching me for the last time.

"She must have been there for you to be here. I should have sent her farther away, to one of our homes on the islands. Not where you could get to her. But my father said he needed Bree closer to them just in case. God, this is impossible."

"So, we figure a way out. It can't be impossible."

"I wish I had the power to send you back but it looks like you were meant to be here, anyway."

"And how did we end up here in this place, exactly?"

"Bree had to be thinking about the consequences of what she would do for me, of our father's reaction to her controlling this. I went to her begging her to send me back before you could cross. Before you found a way. That way I could go back and get Tucker and Alex. Or find you first so my uncle could have no claim to you in this time or the next. After the judgment was made and I lost you..."

"But I didn't marry him."

"Aye, God. Thank you. If you would've married him, I don't know what I'd have done, and I found you first. So, I'm not too late. Well, in one sense, anyway."

"You were never too late. Seth, I wanted to talk to you. To explain why I agreed to marry Colin."

"Let's not talk about that anymore, please. You don't have to explain yourself to me."

"Yes, I do. And I will. I was only agreeing to it to save your life. I understand about the light. You already know the reasons I had to cross. But when Colin showed me what he found... When, Seth? When are you going to die?"

He kissed me on my cheek and whispered, "Tomorrow morning, love. By hanging. It's been decided."

# CHAPTER 14

# At This Moment

"In the morning?"

"I was praying to God to let me hold you one more time. To save me from this death sentence. And then, you were just here, and I can't believe it. I see you. I feel you. Jazzline, I prayed for you."

"And even though I didn't see Bree, I screamed for her to send me back. I had faith that she could take me back to find all of you."

I didn't know what my fate would hold in the morning, at least I could be with him. If I had to die this way, let it be with him by my side. Alex survived somehow. Not sure about Tucker, but if Alex lived anyway, that gave a chance for Tucker to do the same.

"But now, for you to be here and I'm about to be hanged?"

"How can we stop this?"

"I told you not to go to Bree because of her instability but I could not take my warning. I knew that she could control the crossing. She brought you to Scotland just because she knew she could convince you to go after Tucker and Alex, and you would do it. And when she saw how I was...well, after the judgment, she only needed a date. I gave her the date, begged her to do it and didn't care what the price would be, even if I lost my life in the cross. You had him, and I had to come back before it was too late for us all."

I cried. "Why didn't you tell me you would come back? They'd told me you went hunting, for crying out loud!"

"Well, that was partly true. I came to hunt for you. I thought if I could somehow find Tucker and Alex first when you'd cross, we'd be having a little party together. I hadn't considered how to get us back. I just needed to get here before you. Apparently, I keep getting what I pray for. Wonder why?"

"Did you find them?"

"Bree! That crazy girl! She was screaming at me about what Monroe would think about all of this. She has a bad habit of calling our father Monroe when we're alone. I swear, if she ever does it again, I'll throttle her."

"Why would it matter that she called out your father's name?"

I was getting good at following this family, but this one got me.

"It mattered as far as location goes. She sent me to Monroe lands."

"Well, good then. Your father's people will understand, I'm sure. You can tell them all about this, us, and our situation. You couldn't have landed in a better spot."

"What about being hanged did you not understand? Not Monroe MacKenzie lands. Munroe clan lands, rival power clan, past enemy, feuding, fighting, wars... Picture the highland festival for real, multiplied by a thousand. Munroe vs. MacKenzie. Does that paint a vivid enough picture for you?"

I felt anxiety take over my body. My breathing was shallow, and I felt light-headed just at the image it provoked.

"God, Seth. What are we going to do?"

"You'll do nothing. Somehow, I have to figure out a way to get you out of here unscathed. I swear I don't know how to do it. There is nothing in this room except this."

He flung the bread against the wall. It bounced right off.

I covered my mouth with my hand and bit my lip. "I'm sorry I'm laughing. I was just imagining you throwing a biscuit and knocking out that drunk guard."

"So, you're saying I missed my moment when I had the chance? My last night, and I got to spend it with you. A prayer answered."

I heard Celine Dion sing The Prayer in my head and couldn't help myself, even in the death cell. He sang with me, and there was such a feeling of overwhelming calmness that spoke to my very soul when his voice joined mine, and if I could just close my eyes, I could put us away from this madness on a stage somewhere. Living out my dreams. Not living in this nightmare in the middle of a dirty, prison cell.

He held me tighter against him. "How ironic is it that about this time last year I sang with Bree at our church? It was at the Christmas play."

"Christmas? I know where we are, but when are we?"

"Merry Christmas, baby. I just wished that we were in different circumstances."

His voice was wistful as if he were picturing us by the fire at our home. We would have been married by Christmas.

"Christmas? I don't understand?"

It was August. I was still seventeen. Now, crossing I'd crossed over into adulthood, centuries, and seasons.

"We're lucky that we landed in 1745. I took it as a sign that we were not too late to find Tucker and Alex because they...you know...on January 17, 1746." He couldn't say the word die.

"But they don't die. Well, Alex doesn't. I'm sure of it. Something changed when you crossed. Your brother, Colin, he saw where you died in 1745, but he found Alex's name on your family genealogy chart as being a Scottish fur trader and writer. Alex lives. There was no trace of Tucker's name anywhere so I took that as a sign that he somehow went back. Maybe Bree's love brought him back."

"If it would have been that easy, Bree would just bring us all back now. I wished we knew how all of our powers work?"

Without warning, the door creaked open, and I had no time to hide or react, only stare into the eyes of the man I loved one last time. My back was to the person in the doorway and I felt myself hunching my shoulders in some pitiful excuse to shrink my neck from him as if he would hang me up right there in the dark. This was the end? It was already morning? There were no windows in the room. I could see no sun streaming in to give me a clue as to the time.

Seth whispered, "Whatever you do, don't speak."

I heard the voice before I saw the face. "Are ye ready tae go now? Are ye ready tae witness a hangin'?"

My heart jumped, and my hope was alive. I sprang to my feet and crossed the space between us and gasped. "Oh, Colin. You found us. You came. Oh, thank God. Colin."

The hood fell down and his face was just as beautiful in this time as it was in the next. He was inches from me.

He frowned and whispered, "Do I know ye, Sassenach?"

Seth wobbled towards us and winced in pain. By the sound of his discomfort, I knew he was hurt. He hadn't mentioned it or moved from the spot on the floor until now.

He growled, "I told you not to speak."

"They told me a MacKenzie was in the middle of the devil's den, and I'm here tae come an' save a MacKenzie. I hear no MacKenzie in this room. I hear Sassenach. I'll kill ye before ye are hanged and save them the trouble."

That was why Seth didn't want me to speak. I didn't have this accent, this vocabulary. Anyone would assume I was the enemy. I knew nothing about Scottish history but how Colin was now using the word Sassenach at me, I was sure that it was an insult.

I remembered what he'd spoken to me about when we met. That he had doubted that love existed until he touched me. The same way I'd felt before Seth touched me. Now, both of my men were in the dark with me. I was staring at my past, but he felt very present to me again. My blood was racing and out of control. The touch that brought me to Seth in that dark prop room was just a spark compared to the flame that erupted when my hand touched Colin's. I was expecting it. Seth cursed behind me. He'd known what I'd done but I had no choice, yet again, but to make Colin understand that he'd found the right MacKenzie, the right girl.

Seth spoke to him in Gaelic. Colin nodded. Whatever Seth said convinced him to help us.

"Well, come on. An' ye better not speak. Don't say a word."

He threw a cloak at Seth and he slipped it over his clothes, "Are ye a MacKenzie, tae? I wouldn't want tae be helpin' an enemy."

Colin's eyebrows shot up at something Seth had said back to him in Gaelic, and he grinned. "So, I'm yer uncle, huh? An' ye are from th' future? Okay, this will get mighty interestin'. I know I have tae save ye now just tae hear the tale."

Colin took my hand in his, and I saw the look cross his face. He was still confused, shocked, off balance, but he pulled me through the dark corridors with no light to guide him. He knew the place and it was too easy because in just minutes we were free of the room, the stronghold, and lying in a field that apparently had livestock in it by the smell of what was on my shoe and hem of my dress.

Colin whispered to Seth, "Are ye hurt tae badly tae run?"

"I can't run. Take her. I'll catch up." He whispered only for me to hear, "I'll lose you to him, Jazzline. Even now. Even when I found you first."

"I won't leave you. What's wrong with your leg?"

"It's broken, I think." His voice rose, "We have to get out of here."

"I didn't expect tae fin' ye hurt. An' I didn't expect tae fin' her."

Seth's eyes revealed the pain of this impossible situation. "Neither did I. I can manage. Let's go."

Colin began to crawl through the tall grass like a Navy Seal and I looked to Seth. He nodded for me to move after Colin. He was already way ahead of us, and I wondered if in all of his years alive what was his existence like? Was he ever in the military? His movements tonight, his precision, his tone, it all rang like a soldier. We never talked about his past. The time that we did spend together was filled with him kissing me or us fighting over it. Nothing more.

As soon as we made it out of the clearing, Colin stood amidst the trees and leaned up against one, waiting for me and Seth to follow him. I watched the emotions play out on his perfect features, and he shook his head as if to knock him from a daze.

I whispered, "Can you carry him?"

He chuckled. "Can ye not see th' difference in our size? He could probably carry me even wi' a broken leg."

He was right. Seth was at least six inches taller than him, not to mention about fifty pounds heavier with muscle and thickness.

Seth groaned. "I'll carry both of you if you don't stop talking and come on. It's as if you've forgotten I had a scheduled appointment when the sun rises."

He pointed to the moon as if it were about to disappear at any moment. I wasn't sure of the time but I felt the urgency.

Colin held his hand out to me again, but I could not touch him now. I could not allow this to happen again. I turned to Seth and forced his arm to come around my shoulders. He relented. When Colin saw me struggle, he came to Seth's other side and we maneuvered in the forest's darkness with little trouble. Except I had no clue where we were traveling to and I could see that Colin and Seth had no plans on stopping to discuss any of that with me. We just kept moving west through the forest until we came to a small overgrown clearing.

Colin said, "She's cold. We need tae stop, I guess. We need tae make a fire."

I stammered, "I... I... I... I'm not cold."

It was difficult to imagine this kind of cold. I'd never experienced it in my life, even in the dead of winter because by the beach it was still mild. Colin led Seth to a fallen tree and he leaned against it and sighed. Then, he was gone. Seth pulled me close to him and put his massive arms around me like a quilt and rubbed his hands up and down my arms. If he would have just kissed me, then I would have warmed.

I frowned, my teeth chattering like a wind-up toy. "Why didn't you tell me you were hurt?"

"I didn't think that it would matter anyway. The pain was soon to be gone."

"Don't talk about it like that. What do you see? Do you still die tomorrow or this morning?"

"I see nothing right now other than you're here with me and Colin. We'll just have to wait and see."

Colin was back, stacking the limbs he'd gathered and started a fire in seconds. Seth pushed me forward. "Go ahead."

"I'm staying right here."

I forced his hands to go back around my waist again. If this wasn't a signal to Colin to let him know that I was claimed, I wouldn't know what would convince him.

Colin frowned at us. Maybe 18th-century women didn't fling themselves on men in the forest, but I didn't care about all of that.

He said, "How did ye go an' hurt yer leg?"

"Those Munroe's have it down on the torture bit."

"What is this talk about th' future an' ye my nephew? I want some answers. An' I would prefer them before we got back tae th' family."

The MacKenzie family. What would this set of couples be like? Lord, help us all.

Seth looked down to me. Fear and sadness crossed his features.

"Maybe you should try to explain this to him? Your words will be the one that touches his soul anyway."

He looked away then, and Colin's eyes narrowed. I faced Colin, and I couldn't help but stare at how the flames highlighted his hard jaw, his perfect lips red and waiting, his eyes were gleaming with sparks in them. The light was there, and I could see it glowing against the fire. He was magnetic, and I felt Seth shifting his leg then wince, bringing me back.

My voice was not as strong as I wished it to be. "I'm Jazzline, and this is Seth, your nephew from our time. He's my fiancé', a man with gifts. I know what your gift is. I know about MacKenzie's."

His eyebrows raised. I was sure an English girl knowing his family secrets didn't quite appeal to him. "Tell me what ye know, Sassenach."

"You never grow old. You feel no physical pain and heal miraculously. And you never die. You are a youngling."

He threw another log on the fire and the flame erupted, sending ashes in the air. I couldn't help watch them as they fell around him. He was on fire.

"An' ye know this how?"

I whispered, "Because you told me."

He twitched his lip as if he were trying to figure out if I were lying. It was obvious he grew to not believe my words, but he felt the touch between us. I could read that on him when it happened.

"What else did I tell ye?"

He was on the verge of crossing that fire himself, I could see it on him. How his fingers were rubbing against his knuckles. The way his jaw moved back and forth, planning, waiting. Even now he could not mask his feelings from me. His expressions were so readable. I could feel it in my soul.

I wanted to say, "You told me that you loved me. You told me that you would help me find Alex and Tucker, that you would do anything for me. You gave me your mother's ring. You asked me to marry you."

With Seth listening, all I could say was, "A lot."

"What am I supposed to be doing with the both of ye?"

"Are you taking us back to Eilean?"

Colin asked, "You mean Eilean Castle?"

"Yes. Is that where I'll find Tucker and Alex?"

"Th' castle was destroyed in..."

Seth did not let him finish. "1719 by Spanish invaders. Jazzline, I really should've given you a history lesson before you decided to cross. It may have been helpful."

Colin began throwing dirt over the fire and I missed the warmth already.

"What are you doing? I need that."

"Sorry. They already know we'll be travelin' west. They may have decided tae go an' ask their guest fur one last request only tae fin' him gone."

"God granted me my last request. It wasn't anything a bloody Munroe could give me."

"Ye came here fur th' others. Tucker an' Alexander said 'at ye would find a way to come. He spoke of ye so often."

I flew to him, my hands landing on his shoulders, shaking him. "Are they alive? Of course, they are. The Battle of Falkirk hasn't happened yet."

Colin said, "Seth, what is she talkin' about? What battle?"

"Jazzline is Alex's sister. She saw their tombstones and the date. January 17, 1746. The date of the Battle of Falkirk. She came to find them."

He frowned. "Well, who did ye come here tae fin'?"

Seth smiled through the pain. "Her."

He laughed. "Ye folk of th' future are some complicated lot. I hope 'at life gets easier, not harder."

I couldn't help but smile at him. "Don't count on it."

Something caught his attention and I saw that he was looking down at my hands. Before I knew what was happening, I felt a sharp object pressing close to my vein in my neck. The one that with just one slice, it would be over. I froze. The pressure of his hands around my waist, the feel of his rock-solid body at my back, it was more painful to me than the feel of the cold knife blade pinching against my skin.

Seth was up and standing before us wide-eyed. He didn't quite expect this and neither did I. His hand came up, raised in front of him.

"What's wrong, Colin? What just happened here?" His voice was on the edge of a whisper, a panic seizing us both as he said, "Please, Colin. Please, let her go."

I cried out but he just squeezed tighter. "Ye tell me right now where ye got my mother's ring or I will slit yer throat right here an' not feel a bit of remorse fur it."

"Tell him, Jazzline. Tell him everything."

I pleaded with him with my eyes to not make me do it.

He begged. "Do it now, Jazzline. He'll kill you."

"You gave it to me, Colin. We were to be married, but I crossed right before... I crossed after our engagement party."

He dropped the knife from my throat and pushed me towards Seth, his face filled with confusion, doubt, and utter disbelief. Tears were flowing now that Seth's arm came around me in his protective way.

"It's a little hard to take in, I know it. But please, believe me, all I want is to find Tucker and Alex and go back. I don't want any part of this or you."

He still did not speak, just stood there looking at me, turning his head as if he was trying to figure out the truth of things. He was trying to connect his feelings with what I told him about us. But I didn't want him to take it too far, like to soul mate level, so I asked him again.

"Please, do you know where my brother is? Just take me to him, and we'll leave."

"Let's go before we're found. And there won't be any time to get away the next time. I fear if they find us, we'll not have a public hanging but our own little private one right here."

Colin turned and walked away. The conversation was over. He had closed himself away. Seth's typical avoidance style, not like him though. Colin had pushed me from the very second that he could get me alone. He froze here, seeming more like Seth to me. I twirled the ring that he gave me and felt guilt wash over me like a flood.

"Where is my ring?"

"Here."

I held up the chain that Colin had given to me.

"Who would have thought that you'd have three rings in a month?"

"Seth, don't."

"Three, aye Sassenach? Ye a wee loose?"

"No, one was a fake ring in a play, thank you very much. One was from Seth, who I love and will marry. And then, well, this one is from you."

"So, I'm not tae be married after all? I've always wanted 'at. I've always wondered what it would feel like tae spend my life wi' somebody again."

He would be alone until he could find Sarah. "Have hope, Colin. You'll meet Sarah and have Devon and Donnel, twin boys. Adorable twin boys who look just like you, but with darker hair like their mother."

Seth glared at me. "Don't tell him things like that. We don't divulge our secrets about future events. You've already slipped up about the battle."

Colin smiled. "Sarah, huh? When will I meet her?"

I could tell his mind was not on war, but on love.

"Colin, don't listen to Jazzline. She's now learning about our gifts and doesn't realize the full price of it."

"I don't have a gift. I can say what I want."

"Ye have a gift, alright. A gift fur steppin' into trouble."

My eyes adjusted to the dark shadows breaking free of the oaks and tangled vines. I counted three, four, now six rough-edged men in full highland dress, coming at us with lightning speed and agility. The colors were not MacKenzie and the fear seized me. Seth shielded me yet again with his massive frame and I found my hands clutching onto his sweater at the shoulders, digging into him.

One man slurred, "Look what we've got here. Nice tae see ye again, Colin."

Colin seethed, throwing an icy glare at the group of men. I saw no fear in him. Anger and hatred, maybe. But no fear. Then, I realized the power of such a gift of his. Immortality. He could face anything and survive. This was a minor situation.

"Aye, Simon. I was hopin' 'at we would meet up under circumstances such as these. We would ask ye tae stay fur a chat but we are on our way." He hesitated, then smiled a beautiful heart skipping smile. "But I dare have tae ask, how is yer mother?"

Was he out of his mind? Apparently so. Because the fury rose in the man he taunted, and he flew over the tangled mass of vines and fallen trees and came barreling into Colin with such force that it slammed him straight back into a massive oak. I heard it crack with the sound of Colin's body being thrown, and I wasn't sure if it was his back or the tree trunk.

The movement happened so fast that it was hard for me to register the fight around me, with shadows of men flying in the air or cowering on the ground. Seth pushed me back, and I stumbled over a fallen branch, knocking the wind right out of me at the force of my hitting the ground. I rolled, trying to take cover.

Even with Seth's leg broken, he was a warrior. He punched at the assailants with such power that with just a few hits their knees were buckling them to the ground to lie in a heap at his feet. The fury in his eyes was hard to see, and I had to turn away from him to find Colin's opposite reaction, amusement at the fight and the strength of Seth's blows. He had gained respect from this timeless man. But Colin deserved his own respect because he had taken a few blows himself, but gave out more.

The day of the Highland Games played out in my mind. Watching the men and Alasdair fighting a rival clan was like a sport to them.

Seth had called it a competition, but I knew better. They were fighting for blood. Here, they were fighting for survival, and I was glad that I was on team MacKenzie. But then, this skirmish in the woods turned from fists, smiles, and respect, to a different channel. The late-night horror channel that I had blocked from my view. A mature video game with graphic violent was now playing in front of me in 4D.

I saw the flash of silver in Colin's hand and in one decisive flick of the wrist, another Munroe fell. But I realized that this time, the man would not get up. It was the man he had called Simon. Dead. I found the sickness rising in my throat and curled my fingers around my neck as if it had been mine that had rolled. Just minutes before, it could have been when he saw his mother's ring on my finger. Now, the man before me was dead. I'd never found myself near a body before. A body seeping blood from the same place that the dagger had pricked my skin. It was eerie, sickening. I heaved on the ground, nothing left but a gagging sound to replace the moans and begging of the men that were still alive.

"Stop!" My hands covered my ears to block out the sounds of their pitiful voices. "Stop it!"

Seth dragged himself to my side, his leg unnaturally sideways, but he was there covering my body with his.

He whispered, "Shhh...shhh...baby, it's okay. It's over."

I could hear a gurgling sound right near me. A sound of blood rushing out of places sure to cause a slow and painful death. My ears couldn't stand the sound of the last breaths of the men and my body shook with the pain and the violence. Images of their families at home, sitting by a fire, waiting for their man to return, children playing at feet, waiting for their daddy to ride them on their back, all gone at the sound of the cutting of flesh.

No matter what would have happened either way, I felt for the ones that we were left behind, knowing full well it could have just as quickly been the three of us.

My eyes searched Seth's face, which was now only an inch from mine. His eyes were cold, hard, and his body like ice. I could sense a vision when they would come on him now.

He said, "They would've killed us, Jazzline. We had no choice. These are different times."

I whispered, "I'm so sorry."

I was sorry that his life had to be this way. This curse. It's a burden too great for any man to bear. How could he find hope in anything? Whatever strength he drew from, I needed it now.

Colin knelt beside us. He pulled Seth's arm and I flinched, curling myself in a ball when I had the break of Seth's body off of me. I was sure that I was next. I

He sighed, frustrated. "What's wrong wi' her?"

"What's wrong with me? Are you serious? Colin, I just witnessed a murder, multiple counts of first-degree murder."

"What I did, 'at was in self-defense, sweetheart. Those bloody Munroe's don't deserve tae live, th' whole lot of them."

"Jazzline, you realize you've stepped into a different time. There are things here, situations that are not for you to understand. Life is not like it is for us here. We must keep moving. That might have only been one band of men out in a search party. There could be more."

I didn't have to be told twice.

"Wait, baby. You're going the wrong way."

Colin laughed as he stepped over the man that he had called Simon, then turned to spit on him. "Take us right back tae them, Sassenach. If 'at is what ye want. I could take them all on."

How could Colin move so easily over bodies, back on his track as if it had never disturbed him? As if it were an innocent walk home, not an escape from a clan about to hang Seth, who would have hung me if they would've found me in the cell.

"Thank you for saving Seth."

"Aye, Uncle. I haven't formally thanked you for saving my neck. Who was that Simon character back there?"

"Aye, he's a tricky one tae be around. Simon means he who has heard. Hears yer thoughts, danger fur us MacKenzie's. He had tae be disposed of before he found out our secrets. Glad I could do it. This has turned out to be my lucky day."

I wanted to ask him did he know Simon's mother, but the jealousy rising in me was absolutely absurd. Mrs. MacKenzie had told me of

Colin's past. How he had many women but never found the one. Now that I was here, what would he do?

And even though I knew it was wrong a song came but I would not sing it aloud, only heard the melody ricocheting between my ears, an oldie by Luther Ingram.

"If loving you is wrong, I don't wanna be right."

# CHAPTER 15

# I Can't Fight This Feeling Anymore

It was morning. The sun was peeking through the break in the snow-capped mountains, and tears threatened to fall. We were out of danger now. No other search parties found us, and we had a quiet night, moving through the forest at a pace that fit Seth's ability to walk.

Seth was beside me and I wanted to wake him, to witness God's sunrise with him. If I blinked, I swore I would miss the rising so I tried my best to hold the sight of the sun coming up for us. It was morning and he was alive. Thank God.

I was always in love with the beach. The sound of the waves crashing against the shore, the moon playing with the water, the feel of it all was like second nature to me, yet new to me every night since I was a young girl, with Tucker at my side, trying to figure out where I fit into God's big universe.

But this, it was something more. It was more than home. It was like Heaven, and I wanted to tell him. His body was still and that meant he wasn't hurting. His hand was warm against mine, but I wanted more warmth. My body craved warmth. The fire that Colin built for us again was not enough for me.

Colin's eyes were never closed. I could feel them on me. I compared the new dawn with the way I felt when he touched me with his eyes, so warm and inviting. Within reach, but so far away.

He sighed. "Come here, lass. Let me keep ye warm."

He held his hand out to me as if he expected me to take it, leave the side of Seth, and fall into his arms.

"I... I... I'm fine." My teeth chattered, exposing my lie. "It's...so...beautiful."

He laughed as I stuttered out that last word. He wasn't looking at the sun, now moving closer to the cloud line.

"Aye, ye are."

My heart broke against his voice and shattered at his feet. "Stop it, please."

He would not. This was Colin. "I love ye, don't I?"

What could I say to him to take it all away? So, he would not know that I was his soul mate and be a lovesick fool for me for eternity? To wait for Sarah?

"Sarah, remember."

"I'm not talkin' about a Sarah. I'm talkin' about ye. Ye an' me. Don't hide it from me. I will get th' truth from ye soon enough."

Seth spoke then, his body still. His eyes still closed. Thank God that the freezing temperatures made it more difficult to respond to Colin, and I hadn't spoken the wrong things.

"Tell him, Jazzline. He will find out the truth. We can't stop it. Don't you see that we need him to know?"

"Why? No more telling about the future, right Seth? Didn't you tell me that? So, I'm done with all of this talking. I can't tell him. It's not fair. I'm trying to be responsible."

They both laughed at me. Two different laughs, both warming over my soul making me forget that cold ever existed.

Seth looked at Colin with a silent signal that he needed time with me alone.

Colin stood up and stretched. "I think 'at I need tae find something proper tae sit yer leg with. Ye will have a limp fur all yer life from 'at crooked mess, I'm afraid."

He went back into the forest. I wanted him close. Not that I didn't trust that Seth could handle himself in a fight. I saw that he was very capable. But I knew full well Colin would live to tell the tale.

"Don't you see you have to tell him. We need him for the future, to claim you, to force me to cross, so we can find Alex and Tucker together. God had this in the plan from the beginning. Who are we to tamper with God's plans for our lives?"

"You would have come for Bree and only her, to bring Tucker back. It wasn't about me at all. We figured that out right before I crossed."

"I don't know about that. When you found me, I knew who you were and remembered everything. We are missing something here. You still have my ring around your neck. Show me."

I pulled the chain from under the bodice of my dress and held up my engagement ring.

"But that's how we must have figured it all to happen."

"Well, you must have been wrong."

"Do you remember Sarah and the boys being Colin's family now? She was his soul mate in another time. How can this be in God's plan when a family just disappears and you or your family have no memory of them but I do? Wouldn't I have forgotten them to or had selective amnesia? How can I remember them? I swear Seth, I'm not lying. Colin's family is out there, or Sarah is somewhere. He'll find her and then it could change again."

He frowned. "Maybe you're right? Maybe not? We don't have Gillivary here to help us in this situation. We only have Colin asking you a question that you can answer. If you don't answer him, he may have ways of making you talk."

"I won't get near him, then."

"I didn't mean that. There may be a Munroe or a Shamus MacKenzie in the family. There may be someone with a gift that we've never encountered."

"I think I can take my chances."

But the thought of being in front of another clan with powers that we would not know of since we didn't know the full extent or the meaning of every name in the universe was unsettling to me. Colin said he had ways of finding out the truth. I believed him.

Seth was insistent. "But I feel that this needs to come from you. You need to face all of this. Release it."

"Release what?"

He turned from me then, his hair covering his face. "What you have for him. I know, Jazzline. I can feel it from you. You're torn between the both of us. Please, talk to him for me. Make your choice, and let's be done with it."

I was trying my best to be careful, but not enough. He saw through my mask. Torn was an understatement. My emotions cast a heavy shadow across my face.

"Can I at least be alone with him?"

"No." His eyes flickered with the light of pain mixed with jealousy.

"Please, Seth. Trust me."

I hated to speak those words to him because I didn't trust myself. But I could not talk to Colin with Seth there watching my every move and emotion flow through me. Better if he wondered at a distance than to see it right there in front of him.

"If I tell him, I need to make him understand that he can't have me."

"Is that what you want? Is that the truth? You really don't want to be with him?"

I would age. He would not. There was never a possibility that it could last between us. He would have to move on, and so would I. I had Seth for me. He would have Sarah.

"The only man that I want to spend the rest of my life with is you."

He sighed, rubbing his hands through his hair and down his face. I wanted to convince him what I felt was true, but I didn't even know myself. My mind hit Stryper's song, Honestly, but I couldn't sing the words to him. Not yet. I didn't know how much my heart could stand. Even though I didn't speak it, the lyrics were slapping me just the same. But could I do this? Would my faith be enough to hold me?

"What is it? What were you singing?"

"How did you know I was singing? I didn't say a word."

He touched my hand and I shivered in the cold. "You didn't have to. Was it for him or me?"

"Don't do this to yourself, Seth. The song was for you, I just didn't have the power to put the words out there. This is too much. You're alive. Alex and Tucker are so close to me now. Let's focus on getting us all back safe before something else goes wrong."

Colin was back. He secured a limb as a brace for Seth's leg.

"Colin, do you mind taking a walk with Jazzline? I think that it's time both of you talked."

He emphasized the word, talked. At the prospect of it all, I couldn't help but feel my heart begin to race out of control.

Colin reached out his hand to me to help me up, but I refused to take it. I could not stand the thought of him touching me in front of Seth. He didn't know what it did to me. He just shrugged, threw down the brace materials beside Seth and walked off through the trees, stomping as he went, cracking limbs and brushing past greenery. He seemed agitated and irate. Wait until he heard what I had to say, if I could even figure out the right words to speak to him.

The rain began to fall on us and I could see the crystals glistening like glass in a kaleidoscope. I sang as I followed behind him, Here Comes the Rain Again, by the Eurythmics.

He did not speak until we broke free a few hundred yards of Seth. Colin put the distance between us, and it scared me. The more distance from Seth, the more of a pull I felt towards Colin. I felt that in each step that I took. When he turned to me with those eyes, I was aware of every sensation rising up in my body, and it was too much to hold in.

He'd taken me to a setting only conjured up in dreams. A waterfall cascaded against ice and snow, covering the rocks. The snow had left its mark here and the evergreen and white were striking. The smell of the rain was on my tongue and the feel of it sent shivers down the course of my body. He stared at me as if he were trying to pull out the secrets without me having to reveal them to him. He didn't trust me, either. And that was okay. I still didn't trust my heart to be strong enough to withstand this.

He looked around him. I followed his gaze. It was one of the most magical places that God could have created on earth, and it was for me to have to break his heart.

He whispered, "It will snow again soon."

I held out my hand to the rain and watched as the drops landed, one by one, icy then soft. As soon as he spoke it, it appeared. I caught my breath. Snow at Christmas. Another dream.

"How did you do that?"

"I can't control th' weather, Sassenach."

"Oh, I knew that. Sorry."

He was too close to me, and I inched back.

Colin's voice was low and husky again. I prayed to watch out, but he kept talking to me, that voice calling me in. "Why will ye not let me touch ye?"

"Seth."

"I don't care about whoever that Seth MacKenzie is back there. All I seem tae care about right now is findin' out th' truth about ye and me."

"I should have never agreed to this, to be alone with you. I knew that this was inevitable. That you would start this with me and then it would crash against me. I can't do this. I have to go back to Seth."

When I started to turn away, he grabbed me then, pulling me down to him, my knees hitting the earth beside him. One arm came around my back, steadying me, and the other found my hand. I was caught by his stare, by his intensity, and by everything I knew I could not choose.

He whispered, and when he did his breath caught with mine, "I see now. I see what my touchin' ye does tae ye. I feel what it does tae me. Ye love me, Jazzline. I love ye, tae. I love ye like I have ne'er felt before. Like I am reborn. Ye are what they call my soul's light, aren't ye? Tell me the truth. It's happened with ye an' me."

I felt the shifting of his weight and the fingers in my hair now found the base of my neck and his feather touch was stroking me there.

"Stop it, Colin. Please. Seth."

I scurried away from him, wounded and ashamed.

"This has to stop. I love Seth. We can never be."

He put his fingers over his lips as if he were trying to hold on to the feeling of almost kissing me.

"But we are. I am here wi' ye. Seth will step aside."

"You don't know Seth. He won't give up. He is my soul mate from my time. We will be married as soon as, as soon as this is over."

"But it will ne'er be over, will it?"

"It will be once I find Alex and Tucker."

"No, I meant fur me."

"It doesn't have to be this way. There will be a soul mate for you. I promise you that."

"But not yet?"

"I told you about Sarah. It makes no sense to love me anyway so understand that loving me is futile. I have no gifts or ways to stay young with you. Sarah does. I know that. Knowing you'll soon find the one you can live with forever makes it better for me somehow. It should be enough for you."

"There is not another like me."

"There is, I swear it. They're out there, and you find one. That will be what God has planned for you. Not me. I don't understand why He would have given me to you to begin with, unless it's to protect us and lead us all back home."

"I know exactly why God gave ye tae me. He wanted me tae feel what it was like tae die, to sacrifice because yer words cut me more than any natural wound, or blade, or sickness could ever do. All I want is a family to love an' to cherish. Bairns of my own."

"So, wait for them. For Sarah. She'll give you all that you ever wanted. Let this be our goodbye to soul mates. But let us stay friends. You'll one day be my uncle. Can I ask you something?"

"Anything, love."

"Where does your light come from? The gifts?"

"My light can never die out because I don't bleed the same."

He knew more of the MacKenzie's than anyone. The gifts, the potential, the dangers. His mind would be the one that needed probing. Not some internet research.

"Where does the light come from? Why do you have a gift, and I don't? I don't understand how you can exist."

"God gives us all a light. We're all born wi' th' light. My family, well, an a few others, we have th' faith an' th' belief tae bring th' light into a stronger manifestation of th' power of what God has given tae every creature in His universe. We just tap into the light like a faucet. Once we turned it on, it never stopped flowing. An eternal spring."

It couldn't be that simple. "There's something more. I know it."

"I was bestowed th' first gift of the family by an' angel of God. 'At of everlastin' life. I was th' first Gentile tae be converted tae Christianity. God used me an' Peter as a bridge between two worlds."

If only I had Munroe here to pull the truth out of him. To ask him the right questions.

"Peter? You mean, Peter, apostle, rock, denying Jesus three times?"

"Aye, love. Simon Peter. I see you've heard of him. Poor lad could never live down the denying Christ."

"Colin? What are you saying to me?"

It was only a whisper, catching on the snow that was now falling around us like a covering to my soul.

"My birth name was Cornelius. Colin came after th' Roman invasion of Scotland in 71 AD. Some have called me a saint. I wonder, love, what ye think of me? What would ye call me, if you could?"

His voice was soft against my skin and now that his lips were there, I could not stop myself.

"I call you my miracle."

A song flooded my senses. I sang to him, REO Speedwagon, Can't Fight This Feeling.

Colin buried his head against my neck, pulling me closer to him. Tears were falling for this man that I could never have. This man that had more light in him than I could hold.

"I know 'at ye don't see how we can be together now. But I swear, I'll find a way tae love ye. Tae keep ye wi' me."

"Seth has first claim to me. There is nothing you can do."

That was true. When I crossed, I went straight to his arms. He was my connection first, in this time and the next. Thank God that this could not be challenged. I already knew the verdict, and we'd be wasting taxpayer's money and MacKenzie time.

"What do ye mean?"

It baffled me I could tell him something he didn't know. I told him how he challenged his claim to Gilivary, of how Seth left and went to Bree, how he came here, how it all happened in the way we believed it to be.

His face crinkled with a slow smile. "A judge? Our family has a judge? We need one of those now fur a current problem we are facin'.

But, anyway, ye seem tae be forgettin' 'at I don't care about Seth MacKenzie. I will claim ye one way or th' other. I have no doubt."

"Take me to Seth. I have to be with him. To let him know you haven't carried me off somewhere to hide me away."

He caught my hand. "Ye know I could do this thing you say right now. His leg is broken. He is tae far from us. He can't stop me or stop us from lovin' each other."

His voice was edging on madness, desperation. I could see him darting his eyes to the sides as if he were scoping out his perimeter for an escape plan.

"I love you, Colin, Cornelius, whatever your name is. I love you. I can't stop that. But I can face that I can never love you like man and wife, to have a life with you, to be with you. Think of your past, your future. It is not fair to both of us if I give in. So, I will be stubborn on this and just fight you."

I held up my fist at him and tried to make him smile. To break the tension that had seized his body.

He chuckled but let go of me, walking back. "A stubborn Sassenach. I haven't had a challenge in a couple of centuries. I think I'm well-rested fur a fight."

I could not have this timeless beauty. But I could have the man that was made for me. God had blessed me twice. Why did I deserve one true love? Let alone two? Why did I deserve a second chance? I guessed I was living proof we all did.

Seth was waiting right by the tree line, so I was sure that he caught most of what we said. His voice was low, on the edge of anger. I saw the emotions dance across his face and it was severe.

"Well, come on Colin. I'm ready. Step back away from her and fight me."

Colin smiled and stepped back. "I won't fight you, nephew. She has stated her case. I will back down."

But I heard so much behind what he spoke. Now. I will back down for now. I knew Seth was my north, my future. Colin, as strange as it already sounded, was my past, my south. The love felt, consumed, then impossible to hold. It could be a country song. Maybe I should start writing my own song lyrics instead of voicing everyone else's.

"What a predicament we're in, yet again. I can't fight you because I know that I can't hurt you even if I put all my might into it. Jazzline, have you decided?"

His voice was dripping with jealousy and I wished that I could just erase this all, to take away all of the pain. Stick to the plan, find Tucker and Alex, and just go home.

"There was no choice to make. It's always been you, Seth."

Colin answered, "She says 'at even though she is my soul light 'at I have no claim tae her since ye have found her first."

"That is correct. That's why I came back in the first place to claim her. To find her before you."

Colin smiled. "I know why. I see why ye can't live without her. I don't know how ye expect me tae."

I closed my eyes to the sound of his voice and knew I made the right choice. I had Seth. This was enough. It had to be. There could be no other way.

I whispered, "I'm so tired. I just want to go home, please."

Colin frowned as he passed us, heading back towards our camp. "Home. We have no home tae go back tae. If ye didn't realize it, Jazzline, we are in th' middle of a bloody war."

"Where's Alex? Please, Colin. I have to find him. Is it really Christmas? Closer to losing them?"

"Aye, love. It is th' day tae celebrate our dear Savior's birth."

"We only have a few weeks left to find them. Colin, where are they?"

Colin's expression changed for a brief second, then grew soft again. "They're with a unit of MacKenzie militia traveling to Bantaksine or to Perth. Either way on a road away from here."

"My baby is with a militia?"

"We tried tae talk him into stayin' wi' some of th' elders an' th' women, but he refused. He would not separate himself from that crazy lad, Tucker."

"Of course not. Alex would be scared out of his mind."

Colin laughed a deep bellowing laugh that sounded more like a grizzly bear roar. "Scared? Both of them are bampots! They think 'at this is th' best place in th' world, apart from Tucker not havin' his lady, an' Alex not havin' ye. I can account for both of them on this subject 'at they wanted tae fight our war."

"That is what they always said about Medieval Times. I guess I didn't stop to think that they wouldn't want to be found."

"They've traveled back in time before?"

Seth and I laughed. I remembered the night we took Alex as payment for allowing Seth and I to go on a date alone without guilt attached to it. And now, look at us all. Stuck in this place, in the middle of a war. My laughter turned to sadness.

"We've got to find them before they get killed. Seth, can we do this? Have you seen something?"

"Aye, I know something."

"Well, what is it?"

Colin said, "He's mad at himself an' I don't blame him one bit."

But there was a way that Colin had spoken it, the light in his eyes, the smile that was hidden, and like a child he was too excited for his own good.

My patience wore thin. "Seth, what's going on?"

Seth put his hands through his hair and looked down at me. "You'll go alone. You'll find them and bring them back without me."

"But...but...you were right. I can't do this. I can't go off traipsing through some wilderness. Seth, I won't leave you. I can't do this alone."

Colin smiled then, his light radiating from him like the sun melting the snow that had settled at our feet. "Ye will not be alone. You'll be with me, Jazzline. I'm takin' ye tae Alexander an' Tucker. I know exactly where they are."

CHAPTER 16

## At Last

I heard the words in my head, bouncing around like the SpongeBob rubber ball that Alex still loved to carry in his pocket to throw down the Marshwalk and chase like a maniac. I heard them. But it didn't register with me as the words knocked against my ears. I covered them a second to stop the ringing.

It all came down to Colin.

Seth limped with newfound force. I was sure that his anger was fueling him on. "I can't walk through the mountains with my leg like it is. There's no way. I'm sure it's broken."

"Mountains? I can't climb a mountain! I'm from the beach, you know. Seth, are you serious?"

"I'll carry ye, Sassenach. Not ye Seth, but ye Jazzline, if th' terrain becomes tae hard fur ye."

"You'll do no such thing. And stop this talk. Look at what it is doing to Seth. Oh, I forgot. You don't care about Seth MacKenzie. Well, I do. Go get the guys for me alone."

Seth said, "They won't believe him if he goes alone. They'll think he's just trying to protect them and pull them out of the front lines. Those boys seem ready to fight for a country that's not even theirs. I'm proud of that, don't get me wrong. But we know the ending if we let them keep traveling. You have no choice, Jazzline."

Fire blazed in the pit of my stomach. Alone with Colin? Oh, God, help me. Jesus in Heaven, hear my prayer.

"I don't know if I'll be strong enough." It was more than the mountain terrain and the freezing temperatures.

"You'll be able to do this, Jazzline. The mountain passes are used for travel and fighting so they will be clearer than you think."

Colin added, "Before the storms come ragin' in, and the ice makes it impossible. We must go now. They should be near Sterling, about ten miles from Falkirk."

"Seth, where will you be?"

Colin said, "He'll be safe at Brahan."

"The Brahan seer?"

Colin nodded. "Aye, Ye heard ay him?"

"Aye, who hasn't?"

I raised my hand. "Me."

Seth smiled at me and pulled my hair from my cheek, wet with snow. "The Brahan seer was Kenneth MacKenzie, who some say lived from 1530 to 1577 or from 1650 to 1675."

"Both are true. And we know the date now. It's a shame how time can limit people's perceptions of th' world."

I bit my lip, "So, he could cross through time, too?"

"Somethin' like 'at. He had th' power tae see th' future. 'At alone is connected tae time."

Seth's eyes narrowed at that. "I can see death."

Colin didn't seem surprised. "I figured ye saw death by the looks of ye with those Monroe's slain."

"I see other things, images, as well. Dreams. Both of my parents have gifts, so we have a double portion. My sister and I."

"Don't be going around revealin' tay much when ye meet th' family."

"I wasn't planning on it."

I pointed to the castle ahead. "So, you're staying here, while I go off through the mountains?"

"Looks like 'at, love. Don't worry about Seth. Our folk are used to strange occurrences and will take care of him."

Seth said, "I hope better than they did the Brahan Seer."

"Why? What happened to him?"

"One story tells he was burned alive in a barrel of tar."

Colin smirked. "Once he was burned in tar, another he was burned at th' stake. Both leadin' tae a fiery end, no doubt."

I gasped. "Who would do such a thing?"

Seth said, "Jealous women, on both accounts."

"Well, then, Seth, I demand you stay away from any women in that castle. Do you hear me?"

Colin winked. "Whose jealous now?"

Seth cut his eyes and turned his head sharp. "Me."

It was taken over by the sheer force of a battle cry of the MacKenzie's coming out to meet us. They swarmed me and picked Seth up. A brawny man named, John, started to call out for medical attention. He seemed like such a gracious man, with his soft crinkling skin and rosy warmth.

"Welcome home, ye weary travelers."

They literally carried us into the castle walls, my feet never touching the ground. I was floating amidst the beautiful MacKenzie clan. The strawberry-blonde haired women, the darker haired men. I felt like I was swimming around in Neapolitan ice cream. So, instead of Eilean, Alex had been here, at Brahan. My castle was more grandiose than this one, but still, who was I kidding, it was a castle, and it was magnificent. I was in awe of this place. Alex would have loved this family. I knew that.

I already did love them because they took care of him and Tucker for me. They held out hands to me and pulled me one to the next for a round of quick introductions as if we were in a roundabout dance.

They went on to tell me all about what they loved about Alex and Tucker. Alex taught ball to the younger boys who went off with the regiment. The conversation was light at first until the talk turned to war. Sadness flickered across the women's faces. I knew the feeling.

Tucker was quick to learn the moves of a soldier. John seemed most impressed with him. I was sure Tucker wound them all around his finger. Oh, how I had missed them. But I was just thankful to God they were alive. They'd left in late August with the regiment and already defeated the royal troops of King George II at the Battle of Prestonpans. They had received correspondence with a list of the wounded or deceased, and my men were unharmed. Up to that point. Thinking of them showing up on a list was devastating to me, and I felt my feet begin to give way.

Colin was there, his hand moved around my waist. "Fur all I know, she has not eaten in days. I know 'at she has not slept."

He was right. I could not sleep with Seth beside me, and Colin across from the fire. I would never forget as we watched the sunrise, never speaking a word all night, just staring at each other from time to time. He'd whispered to me, "I love ye, don't I?"

Two of the elderly ladies took me from Colin and began gushing over me. They smelled like apples and cinnamon. I leaned my head against one of their shoulders.

"You smell nice."

She roared. "I know ye've not eaten. But don't be thinkin' I'll be th' meal."

I didn't know where they were carrying me and didn't have the will to stop them. I was placed into a scalding hot tub of water steaming, thawing out my senses. I dove lower and lower until I was submerged. It was peaceful there. I could not hear their voices or see their faces. I was not crashing.

Then, I felt a tug on my head, pulling me back up. It was one of the younger ladies. "Ye look like my size. I've got ye a set of warm clothes waitin' by th' fire. Yer food has been brought tae ye, too. Colin said 'at ye would not be up tae celebratin'."

I wondered how this household even had the stamina to celebrate when members of their clan were out to battle.

"Celebrate what?"

A smile lit her face like no other. These people were models, cover girls, and superheroes. The whole bit. God had surely blessed this bunch from this time to the next.

"Don't ye know what day it is? It's Christmas."

"I'd forgotten. Colin told me." Or was it Seth. Oh, both of them had me so confused.

"Well, if ye change yer min' we'll be down in th' Great Hall. I'll be singin' soon. I'd like ye tae come after ye rest up a bit."

"I'll see."

"Best get out now. Th' water is gettin' cold. You'll catch th' death."

She handed me a towel, then disappeared. The sharp pains of loneliness stabbed me. The fire was crackling. I heard what sounded like a trapped cricket, near the corner of the darkened bedroom. This place was lovely, with lavender and cream accents. They painted Wisteria along the walls and I felt as if I were in a garden.

I pulled on the wool dress, burgundy, thick, billowing right down to my toes. It covered all of my skin, rising high to my neck, with soft white buttons down the back and little white cuffs on the sleeves. The border was a dress MacKenzie plaid and it swooped across my waistline and trailed down my side in a perfect wave of material. She'd given me such a beautiful garment to wear and I acted as if I couldn't return the favor of hearing her sing.

I didn't want to leave the fire, slurping down my soup with no spoon. And it wasn't about the cold anymore. I was beyond that. It was the chill that ran down the very core of me, straight down my spine, that revealed the knowledge that tomorrow morning, early, I would set off trekking a mountain with Colin MacKenzie at my side.

There was a light tapping at the door and my heart sighed with it. I knew it was Seth. Colin would've beat the door down before realizing he was so heavy handed. When I flung open the door, my dress swirled at my feet and my eyes caught fire as the striking blue orbs were staring intently at me.

I was wrong. It wasn't my Seth. It was my Colin, looking stunning in full Scottish dress. I blushed with my thoughts and bit my lip. He did something to me every time we were close that was not rational.

"I thought...that...that..."

"Expectin' Seth? No, love. But if he gets tae travel in time wi' ye an' love ye fur all his life I have ne'er wanted tae be anybody else but him."

"Colin, please don't do this anymore. How am I to go with you in the morning? Can we bring someone else with us? A guide? A chaperone?"

Funny how all of this started. Me being a chaperone for Bree and Tucker. Now it was my turn to need one.

"I will not do anythin' tae ye 'at ye will not ask me tae. I swear it."

"That's what I'm afraid of. Where's Seth?"

Bringing Seth into the space between us always made me focus. Mind over body. That would be my new mantra.

"He's gettin' his leg set. Heard 'at could be painful fur somebody 'at felt it."

"Can I go see him?"

"Nae, not like 'at."

"You really feel no pain?"

"Apparently, I do. In th' past couple of days my body has felt no blow, but my heart has taken th' brunt of it. I haven't told ye how bonnie ye are tonight."

I whispered, my voice a shaken reed in the wind, "Talk about something else. Why is it so dark? Have we skipped more time?"

"Weil, it's dark at midday this time of year. We've called it night already an' have begun th' festivities. Would ye please join me?"

He offered me his hand. His presence alone was enough to bring me under again, and with Seth away from me, the feeling was peaceful and so warm. Not tearing or confusing. An uncomplicated love in a complicated situation if I ever did see one.

"Please take me to check on Seth." I bit my lip. To get away from you.

"He's out. He's filled wi' whiskey about now an' wouldn't even know ye existed."

He seemed to like that idea, and the amusement danced on his face.

"I can't be too close to you."

"Do me this honor. He'll be able tae spend every Christmas wi' ye fur all of yer life. Can I at least have a day?"

"Supervised."

"Ye don't trust me, lass?"

"I don't trust my heart when I'm near you."

"Okay, then. Follow me."

And he did not wait for my hand because by now he knew that I didn't have the power to reach out to him, and his strong arm circled around my waist. He brought my hand against his lips. It still held the ring he'd given me. I had to collect myself. No matter what the consequences were or how revealing myself to him might destroy the both of us, I had to let him know just how he made me feel. And since I was sure we were to be supervised in the Great Hall down below, I let go.

I couldn't have held the song within me if I tried. It flowed from me without inhibition, fitting who he was for me, an Eternal Flame.

He pulled me close to him and whispered in my ear, "That was th' best Christmas present I've ever received. An' I have nothin' tae give tae ye. Ye already have my ring. Will it be enough?"

"No."

He put his hands across my cheeks, wiping the tears away. "Don't cry. Tell me what I can give ye, love? Ah would give ye anythin' in my power tae see ye smile again."

"Take me back to my room."

His eyes narrowed at that, and his head cocked to the side. His jaw clenching back and forth. He was searching, hoping.

"Aye, love."

I could not go down there with him, in front of his family, for them to see my adulterous stare at a man that I loved while the other man that I loved lay hurting with a broken leg. He wanted a Christmas with me. He would have to just take me alone. Against all of my better judgment, it had to be this way.

When the door was closed behind us, he went straight to the fire. I leaned against the door, my hands pressing against the wood. When he turned to come towards me, I held out my hand in Seth-fashion.

"No, stay over there."

His voice was soft. "Ye choose to stand there freezing by th' door? At least come over here by th' fire."

I bit my lip and pointed to the other side of the bed, separating himself from me by an object seemed hopeful. "Only if you go over there."

He laughed. I amused him. Glad I could be of some comedic relief.

I couldn't laugh in return. Only stare at him as the fire danced across his perfect face.

"But 'en I'll be freezin'."

Here we go again with the asking and not doing which would lead to doing. "Then, I'll have to ask you to leave. Go. Go be with your family, where you belong."

Colin's hands crossed his chest. He was prepared for a standstill. "Nae. Ye already promised me a night wi' ye. I will not leave."

My arms crossed next. "Then, promise me you won't get close to me."

He threw his hands up in the air in surrender. "Aye will not compromise ye. I would never do such a thing anyway. I will be close to you, but only when we are wed with the seal of God over us will I do what I want to do tae ye."

"Fine then. Stay."

Colin's eyes sparkled. "I think I will."

He was right there waiting for me. I could reach out and touch him. What harm could it do? And I trusted him. I took his hand then, and he was shocked at my willingness, and I knew that it pleased him.

I sat down by the fire and pulled him beside me. "Just sit here with me."

"Aye, I would not want tae be anywhere else."

His hand came up to brush my cheek.

"What's got ye like this, love?"

"I've got a promise, and I'm already knowing that I'm going off with you alone to find them. I might as well try my best to make myself immune to you."

"Promises are made tae be broken."

I caught my breath and pulled my hand away from his cheek. "Not for me. You wouldn't dare. Colin, I need to trust you. I need to...to... I need you to understand."

I held on to the fact that God had made Colin for me, too. So, my excuse was to just let God's plan work. I knew I couldn't hold on to Colin forever, but God gave me Colin now. Right now. In front of me with all of his beautiful soul.

I said, "I love Seth MacKenzie. And I will marry him. And I will be a faithful wife to him. But right now, with you here, it makes it very difficult for me to stay at arms length, because I want to know everything all at once."

"What do you want to know?"

"I want to know you."

To remember you for the rest of my life and lock you inside my heart and throw away the key. He whispered the stories of his life to me. Those times that were to stand out in his memory forever, his coming to Scotland for the first time. How he felt that God had taken everything from him when his family and brothers in Christ were being persecuted by the Romans in the siege of Jerusalem, which sparked the beginning of the First Jewish-Roman War of 66 A. D.

He told me of founding the first churches when he could escape with a Roman garrison, then abandoning them upon arrival to gather new missionaries and converting new workers for Christ.

"I love you, Colin, but how do you think that I even deserve you? Me? I'm so simple. And God wouldn't give me to you to cause you pain. I can bring you no joy."

He pulled his hands through my hair. "I know 'at God created ye fur me. An' ye do give me th' greatest joy. Just yer light, it's a powerful one ye have, lass. Yer presence alone rocks me to my core and sends my mind to all places past and future. This one night will be enough tae last me ah few more hundred years or so. However long it is until I see ye again."

"But when I see you again, you will be with Sarah and I will still be with Seth. Seth is mine now and then."

This was insane. Couldn't he see that he needed to let me go now? There would be no hope for us. No time would be ours. But I could neither let him go, like the moon could not lace itself from the night sky.

"Seth is sick. Do ye know 'at?"

I was sure that he didn't know about Lupus, but he knew he was sick. Could he sense the hurt in him? I prayed that it had not progressed.

"I know that. He has been sick since, well, since he touched his other uncle with a disease, and it passed through him. Is that how it works?"

"That's why when I killed those men back there, I had to make sure they were done with. It doesn't transfer the gift. Not th' light. But th' parts left behin'. Th' sickness, th' jealousy, th' hatred, or th' disease, or th' hurt. Th' darkness of th' body stays behin'. It doesn't enter into th' Kingdom of God because God can't accept th' darkness into th' light."

I didn't want to talk about Seth's illness. "I'm so tired. I feel like I will go to sleep sitting here."

Colin pulled the quilts off the bed and laid them by the fire for us to stay warm. It wasn't long before I drifted off, knowing I was being protected was enough.

I knew I was dreaming because Seth was there. He was there and Colin was not. I found my eyes searching out through the fog as if I were missing him. I wanted to call out his name but Seth was there, watching me, waiting. I cried out to him and held out my hand but he would not come. I watched him slipping away. Time was slipping away and I knew it would be too late.

I woke up screaming his name.

"I'm not Seth, love. Ye were dreaming."

"Where's Seth? Does he know?"

"Know what? 'At I am here wi' ye? I don't see how he could know it. I locked the door but he said he has th' sight."

"He can't always see me, though. But you, I'm worried about that."

A puzzled expression crossed his face. "Why can't he see ye? Th' visions should come tae him as he wills them. He might not have control since he's so young."

"Technically, he's only three years younger than you, Uncle Colin."

He smiled tenderly at me, brushing off a tear that had settled on the tip of my nose. That brought me closer to him and I found my body instinctively inching towards him. Just a touch more from him and I would kiss him. Morning breath beware.

"I was given the blocker from Mr. MacKenzie before Seth...well, before he proposed to me."

"What blocker?"

He didn't know. I remembered Mr. MacKenzie saying that Gillivary had found this for his wife, Munroe's mother, then it was passed on. Knowledge like this could be useful for Colin.

"This." I touched the comb in my hair. "There is a property in the shell that serves as a shield against other gifts, such as mind reading, future sight, truth serums, all of that."

"Truth serums?"

"Mr. MacKenzie, or Munroe, who will one day become your brother, he has the ability to seek the truth in others. Wait, shouldn't you know that about the clan? Your enemy? The ones that tried to hang Seth and would have killed us if you hadn't...."

My voice trailed off. I sat up at the thought of it and it broke our spell.

"Munroe means mouth ay th' river. They took the name from th' River Roe. It is a land association only. Just as MacKenzie means son of the fair one. We all seem tae be handsome if ye ask me and took after my fair looks."

"I know this to be true. Munroe can just look at me and I can't help myself but to allow the words to spill out all around me like a river of truth. It just comes out, as ridiculous as this might sound. That is the meaning of the name."

"Tae know 'at someone would name their bairn Munroe is beyond me. Ah can't believe it would have been a MacKenzie tae do 'at."

"Oh, the enemy thing. That doesn't exist in the future. I don't believe so anyway."

He chuckled, but his eyes were not laughing. "I'm the first one to believe in forgiveness an' all 'at, but God must challenge us in th' days ahead. I can see truth by what ye say though. Any time 'at I happen tae be around a Munroe I can't help myself but tell them how much I despise them. It usually ends bad fur them. I always seem tae come out unscathed."

I looked from Colin long enough to notice that the sun was casting light through the lavender curtains. "When do we leave?"

He stretched. "Now. I was waitin' on ye tae ask me. I promised ye 'at I wouldn't do anythin' 'at ye didn't want me tae do."

"I didn't mean you to take me that literally."

His eyes gleamed as he came in and kissed me lightly on the lips. "Aye, 'en I won't. Come here an' tell me ye mean it."

"I need a few minutes to get ready. Then, I must find Seth."

"I'll go fin' him fur ye. Make sure 'at ye have warm provisions. Ben Nevis snows all year."

He turned and was already unlocking the door. "Wait. Please Colin, don't tell him about last night?"

"There's nothin' tae tell."

Was that true? It was nothing? To me it was complete bliss. But I couldn't say that to him. His eyes betrayed him. I knew he felt it, too.

He left me there to rummage through closets and dressers, finding wool sweaters and long riding pants, wool socks, plaid coats. I dressed as quickly as I could by the fire. I was just pulling the last of the layers of a sweater down over my head when the door swung open.

It was Seth. He looked like I felt. "Seth, are you okay? What's wrong?"

He grimaced, holding onto his stomach. "For one thing, my leg hurts. Another, I don't drink, Jazzline. And well, I drank last night. Not a little, but a lot. Now, I'm paying the price."

He smelled of it still. I whispered as I kissed his tangy lips, "I love you, Seth. I was so worried about you."

He frowned. "Were you?"

He glanced behind me and saw the quilts thrown over the bed haphazardly. I tried to make them look as if they were tidy and neat but I couldn't seem to get them straight. I had other things on my mind, like the way the blankets still smelled like Colin, and how it felt to be held by him. I wanted to take the quilts with me and was going to ask Colin if we could somehow manage.

"Seth, I'm scared." My voice broke into sobs and I cried against his neck.

"Of what? Going off to find Tucker and Alex, or being alone with Colin?"

"Of both. If you want to know the truth. I can't help this soul mate connection with him. I never wanted this. You are the only man in my life that I can be with." That was carefully chosen. "But I'm scared I won't find Tucker and Alex. That we'll search and miss them and be too late. Will it be too late for us?"

"Don't doubt. I have full confidence Colin knows how to find and rescue them. He'll protect you at all costs, so I'm not worried about that either. I love you. I'll wait for you."

"Please trust me while I'm gone. I have his word."

"I know that. I heard."

"What? Did you hear us?"

"No. Colin came to find me this morning. He told me I could trust him and said he wouldn't push you. That you explained the situation that we were to be married and you wanted to wait for me. Is that true? Did you really tell him that?"

"I will not spend the rest of my life with Colin. You are my best friend, my love, my heart. Once this is all over, I will give you every-thing. If you can wait for me, and forgive me all this."

"I'm the one that needs to ask for forgiveness. I've put you in this...this situation. It's because of me that you must go out in dangerous territory, in the middle of a war, to bring them back. I knew better than to touch you. I should have never..."

I put my finger across his lips. If it was true what Colin said and our gifts were materialized by prayer, I didn't want him to ever speak it again for fear we would just disappear.

"Don't speak it, Seth. I love you. I wouldn't change us. Except the part where you had your leg broken and you can't travel with me. I'll be back before you miss me."

Seth crushed me against him and held me until I couldn't breathe. "You better be. You better come back to me, Jazzline. If something were to happen to you...if you... You know that I love you."

"I know."

I had almost forgotten the warmth and the love that just flowed through me at his presence. I'd forgotten because I'd had other feelings to wrestle with. Seth made sense. We worked.

"How long do you think this will take?"

"It won't be long. A few days. It'll only take two days for the moun-tain, then you'll travel to Fort William. They'll be there. I've told Colin everything I know to try to help you both."

That wasn't like him, to divulge what he knew. But this time, maybe he felt the need for an exception. "And then, what will I find in Fort William?"

I pictured an old-timey cowboy fort in my mind, probably wouldn't be that way at all. It was more of who will I find, not what it would be like.

"They are there. Cold, but safe."

"Thank God they're still alive. I pray to God I find my way back to you as fast as we can. That I find those crazy boys and beat them upside the head, then throw Alex over my shoulder and spank him one, and run back up that mountain straight back to you."

"It won't be exactly like that."

Before I could ask him any further, Colin burst into the room. I guessed he figured this was now his room since he'd slept in it all night. He stopped short at the door when he saw that Seth was holding me and turned away. He talked to the wall, and it broke my heart. So, I kissed Seth lightly on the lips and backed away from him. That would be my goodbye to him.

Colin's voice was strained and his jaw tightened. "Are ye ready tae leave? We are wastin' precious daylight. It will already take one camp overnight."

Seth pulled at my baggy clothes. "She's going to be warm enough without you smothering her. Hands off, Colin."

His eyes twinkled but he still did not look at us. I could see them in the corners, crinkling with amusement. "I told ye I would take good care of 'er. I won't let nothin' happen tae 'er. I'd die before then, and ye know that won't happen."

"It can be dangerous on the Ben. You better stay close to him and don't be daring. Don't be foolish. You listen to him, and you be careful."

"I will. I'm scared."

"You'll make it. Just stay close."

"We need tae go now. Seth, remember what I told ye."

He frowned, then turned to me and brushed his hand against my cheek. "Aye."

I hated this. I wanted him. I wanted the man at the door. I wanted my boys back. So, many things that I wanted in life. And it was Christmas after all. My list seemed to be mounting immensely. Shouldn't a girl have it all?

I wanted to say so much to Seth as I watched Colin and him turn and walk out the door, with me trailing behind. I wanted to tell him I was sorry for feeling this way about Colin, for kissing him, for wanting more. I wanted to tell him I was sorry I allowed my heart to be weak, and my voice to sing for him. There was so much that I wanted to say but I couldn't. He told me that we would make this. I knew there was an end to this, soon. But that alone, was the saddest of it all.

I hadn't even noticed the way that the castle had been decorated for Christmas when we were practically carried in the day before. There was holly sprigs and Christmas trees reaching at least twelve foot awaiting the MacKenzies in each room. Candles were still burning even in the early morning, and by the looks of things it had been a long one. There was a twinge of regret that I'd missed a Highland Christmas. One that would never come again. But then again, I had Colin with me. He turned to me as if he knew what I was thinking and winked at me. He wasn't regretting anything.

The beautiful girl that let me borrow her clothes was in the Great Hall. She was smiling at us and cooed, "Colin, yer just in time fur boxin' day."

Not another fight. No more bloodshed. I couldn't stand the thought of it and grasped the doorframe, my knuckles turning white. Seth's soft laughter filled my head, and I tried my best to memorize every rise and fall of it.

"No, baby. It's the gift exchange. They pass gifts in boxes, boxing day."

I smiled at him, trying to gather some strength about me. I thought of Bree and wished that she were here to touch me when I needed her the most.

Colin said, "I'm sorry, Sirena. We must be on our way now. I will share wi' th' family on our return."

"But I have somethin' fur Jazzline."

"I'm sorry that I have nothing for you."

"It's not about what I receive. It's about my givin'. I want ye tae have this."

She handed me a worn copy of a book, the binding was creased and old. I held it gently in my hands, the weight of it light but the meaning behind it heavy. I felt the tears well up in my eyes and I wanted to refuse the gift but I knew that it would be rude and so hurtful to do so.

"I... I...don't know what to say."

I turned it over in my hands and flipped to the title page. My fingers crossed over the beautifully scripted pages. The handwriting looked strikingly familiar, somehow. It was a handwritten transcription of the Book of John, an old version. A King James Version, but I knew enough about Bible history to know this was an earlier one. I always had a Bible close to me in my home, and even at Seth's house, I would flip through his worn Bible. But this was different.

"How did you know this was my favorite book of the Bible?"

Seth smiled at the young girl. She looked to be fifteen or younger. She had not come into her gift yet, I was sure. But she was already an angel.

"Sirena, that was a very lovely gift. Jazzline is very appreciative."

She blushed. "I felt 'at ye needed all of th' protection ye could get. From weather, th' Sassenach, an' Colin."

Colin laughed at her and then John appeared. "Sirena, hen. It is time tae come wi' th' family. We will see ye both off."

He saw what I was holding in his hands and reached out to clasp my hand on top of it. "Was this yours?"

"Aye, it was mine. Ye need this now more than me. Learn it. Colin will show ye."

His name meant God is Gracious, I had asked Colin the night before because I was curious at that simple name John.

I turned to him and Sirena. "Will you both please look after Seth for me?"

"Even wi' a broken leg I'm not tae worried about him."

I felt the threat of the Brahan Seer's story all over again. "You better be the one to stay put waiting for me. Hide yourself away and read yourself. Do something extravagantly boring." For his ears only I whispered, "Stay quiet and don't go making any women jealous or mad."

His face broke out into a brilliant grin. "I can't believe that you'd even think I was in danger among my own family. Go on and find your brother and Tucker. I love you."

"I love you, too."

A cloud-filled sky loomed overhead, already with the threat of rain. By the doors stood the small band of women and a couple of the elder men. John seemed to be the middle-aged representative to stay behind to protect this keep in case of a raid or an invasion by another clan or English army. At least he'd have Seth now to help fight if need be. Then, I shivered at the thought of that. It seemed that no matter where we were, castles, forests, mountains, forts...we were all in danger.

You could almost feel the unease and desperation behind the faces of the women. Their men were out there. Their children. My child with them. And then my mother's image flooded my mind. Her only concern in life had been a shipment arriving late or a waitress calling in sick. These mothers were filled with fear every waking second but tried to mask it for the sake of breathing and moving on in a day's time.

Each family member gave Colin something to carry with us. A bag was slung behind his shoulder. I was also given a bag, and it pulled down on my shoulders but I didn't complain one bit. Whatever supplies were loaded in there, I was sure we'd need them. The family had climbed this mountain countless times before. Even Seth had climbed this mountain on one of his summer trips here. It was possible.

Who was I to think I could possibly be prepared for this? Then, I remembered the jump off the bridge when the cab driver had dropped me off. Thank God it hadn't worked. There was no way in this world or the next I could've been prepared to end up in this magnificent place and be able to trek the terrain alone. It would've been death for me the first night. God knew that. God had orchestrated all of this, and I praised him for it.

Colin whispered, "I won't put ye in danger? Ah have faith 'at we'll be safe. My faith will be enough fer us both."

"Faith? Where does it truly come from? You should know this by now."

If he talked to me then I wouldn't dwell on the fact that my feet were getting closer and closer to a forest that led to a glen that led to a mountain.

"It comes wi' knowin'."

"Knowing what?"

"Knowin' 'at God exists. 'At God loves me. 'At I am His light. God supplies all needs. Do you know Psalm 89:1, I will sing of th' mercies of th' Lord furever: Wi' my mouth will I make known thy faithfulness tae all generations."

"Have you memorized the whole Bible?" I felt for the book in my bag that Sirena had given me and then, it hit me. "Was that John back there, the John? Is he like you? From that time?"

His face turned gray a second, grayer than the clouds I swore would overtake us any second. I prayed for it not to rain just yet. My body needed to adjust to the temperature before getting a dose of the rain or snow.

"I've had many years in God's word. It's my callin' tae speak it, so I needed tae learn it. How else could I carry out th' light fur eternity fur our Savior? An' second, no, 'at was not John from yer Bible. But Ah did know him and loved him. We all loved him. Ye know he was one of Jesus' favorites."

I had remembered reading that in the Bible and then marveled that I was here, walking through a pine forest with the birds chirping, the sounds of the animals around me, the wind picking up my hair, the snow now beginning to fall around me, speaking of characters in the Bible that many thought were just that. Characters in some story that man created. The realization that John was a real man. Jesus was God in the flesh was amazing to me. Funny how it never felt like that before Colin. Names on a page, words written in red. Truth.

"I heard that before, about John. What happened to him?"

"Do not ask me about th' death of my brothers an' workers in Christ. I can't do 'at. Ask me somethin' else tae get it out of my head. Time is different fur me than it is fur ye. Vivid like it is this day. Vivid like yer beautiful face."

I knew what he meant, somewhat. I sat on a back pew with Momma after Daddy left us and I pledged my heart to Jesus and asked him to protect me from life, hurt, and pain. And even though I turned in myself and stopped using my voice, I never turned from God. I felt the goosebumps rising on my arms just at the thought of my own experience, as filling and wonderful as it was for a thirteen year-old-girl. I felt it now, and it was only five years before. With Colin, we were talking over two thousand years.

"Did you know Jesus?"

"No, but I wished 'at Ah did have 'at chance tae hear him preach God's kingdom. I knew him by his followers, by Peter an' his disciples. By brother Paul. I felt His power, received my gift from th' angel of th' Lord. We all have seen an' heard Jesus by God's word. Ye know him, tae. We didn't have tae be there, just believe 'at it was. At' is faith fer th' believer."

"That's harder for people like me. You don't have many eyewitnesses walking around, first generation Christians. Many have a built-in blocker."

"Aye, ye are not wrong. 'At is th' problem there. Th' attitude, th' misdirection, th' nonbelief. 'At is what hinders yer light. Satan hinders yer light. When ye are open tae truth, yer light shines. When ye are in God's presence, th' light shines. When ye subject yerself tae th' world an' begin tae let it strip ye awa' wi' doubt, th' light fades. Don't ever lose sight of th' light. Th' faith. Hope springs eternal."

I smiled at him, already filling the light within me begin to burn. "I think I'm going to get that on my license plate. Hope Springs Eternal. Perfect."

He frowned. "License plate? Whit is 'at?"

I laughed. It was amazing knowing something that he did not. Then, it dawned on me of all the worldly things I did know, all of the futuristic technology and advancements he'd have to look forward to. I couldn't help but think of a car getting me into all of this mess, and I told him about that time before, the play, the reward waiting for me for speaking, having a lead role. It would have to be called the Time Machine, compared to Tucker's Jeepers Kreepers that would never be operational again thanks to the crash in the inlet.

I would get it painted just like Scooby-Doo's van, green with flowers, the whole bit. I'd have the Time Machine painted across the sides. Momma would be surprised at my request but she said I could get whatever I wanted. That was it. But would that hurt Seth? Would it be a reminder of my time with Colin? I was afraid that everything from now on would remind me of Colin.

"Tell me everythin' about ye. It would take ye another thousand years tae know about me. An' we know 'at ye don't have th' luxury ay time or ye would be mine forever."

"If ye had my gift of eternal life, would ye choose me? Would ye leave Seth like ye will be leavin' me soon?"

"I fear I'll already love you the rest of my life."

"Aye, lass. My life fur ye. Tell me about ye."

I sighed as he pulled away. He was walking again, and I followed. Not caring about my lush surroundings straight out of a picture book with all of the snow covering our world. I only focused on the movements that he was making. The turn of his head so I could memorize his jaw line. The way his hair curled down and around at the nape of his neck, itching me to put my fingers there to touch his bare skin. The broad width of his shoulders and his swagger walk on the forest trail. Nothing but him. God, I'd see Scotland again, I was sure of it. But not Colin. Not this way. Not alone.

"There is nothing really to tell. I'm just a boring girl where nothing exciting ever happened to me, that is, until I met your family."

"Where did yer name originate from? I've studied names, ye have tae, tae know what I know about th' power of a name. But I've ne'er heard of a Jazzline."

"My father named me that. After his favorite kind of music. Jazz comes around in the 19th century. You have a long way away to hear it. They say that it was started by slaves in the south, from where I'm from. My father was always in love with the lyrics. But they are so sad to me."

My life was becoming a jazz song mixed with twangy country music undertones. My 80's was slowly being replaced with songs of loneliness and cheating hearts.

"What is your favorite Jazz song?"

"I have so many favorite songs, it's hard to narrow just one. I do love Ella Fitzgerald the most... I think...it's so hard."

My mind raced with lyrics but I kept going back to one line from Etta James, At Last. Especially since we hit the clearing and the highest mountain in the whole United Kingdom was before me, it's deadly and overwhelming magnitude took my breath away. The words were still burning me, and I had to release them.

I sang the song for Colin.

Colin kissed me, then put his arms around my shoulder as we walked on. The mountain before us, beckoning us with its snow and cliffs, and rocks. Oh God, help me.

"Alexander is sure lucky tae have ye in his life. He's such a braw child. Fur ye tae travel through time, tae cross Ben Nevis fur him. Tae fight me off. 'At is love."

The image of my baby was there before me, calling me over the mountain. "I love him more than my own life. I would do anything for Alex, for Tucker, too. They are my life. Now with Seth...and...and...you..." I couldn't help but know that he would be woven in the threads of my life's story. "It's love."

"So, Jazz means music. Yer name is a musical one which makes sense since all ye do is sing all the time. A name meant fur one thing only."

Mrs. MacKenzie told me my gift was my voice. Gillivary said he understood why I was named the way I was by my father. They believed in this name business. Apparently, God did, too.

"What do you believe my gift is?"

"Yer gift is tae sing, tae use yer voice fur tae bring folk tae Christ's love through music?"

"Are all gifts made for sharing Jesus' message?" How could Seth's ability to see death be so?

"Aye. It's all fur Jesus. But there are some gifts 'at your given tae us fur th' choosin'. Some names have double meanings. We don't know th' course of action 'at th' heart will take until they manifest th' gift, either in th' darkness are th' light. We try our best tae live in th' light. If ye bide in th' light, darkness can't prevail. Always live in th' light, an' yer gift will grow an' protect ye fur good."

"Why is the light connected with the name? What makes a name so important?"

I thought about all of the expecting parents out there buying alphabetical baby name books or searching on the internet for the perfect name for their child. Could it be more than just a random desire to call a child a name? Could it be God whispering it into the soul of man?

"Th' name is connected tae th' light. Th' callin."

"But how can a parent know that? Just because my Daddy liked Jazz music and my mother's favorite writer was Alexander Dumas, they named us this. It's more like a random name out of a hat to win a door prize. Chance."

I could tell he had no clue what a door prize was, and I smiled.

"It's nae th' parent 'at knows th' light. It is the Spirit of the Living God. God speaks tae them through the Holy Spirit."

"So, you're saying that God spoke to my parents when I was conceived? He gave them the name because He knew our gifts?"

Amazing. Supernatural. But it made sense, somehow.

"Aye, love. Why do ye seem so shocked by this? Ye did know 'at God speaks tae His folk? God has ne'er spoken tae ye?"

The look on his face showed his shock. He took for granted the power of his own gift, from his own walk with the disciples, his visions of the angel.

"I've never heard God speak."

But I knew that sometimes in my life when I'd hear a voice inside my head, urging me on to make a choice. A choice that was the right one for my life, and I attributed that to the Holy Spirit. I'd learned about the still small voice of God. I'd heard that from a Bible lesson once. I'd read about characters, I mean, people, in the Bible visited by angles', Jesus as well. So, if I confessed the Bible to be true, why did I doubt those things could happen?

My faith was being challenged. Just as my coordination, strength, and focus were coming into question as we started the incline on the wet rocks. The snow was continuing to fall, and without a break in the clouds, it let me know I needed to be careful of my surroundings. And for as many steps as we could take Colin was right there with me, holding my hand, my arm, practically lifting me along beside him when possible, or shoving me in front, as if just by mere believing he could catch me if I fell. It was almost like an angel was right there with us, too. Because the cold was not biting me, the snow was only a beautiful reminder that I was in a dream.

He was silent. I wasn't sure if he was contemplating my response of not hearing God speak to me, planning the best Christian response through his own index of Bible verses, or he was trying his best to maneuver us both up the mountain without getting us both killed.

Then, he came out with a Bible verse and I smiled. "Do ye know, Jeremiah 1:5, Before I formed thee in th' belly I knew thee; an' before thou camest forth out of th' womb I sanctified thee, an' I ordained thee a prophet onto th' nations."

I remembered God showing me a Bible verse in Seth's room one night about how God had plans for me. My heart lifted and I was no longer afraid. No longer afraid of the heights, falling, dying. God knew. He had a plan for me and had called me from my mother's womb. I would just have to trust in that. I sang, my voice to his scripture. Up Where We Belong, by Joe Cocker, flowed through me like a verse from him, and it carried us further on.

His smile broke across his face like the sun now breaking through the clouds. "An' ye wonder how I can learn Bible verses? How do ye know all of yer songs?"

"I guess it's my gift."

He laughed. "I guess so. A lovely one, indeed."

The sun was now in line with us. I could feel the warmth of it. It was breathtaking. Tucker, my sun, I'm coming for you. Alex, my son, I'm almost there.

"How long now?"

"We'll stop tae rest soon. Just a wee bit ay daylight hours left before it's tae treacherous tae climb."

He was still looking to the sun as if he were in awe of it. Like he knew another secret that I did not. My mind was too caught up knowing that God knew me. And the climb was getting a little trickier as we went. My lack of hiking experience was showing but Colin was so patient with me.

"I'm just a beach girl. That's all."

"Not all. Ye are my girl."

My heart was warm and my cheeks were feeling a burning sensation. I sang, My Girl by The Temptations.

Colin pulled me closer to him and held on tighter than before. "Is everything okay?"

"Everythin' is so right. I love ye so much, Jazzline. I can't explain th' feelings 'at wash over me just by bein' wi' ye, love, fear of losin' ye, hope, grief, warmth, all of it in one heartbeat to the next that brings fire to my bloodless heart."

"You know that we can never be. You know that it's impossible for us but I'll never forget."

"Nor I. Tell me tae move or I'll just stand here."

"Move."

He did and smiled at me as he pushed me forward, his hands circling my waist as he hoisted me up on the next ledge, my arms straining with the movement of it all.

"Yer wish is my command."

But what would my one wish be if I had the power, the control. I let it play out in my mind. The possibilities as we moved upward into the clouds. The fog became denser with each edge passed. My brain more of a fog than before. If I could just live out my life with Colin, I would grow old and die, he would be the perfection of a youthful spirit. I couldn't hold him forever.

I believed in all of the words of the Bible and for some reason, I couldn't wait to get my hands on a Bible in the night's quiet and just read the words again. Next read, I would study knowing that these people were not just characters in a fictional novel, but of real life, flesh and blood, just like me, chosen by God to fulfill a promise.

Colin broke my sudden peacefulness when we were now in a flatter spot than I remembered since we started the climb. He pulled the bag off his shoulder, then took mine from me.

"We must stop here. Th' sun is disappearin' an' th' fog is makin' it nearly impossible tae see."

I hadn't even noticed the sun setting, since we seemed to be sitting on it.

He fixed the camp and when I sat down, I felt the burn coursing up and down my legs. How could the soreness already begin to settle? I figured I'd have to sleep on it and pay for it in the morning, but my body was screaming with the throbbing pain of lack of mountain climbing experience.

He pulled me close enough to shield me from the cold and wrapped his arms around me. Crash. Riptide. Drowning.

"You are too close."

He whispered, and I felt my body inching closer to him in response. "Aye, love. I can't have ye freezing tae death. What were ye thinkin' about just now."

I murmured, feeling his warmth around me was like Heaven. "I want to study the Bible more. I want to learn about the meaning of names."

"Think of names in th' Bible, their meanings. God always lit his folk know their name or gave them a new name tae fit their callin'. Do ye think th' ways ay God have stopped just because it's sealed in ink? God's ways are eternal, everlastin'."

I scooted around to snuggle up against his chest. Better. I kept my arms folded between us, as if that small barrier could remind my heart where it belonged.

"Give me some names. Let me hear them."

"Easy. I'll start wi' my name, fur instance, Cornelius means horn. I shall blast forth th' words of th' Lord as a trumpet of victory fur all eternity. 'At was whit th' angel of th' Lord revealed tae me in my vision before Peter found me an' converted me."

"You know your story is amazing. You know that you are truly a miracle to me. To know that you exist means that Jesus existed. I see it that way."

"I guess 'at was how my gift was meant tae be from th' beginnin'. Ye know th' truth of it, an' only ye. I have ne'er told my story tae another."

"But why? If I were you, how could you keep that in? All of it? Knowing the disciples? I couldn't hold something like that in. I would go around dropping names like I knew celebrities."

"Thomas did not believe 'at Jesus stood before him after th' resurrection until he could touch th' holes in His hands. He only had faith wi' a touch. We only now have faith wi' your ears, tae hear. Faith in your hearts, tae accept Christ as our Savior. If I go tellin' what I know, faith will be in me, not in Jesus Christ. Or people won't believe me and call me a lunatic."

"Why can't you share your story with them, the family that you have claimed as your own?"

"I had tae flee Jerusalem, my family, my babes. Not somethin' I can talk about. Let's talk about somethin' else. Think ay th' one name, Messiah, anointed one. Jesus Christ, th' Messiah, th' one name tae brin' salvation."

His voice came out in a rush, running from all he had held inside for years. It seemed, years of holding his story in had left him fleeing from that part of himself.

"Moses, taken out. He was chosen tae take out God's chosen people from th' Egyptians, from slavery. David, well beloved, and God loved David tae give him th' birth line of His Son, Jesus. Abraham, father of a nation, tae be chosen a gentile tae father a nation of th' Jewish belief."

I put my hand over his lips, "I understand the Bible names. No more trivia. Why did you really leave Jerusalem behind? Why Scotland? You could've gone anywhere."

"Please tell me about ye. Tell me yer dreams. Teel me what ye like? An' how ye feel about yer folk an' yer learnin' of th' Lord. No more about me. I want tae know everythin' about ye."

"How could a Roman soldier end up in Scotland, of all places?"

"Seth was right. Ye don't know any Scottish history. I came in a Roman invasion of Scotland in 71 A. D. I could not be there anymore and took it as my time to escape it. My family an' beloved friends an' missionaries were bein' persecuted. I had seen enough. Killed violently. Posted up on th' walls... Th' Jewish temple was destroyed in 70 A. D. Christians were massacred. Enough. Please sing me a song."

"Who would do that? I'm sorry that I don't know about the history. Sitting here with you it is shameful and embarrassing that I claim to be Christian but I don't know the first thing..." About faith, or God's love for me, or the plight of His people. The word massacre would not leave my brain. I thought of the Holocaust and shivered with the pain. I would not tell him any of that.

"Th' Romans."

I understood now. He could not kill his own believers, his friends. To be in a place to make a choice. I was ashamed. I was seriously caught up in my own little selfish fantasy of who to love, how to choose between these two men, and he was in a mammoth choice of birthright, duty, faith, and love.

"Oh."

"My garrison but not me. I ran after my family was killed. God was wi' me, even in th' darkest of times. Th' angel ay th' Lord spoke tae me tae come tae Scotland. Tae convert as many souls as I could in this majestic an' powerful land. He brought me tae this place. I helped build th' Hadrian's Wall, even Fort William, where we'll be in a day's time, there was my Roman settlement. I was with th' first MacKenzie. So, I kinda adopted 'em all. Now, sing me a song, please."

His voice was pleading with me and I prayed to God to give me the right one. To somehow take away the pain that had overtaken him and was making him crash.

I prayed to God to give him what he needed, and I closed my eyes and found a country song, It's Your Love.

"Aye, love. 'At's better."

I looked into his eyes and saw that his past had melted away, and it was replaced by a desire that was for the present. For me. "Don't love me forever. It's not right."

"It's tae late fur me. I'm yours. Forever. So, stop talkin' an' let me stare at ye until 'at sun comes up. Ye will have th' rest of yer life tae sleep, an' so will I. I fear this might be my last night wi' ye."

CHAPTER 17

*A Time for Us*

"Hey are you expecting me to move after having no sleep?"

He stretched out, putting the blankets back into the bags. "What are ye talkin' about? I just woke up from th' best dream of my life. I'm ready tae go."

My legs hurt. My arms throbbed. My head was on fire. And my heart was broken, slipping down the side of the mountain like a landslide. Broken pieces of debris never to be found, even if I crossed the mountain once more. I was so fixated on the way that his smile lit up every feature of his face, every way that he was so flawless. After my time with him, I could find no fault in him. Then, the fault crashed against me, bringing more of my heart down the side of the cliff. I knew what it was. The one fault that my man had was that he was eternal.

He reached for my hand to pull me up but I couldn't move. One, the soreness was just too much and the second, the pain of knowing that I'd never hold him again wrecked all of my senses, drowning me. I was slowly suffocating, losing all hope of moving. All hope of loving.

His voice was soft, "Aye, love, I know. But think of Alexander an' Tucker. We have this time frame from Seth's vision. If they move again,

156

they may go in a different direction an' it will be like searchin' fur a needle in a haystack."

I frowned, "Is that saying that old?"

"Whit saying?"

"A needle in a haystack? I hear that in my time."

My time. His time. What happened to our time? I thought of Romeo and Juliet. The song that played from the old version that we had watched in ninth grade English, A Time for Us, by Johnny Mathis.

We started on in silence. The words still holding onto us, tighter than his grip on my hand. My eyes were rimmed with tears as I somehow found the strength to pull myself up to the summit. We were standing above the clouds. Not below. Not in. Above. We swayed back and forth on the rocky dance floor, to a song with no lines. I didn't know what was playing in his head, but my head was now caught up in the clouds and I could not register a single, comprehensible thought, other than my life was complete when I was with him.

He pulled me down again and there was a trail, carved out in stone. Markings designated places to put my feet where I was sure that I would not lose balance and fall. I'd always heard that it was always easier to come down as it was to travel up, but this was a little too easy, and I was happy and sad, all at the same time.

I couldn't speak with him on the way down. And he didn't attempt to try. We were both spent, emotionally more than physically. Even though not having any sleep the night before did us no good. I'd lose a sense of where we were when he touched me on the side, or pulled at my shoulders, or circled my waist. Even with my layers of clothing, it was so intimate to me.

As I was traveled down, I could see the place Colin described to me. His past Roman settlement, Fort William. It took us half of the time to move down the mountain and I wanted to pull him back. I wanted him selfishly to myself once more.

I whispered, "Can we find a place to camp one more night?"

"Are ye hurtin'? What can I do?"

"I need you. I can't stop this. I don't want this to end. And when they come, and when they..."

There will be no more us. I could not let Tucker or Alex see it. I would have to hide every emotion that was so raw on me right now. I needed more time. Like an eternity to get my emotions in check.

"Prince Charlie will be on his way to Perth soon. He'll be out an' about lookin' fur recruits. I only sent our MacKenzie's here tae th' fort. No other clans will be here, not yet anyway."

"You sound as if you have some control over battle plans. What's your role in all of this?"

We hadn't bothered to ask him how he barged into our cell and rescued us like that, sneaking in unawares by the Munroe's. Seth and I were just so grateful to have him come for us and escape a hanging that it was irrelevant. For some reason, it was pressing on my mind now. And all it was, was the urgency to keep him preoccupied and standing still. That meant stolen time. Minutes were better than nothing.

"My expertise is in war preparation an' battle. Not just th' gift of no pain, but wi' so many years of experience on th' battlefield, I seem tae be th' one 'at always leads th' clan tae war. I am th' fearless one."

He seemed more alive now, with the scent of conflict flaring his nostrils than I'd ever seen him.

"How did you know about Seth in prison?"

He came right in time. Ironic. Coming in like a hooded crusader, a superhero. He didn't have the power of sight, and I knew by the Brahan Seer story that having Seth's gift was rare. Colin's lip twitched and knew he was hiding something from me.

"You better tell me, Colin. We can't have secrets between us."

"It's no secret. I've told ye before. Whether ye heard it or not, 'at is up tae ye, now isn't it."

"Don't play word games with me. Just tell me what you're hiding. How did you know to find Seth?"

To save me. It was more than just Seth. Since I'd heard him repeatedly say that he didn't care about Seth MacKenzie and I knew that he cared about me...how would he know when I'd crossed? Unless...

"Ah know th' power ay th' cross."

"You mean, Jesus and the cross? The crucifixion?"

"That, tae. But I'm talking about th' cross through time or place."

"I have to know it to get back."

That is, if he wanted me to go back. Is that why he was so secretive? He wanted to keep us trapped here? But what about Bree? And the war? I needed to get Tucker and Alex's little vigilante butt's out of here.

He pressed his lips firmly together, his eyes intent. "If I tell ye this ye have tae swear tae me here an' now 'at ye will not use it fur folly. Ye will not tell it tae another livin' soul."

"But Seth. I can't keep secrets from him."

"I am not bound tae time as ye are. So, it is simple fur me. I pray. I cross. From here tae th' next."

He had talked of the power of prayer before, the hope, before. With Aunt Shea and the family. I knew that it was prayer. I knew it. He took out a folded piece of paper that seemed to be worn with the crease of it being opened and closed many times.

"What is this?"

But he didn't answer. So, I opened it. In perfectly scripted handwriting were the words:

Colin,

You must leave your troops to Munroe prison. A MacKenzie will be hanged on Christmas Eve and you must rescue him at all cost. Leave now and do not stop. In doing so, you will find your wife. Trust this letter.

Yours,

Cornelius

My eyes circled the names Colin to Cornelius. He'd warned himself. He'd been aware of Seth's brother, Colin's, research. When I crossed in the room that night... Wait.

"I crossed. I crossed when I touched your hand. I was screaming for Bree. And I thought that Bree was there."

It wasn't Bree after all. Not with me, anyway. She had helped Seth to cross, didn't she? Seth told me he went to Bree.

"Ye did not need Bree tae cross. Don't ye see all ye need in your life is Jesus?"

"Do you have all of the answers in the universe?"

"Ye didn't know ye were wi' one of th' most powerful clans in all ay Scotland?"

"I kinda figured that out already. But I still don't understand the power of the cross, like you say it. Prayer? I prayed. I came. It's that simple?" It couldn't be. Doubt flooded my senses and made me sound ridiculous. But wasn't crossing through time more ridiculous than a prayer to God. Sure.

"Aye, ye've got a gift. Ye prayed. Ye felt it in yer heart, yer soul. Yer min' was free ay th' world. Ye asked, therefore ye received. Seeking ye shall find."

He was definitely quoting the Bible on this one. I'd heard that before.

"How did you get hold of this letter?"

"Aye, Ah don't know what happens in th' future. I only found this letter here in my time in August. Ah held on tae it fur months. When Tucker an' Alex crossed, an' I heard about ye...well..."

"What? What did they say?"

"It wasn't all about what they said. It was th' way my heart leaped in my chest when they spoke yer name. An' now ye are wi' me."

Tears fell like a sudden rain. When I thought I could cry no more, I did.

"So, you came to find Seth, to find me."

"Aye, but I was tae late. He had th' claim on ye. I know 'at but it didn't stop me from lovin' ye. Nothin' will ever stop me from lovin' ye."

Minutes had turned into a sweet hour. Could I keep prolonging this?

"So, to get back. I pray. I believe, and it is done." His eyes brimmed with tears, the blue a liquid fire. "Ye know Matthew 17:20, If ye have faith as a grain of a mustard seed, ye shall say unto this mountain, remove hence tae yonder place; an' it shall remove; an' nothing shall be impossible unto ye."

"I never believed that Jesus meant that literally. I thought that it meant just like an obstacle we might be facing in our life the size of a mountain. I could get through it with faith."

"No, love. Jesus meant a mountain. A Ben Nevis. If ye want this mountain tae move, ye can cast it into th' sea wi' prayer an' fasting."

I seemed to have the fasting down pat. It seemed like any time I was around a MacKenzie my mind was far from food. Prayer came a lot, but the faith behind it had been wavering like a candle in the wind.

"So, if this is all true, then why didn't you just pick up Ben Nevis, throw it into one of these loch's, and just take me to Fort William instead of making me climb like a maniac?"

I rubbed my arms. They were still throbbing ridiculously.

"Fur selfish reasons, I guess. I did want tae spend th' night wi' ye again. Th' mountain provided me 'at. Secondly, I could not explain th' loss of life 'at a massive loch tidal wave would produce tae th' glens surrounding us. Imagine 'at disaster. But most importantly, Ah wanted ye tae feel th' struggle. Tae know what it felt loch tae conquer yer fear. Tae overcome 'at obstacle an' believe. Tae have faith in yerself an' most importantly in Jesus Christ."

"Thanks a lot. I could have learned a life lesson with a lot less pain attached to it."

"If th' road was always easy, no struggles, no hardship, ye could never appreciate th' light or th' blessin'. Ye have tae travel th' stonier way sometimes tae enjoy th' other side."

Keep him here. Stall him more. "The MacKenzie's believe that it was marriage or babies that kept them together through the cross. You even made them believe that in the future by forcing my hand to marry you. Why would you do that?"

He seemed ashamed by having to play that role of a secret keeper. "I don't want th' family knowin' th' truth because some family manifest their power fur darkness. Well, if they got a hold of this, they could go back an' forth, commit crimes, without fear of restitution, we have at' now. Back at Brahan. Do ye know 'at? Do ye hear me? They need tae believe 'at it is a family connection. Th' blood. Th' bond. Not just a prayer. This is a truth 'at can only be shared between us. Tae get ye home safe, back tae yer time since 'at is whit ye want." His voice turned optimistically hopeful. "Is 'at still what ye want?"

What did I want? I knew I had to take Tucker and Alex back with me. I had to get Tucker to Bree before she delivered. Just in case...what his family claimed to know about Aunt Shea didn't have a second chance to recreate itself with Bree and the baby.

"I want to go home with everyone."

The choice was too much for me. The words that I would have to speak, to break one heart and take another. Words. I'd always hated words. Hated the way that they destroyed and cut out the heart of a person and threw it away in the dark. Words that tore my family apart still would haunt me out in the daylight, when I was doing absolutely nothing. A word she would say to him would sting me in the face. A word that should never have been spoken in reply, burning me, causing the worthlessness to overtake me in a violent flood. One, like I should have never been born or they wouldn't have been married in the first place. Those words always did the trick at barreling me over some bridge.

He took me by the hand and we continued walking. I heard him call out in Gaelic, and I realized that I wasn't the one he was talking to but I saw no one. I saw the fort, and it looked like a civil war battlefield that we'd traveled to at Fort Fisher, in Wilmington, North Carolina, with hills and valleys, and wooden posts.

Then, I saw someone. A face of a young boy. He was not Alexander, but he could have been his age or close to it. He was peeking from behind a barricade and I couldn't help but smile at him. Where he was, so would my baby be. My baby. My heart sped in my chest knowing I'd soon have him in my arms.

The Gaelic continued between the two, then hollering could be heard and out of the dark hole in the ground popped out my sun.

Tucker Lane. In all of his glory. His face bright, eyes shining with excitement. His perfect smile spreading clearly all over his face making me stand frozen. I needed more. I needed to see Alex. I found you, Tucker. Now, go get my baby.

It didn't take but a few seconds more and there he was. Crawling. Scrambling out of the foxhole like a little rabbit on a mission. He was crying already, but I knew by the look of him, Colin had been right. He wasn't scared. Just dirty and smelly. He was just happy enough to cry at the realization that big sis came. I prayed again, I found you, Alex. And then, it was black.

# CHAPTER 18

# My Immortal

Tiny hands grabbed onto my sweater and shook me. My baby. My arms went around him and crushed him. I'd make him feel the way that I felt when Seth hugged me.

He groaned but the smile across his face let me know he didn't mind a bit. "Ugh! Jazzy, that's enough!"

He didn't die over the bridge. I knew it. He stood before me, talking a mile a minute. My hands went through his hair, down to stick in his ears and wiggle them around. Alex's face had already turned red at all of the attention he was getting, and I was sure that all of these MacKenzie men thought that I was insane as I was doing a physical check-up on Alex's facial features. He was alive. I knew it from the start. Thank you, God, for all of my miracles.

Tucker was right over him, his head resting on top of Alex's curls. "Where's Bree, baby doll? Where's my woman?"

I bit my lip. What should I say? How could I tell him? Should I be the one to tell him that she was pregnant? Colin must not have thought so because he spoke for me.

"She didn't cross. Only Seth an' Jazzline. So, it looks loch yer ride home has arrived, boys. Get yer things. Change of plans."

That was when Alex began his whine, "What? No! We're going to Perth when the sun rises."

I saw the look that Colin gave me. It was one of those, I told you so, ones. Alex wanted this. He wanted to go to Perth. I knew that Colin had told me a little of the Jacobite cause and their support of who they called Bonnie Prince Charlie, but for Alex to want this? I didn't understand.

Tucker was already running away from us to grab whatever he had. He came back still stuffing things in a bag, similar to the one that was still draped over my shoulder. I was sitting up now in the snow, my hands crossed over my legs, my eyes taking in every part of Alexander Dumas Chicand.

Tucker's voice rose above it all, in that sing-song silly way he often unleashed without warning, "I'm going home to Bree... Bree is waiting for me...."

Colin went to talk to the men, hugging each one, giving news of their families. He was wishing them all a safe trip, pointing out landmarks on a map that was folded out before them as the men huddled in the snow. Then, the men disappeared back down into the hole. Gone. It was a shocking hit to my system. Colin. Alex. Tucker. Me. In the world, existing at the same time. Alive.

Tears fell again as Tucker embraced me. His warm smile reverberating down my spine, warming me. "Come on, Jazzy Jeff and the Prince. I've never brought you to a loss of words before. I need you to talk to me. Tell me everything about Bree."

"Oh, Tucker. I love you. Oh, Tucker. Alex. You guys scared us half to death, jumping bridges."

Alex had grown up in 5 months. I left him eight, he was now nine. With his boyish life behind him. I never would've imagined how much until the minute I stood in front of him.

"Alex, I missed your birthday."

He smiled at me, "That's okay. Colin actually made me a cake and taught me some battle moves that day. It was the best birthday that I've ever had."

His voice trailed and I knew. I knew it then. He chose Colin.

I turned to Colin, my eyes betraying me. "You...you...you never said you took care of him."

Colin grinned, beaming with pride as Alex came to step beside him. "This has turned out tae be one braw child, Jazzline. I love him like a son. I see why now an' it all makes sense. He's like yer bairn. So, he was mine from th' beginnin'. From th' day he crossed, I found him, an' Tucker, too."

"I don't want to leave, Jazzy. Please, please let me stay."

God gave Alex to Colin. God's plan was to bring them to Colin. For Alex's sake, more than my own. Especially now seeing the way that Alex was looking at Colin. The way he needed a father. The way my father had abandoned us. Colin would never leave Alex. Colin would outlive him.

"I can't let you, Alex. There're things you don't know that I do. Trust me when I tell you, you need to come home. You're too young to make this decision."

Colin began to walk away, motioning us to follow him. I stayed put. The guys started to move on command. General Colin was now in the vicinity, let everybody stand alert. Not me. Tucker turned to me and held out his hand. Colin and I were over. Breaking up was so hard to do.

Tucker waved it in front of my face. "Okay, all that Jazz. Snap out of it. The Sassenach could be here any minute."

I swatted at him. "Technically, you are one of the Sassenach's."

He didn't grin and I found him growl instead. What had happened to him here to bring on such a response? He spoke to Colin in fluid Gaelic, even the hint of the accent was there and I knew that Bree would be proud. I was sure I didn't want to know what swears that just flew out of Tucker's mouth. But Alex managed a laugh.

My hand raised at them all, "Wait. You know Gaelic, too?"

"My best friend, Jimmy, he's teaching it to me. Figured I'd be here for the rest of my life so I might as well learn the language. Fit in."

But there was more behind his words. He shifted from one foot to the other as he spoke. He chose Colin.

He chose Colin when I couldn't.

"We need tae hurry back. We can make it part way before a camp is needed. 'En, we will be back at Brahan tomorrow night."

"Can I tell Jimmy bye?"

Colin waved him back and Alex took off down the trail and hopped in the hole with no fear. He had grown at least two inches since I had seen him last, and another tooth was gone. But there was such a difference in him that was striking. Tucker, no. He was the same. He had the same feel, the same demeanor, the goofy was there. But with Alex, he'd had a different sense of maturity about him, and I couldn't help but feel sad at all that I had missed. I had never missed a thing.

I sang softly, but I saw my men step in closer to hear. Tucker's eyes shown bright with hearing my voice again, and Colin's eyes were closed as if he were trying to hold it in. I sang Aerosmith, I Don't Want to Miss a Thing.

I wanted Colin to come to me and whisper that everything would be alright. But it was not to be. He distanced himself from me, putting the sun between us. And now, I would miss my life with Alex. Not just when the teeth would go, or how tall he would grow.

After I sang, Tucker picked me up and spun me around. I couldn't help but laugh back at him. He always had a way of melting me.

"How's my baby? Is Bree frantic? That sweet girl of mine better be waiting."

Colin coughed then and I couldn't help but giggle.

"Where is Bree? Tell me or I'll dump you upside down."

I looked at Colin before speaking and he nodded at me. His eyes told me to choose my words. I didn't want to reveal too much or start to pray about it. I couldn't travel through time the rest of my life picking up the pieces of Tucker.

"She's back in our time waiting desperately for you. We both knew you were still alive. And once we get back to her, you'll see. That's all I'm going to say."

"Nothing could stop me here or there from finding my way back to Bree. I'm the superhero with powers. I've just been in the war until the time comes for me to somehow jump back."

"No. Apparently, you're not. Because if you stay here, you'll die at a battle in just a few weeks time. We have to get you and Alex back. We have to before January 17th or..."

Tucker turned to Colin and winked. "Die? Really? I didn't think that could happen here."

Colin laughed. "Tucker here has already died once in this place at th' Battle of Prestonpans, where I found him an' Alexander. They were a sight let me tell ye. Among all th' men there, they stood out, but fought our cause for freedom anyway."

"And he taught us how to fight and survive here. I tell you, Jazzline. I'm better prepared now for the next military advancement. If I ever get back, I'm joining the Army. I've been called to serve my country and fight for those who can't defend themselves."

"There is no, if you ever get back. I'm sure you must. We have no other choice. I saw your graves, Tucker. Now, I'm not hearing any more of this. Let's get on home before something else insane happens."

I turned to look for Alex. He should have been back by now.

But instead of Alex trotting along with his too short pants, came a kilt-wearing MacKenzie, six foot five at least, carrying his weapon and on full alert.

He called out, "They took th' map. They're gone. Both of them."

I knew in an instant that Alex was gone. Alex and the young boy. They had left to go to Perth on their own.

I yelled, "Alex!"

Colin was there in a flash cupping his hand over my mouth and whispering a warning, "Shhh...." in my ear.

Tucker started marching off but Colin stopped him. "Perth is 'at way, Tucker. Alexander isn't tae far. I'll fin' him. Ye take Jazzline back tae Brahan. Go over th' ben. There is a pass there now, it'll be easy tae cross." He winked at me.

I whispered, his hand leaving my mouth when he knew that I wouldn't give away our position. "Why don't we just pray him back? Please, Colin."

He smiled, then kissed me quickly on the cheek in that brotherly way that Tucker had done a million times.

"Ye don't know what he's prayin' fur."

"I can't leave you. Don't do this. I have to be with you." I felt Tucker's presence near me and I added for his sake, "To find Alex. I have to find Alex. I can't go back without him."

"Give her what she wants, Colin. She's a stubborn one, I tell you. Just let's stop talking and go get Alex." He paused, looking around as if he just remembered my other half. "Is Seth okay?"

I knew from reading about his DLE, stress could bring on the Lupus symptoms again. But stress was not the word to describe what we had been through since the accident.

"It was like I crashed when you flipped over the bridge. What were you thinking?"

"I knew that was coming. Don't hate me, Jazzy. It was truly an accident. And I saw what we were talking about head on. When we crossed, we landed right in a battlefield."

"Colin, will we find them?"

"I don't have th' sight like Seth, but I do know my way."

Tucker let go of me and began to keep up with Colin, as I trailed behind. We were making our way into another forest. We'd never be able to track Alex. He'd be lost forever.

Colin stopped, then pointed to his left. It was an abandoned cobblestone hut that had its day in a past war. The structure was crumbling and overgrown with trees shooting out where a roof once was. He took off as fast as any person could possibly run. We tried to keep up but it was no use. He disappeared behind the hut and before we made it was dragging both boys by their shirt collars out from behind. Alex and Jimmy were both sullen and teary-eyed. Hopes abashed. Exactly how my heart felt.

I tried to count to ten before reaching Alex, but it was no use. My anger was hot against them both, Tucker and Alex. And Colin. The world.

"What were you thinking? Running off like that, Alex! You could've been killed! I'm telling you boy when I get you home you are grounded for a month."

"I don't want to go home. I want to stay here with Colin, with Jimmy, with the MacKenzie's."

I do, too. Baby. I do, too. But...we don't belong here. We have other people depending on us, loving us. Wanting to know that we are safe.

All the words danced around in my head to say to Alex. To Colin. All of the words formed perfect images of all of the same reasons why this would never be our time. But it would not come.

Tucker stepped closer to Alex and took him by the arm. His legs and arms were flailing like a rag doll and I wanted to weep right then and there. This wasn't how I pictured it. I pictured him running through a field of flowers, holding out his arms to me, screaming how he'd missed me and he wanted to go home. I'd pick him up and spin him around and we'd pray ourselves home just like in the Wizard of Oz. But there was more than just a bunch of hay and tin that could keep us both tied here forever. It was flesh and blood. Friendship and love.

More than I could even hold. Alex cried, the whine reappearing. "Please, Jazzline. What do I have to go home to?"

"Momma. Luke. Daddy. Your friends. Your school. Church. Me."

I was last even though I should have been first in line. I'd always been the one to take care of him from changing diapers to finding pacifiers all through the house, to playing video games and taking him shopping for clothes and everything he needed. He was mine and I knew that I'd lost him. Lost him to a man that claimed me whether he saw me first or last.

Tears were steadily falling. I'd never seen him cry this much, except when Daddy promised us a summer at Carowinds in Charlotte with season passes and the water park and he never came to pick us up. That was three years ago. Now, so much had changed from wishing on rollercoasters. Nothing would phase Alex now I was sure, for all that he had experienced these past months. It seemed like he had taken the ultimate thrill ride and was not prepared to get off.

"They don't love me. Not like this. Not like how I've felt here. I belong here."

"I love you. I love you more than myself. Alex, you have to know that!"

He pushed away his tears with his hands, making red marks streaking down his cheeks in raw pain. "I know you love me, Jazzline. I knew you would come for me. And I know it hurts for you to hear that I don't want to come back with you. But you have your own life now. You have Seth. You'll be going off to school somewhere. Tucker will be with Bree. You can't take me with you. I have to stay at home with Momma and Luke and you know what that means for me."

Tucker said "He's right, Jazzline. You know that they don't take care of him. They just leave him to be. Colin will look out for him."

"But he would be with me."

He stepped closer to me. "I will always be with you but I need to be here."

That was an adult thing to say. A song. A song to me. Not something that a child would say to his big sister as she begged him to stay. "Please let's just go back to Brahan. I can't do this here."

I needed to talk to Seth. To talk to Colin. To push Colin around or off of a cliff for taking my baby from me. But I couldn't hate Colin. I could only love him more for taking care of Alex, and Tucker, too, when they crossed into this blessed place filled with war. My boys had found the light. Literally.

I'd heard every word that Alex spoke about Colin and all the ones he hadn't. Colin, the father that he never had and always hoped for. Colin, the protector against evil forces. Colin, the one that swooped in and saved him in the middle of a battlefield and brought Tucker back from death.

I couldn't help myself but to wish, not pray, that things could somehow be different for us. That Colin could be the one and only love of my life. That we could spend our eternity on earth and in heaven loving each other, and taking care of Alex. I thought of how that had once been a thought for me and Seth. Stashing Alex in our suitcases or in the trunk as we drove off on our honeymoon or to college...whichever came first.

But now. With this new emotion in me. This division. What was that I read once in the Bible? A house divided against itself could not stand? I believed it to be so true because the split in the earth beneath my feet, traveling through the core of me was more damage than any earthquake could do to me and I was on the verge of falling through. Feeling the crack divide farther and farther the closer I stepped towards our mountain. Colin's Peak. That should be the name for it. Not Ben Nevis.

Colin was purposefully walking strides ahead of us, separating himself farther from me. My emotions were a mask of confusion, my head dazed as we trekked up the rocky, yet tolerable path that Colin promised.

Tucker rambled on in his usual style about wars and Perth and Bonnie Prince Charlie, making it even more convincing to Alex as to why he should stay. Alex didn't speak much about anything. His silence was killing me. Just like Colin's distance was. At least with Tucker around I would have no use for my voice and it gave me time to just let it rest. As the hours crept by, the more hopeless and out of control I felt. My heart was racing, and not just from the incline, it was a thoroughbred overworked and tired, yet being pushed to the brink of exhaustion.

There was no way around this. No way that I could stop myself from crashing. Either way. Someone would get hurt in all of this, and I was sure now that it was to be me.

Colin stopped quick, making Tucker stop midsentence. He put his hand around Alex as if to protect him from attack. The tension was mounting between the three and I just knew that something awful or someone awful was about to make their way down the pass. But nothing happened.

"What is it, Colin?"

"We must camp here fur th' night. We'll see Brahan tomorrow."

Now we were forced to make like we didn't exist. I knew I would have to live the rest of my life as if we didn't exist, but I would live a lie. Maybe over time wounds could heal. He didn't bleed. He couldn't feel physical pain. Maybe it would lessen, then disappear, and I would be just a distant memory. Maybe that would be how it would be for me, but I doubted every word of it.

He walked away to find brush to start a fire and left me there with Tucker and Alex. I fell to the ground next to Tucker who'd already began a new story about how he'd met John MacKenzie, and he'd been so kind to them. Just like a man named God is Gracious to take them in. Colin had a lot to do with that, I was sure. I remembered the book that Sirena had given me, the handwritten copy of the Book of John. I'd read the New Testament in a Bible challenge course just last summer with our youth group. We'd tried to read it through as fast as we could and answer jeopardy questions. But reading it here, with my knowledge now, was somehow so different for me. It felt real. Alive in my hands.

Before Colin came back, I flipped it open to chapter one and began to read. "And the light shineth in darkness; and the darkness comprehended it not."

God put the light of Jesus in each one of us. How could I have missed this truth? How could I not see that the MacKenzie's were bearers of the light, but so were we all? I tried to explain all of this to Tucker as we sat on a blanket of newly fallen snow but he seemed to be only concerned about one person. Bree. Not a sermon on the mount. Alex seemed to be anxious about one thing, convincing me to stay.

Alex waited anxiously for Colin to come back and as soon as Colin returned with his arms full, he ran up to him to help. Enough distance to try to speak to Colin alone. I watched their heads together, turned in that way that Colin does when he is contemplating a situation. He was listening to Alex's reasons to stay. I saw a smile flash against his beautiful features and the love in his eyes for my baby. He'd won this battle. I somehow managed to lose the war, and I was sure it was because I had lost track of what I was fighting for.

"Tucker, I've lost him, haven't I?"

I meant Alex and Colin both but he would not know it and I would never voice it aloud to him. He was my best friend and throughout my entire life, I had told him everything. But not this. Never this.

"You can't hold on to him forever. You need to let him make his own choices. I would stay if I didn't have Bree."

"How can you say that? What would make you want to stay here, in this country, with no future? You died on a field, Tucker."

"I've been more alive here than I've ever felt in my life. And it isn't about freedom. It's about the connection to a place, to a people. The MacKenzie's are truly special people, in this time and the next. You know my story. I never had that. Alex would find a wonderful home here. And Colin, well, he is like a dad to us and he's only a few years older than me. Crazy, huh? Do you know his story? I wish I knew how old he really was."

His eyes turned to Colin with complete and utter admiration and respect. He'd saved their lives, took them in, and guided them. But if they stayed, they would be led straight to a tombstone. And I couldn't live knowing that I'd let them stay behind to die.

"Alex has a home with me."

"It's different, Jazzline. You know how Alex feels. You see him with Colin. Colin will never die or leave him. He'll take care of him."

"What if Colin doesn't want that responsibility? I'm sure he wasn't expecting on raising a kid from the future with a demanding, stubborn, and whiny personality. Well, kinda like Colin himself."

Alex twitched his lip. Another Colin move. "Hey, watch it, sis. I heard that."

"So did I."

"So, are we really out of the war? Is this it?"

Colin patted him on the back. "Don't sound so disappointed. Bree seems tae be waitin' fur ye, fur some reason I don't know why since women these days can't seem tae be patient enough tae wait forever. She must love ye enough tae withstand th' test of time."

The way he spoke his words. Never looking at me. Speaking right to me, about me, not Bree...another angry notch up the richter scale.

At the mention of Bree's name, Tucker's mind went off racing around the Nascar track again. Wanting to know a thousand questions, me not answering any. I felt it best not to speak at all as the sun was below us now and I was faced with another realization. Now that I'd found the boys, this would be my last night in Scotland. My last request would be to get Seth, pray for our safe return back to Bree, and cross my heart... I'd be back. I'd be forward. However, I took it in, I'd be gone from this Colin. To find the next Colin possibly waiting for me or moved on with a new love.

Alex settled in, yawning.

"Don't tell me you're tired! It should be around four in the afternoon. I couldn't get you to take in a decent bedtime before eleven o'clock at home."

He shrugged as he curled up beside Tucker. The way they positioned themselves for warmth and comfort let me know that they'd done this over the past five months.

"It's different here. I don't wake up when the sun rises to go do drills or learn techniques or broadsword or Gaelic. I just played my game or was stuck in the corner of the restaurant."

Reasons to stay. Adventure versus boredom. Boredom was safe.

He was still, and now, asleep. Tucker chuckled as he stretched and moved in closer.

"Sorry, Master J. Gotta get my beauty sleep for Bree. She's never going to get rid of me when I get back to her in the morning. We'll be waking you up when the sun comes up. We have an internal clock thing going on. Early risers we've become."

"Thank God I found you both."

I managed to smile at them as I watched their soft breathing, the in and out of their chest, turn into monster snoring. I turned to Colin then. It was safe to just look at him and his eyes had already found me. Tears were there. I found myself crawling closer to him and stopped in front of him, reaching out my hand. His hands entwined with mine and I stared at the man that had taken everything from me.

I whispered and it was not just because I had them to worry about behind me, but because that was all I could manage to do. "Do you want him?"

"Aye, love. He is a piece of ye. I'll have somethin' of ye fur th' rest ay his life on earth. If ye decide tae lit him stay ye know 'at Ah will protect him as my own bairn."

"But, he's just a baby. He dies at the Battle of Falkirk. Don't let him fight, Colin. Teach him protective skills, but don't let him fight. Keep him back at Brahan."

"He's not in any danger when he is wi' me. Tucker, on th' other hand, I see danger sprouting out of his ears."

He loved Tucker as well. Who couldn't with his charm and the overwhelming love that just came out of him for every human being he ever met? His name did mean all heart.

"But he dies if he stays here. Remember the tombstone. I touched it. I stood right there beside it."

But Seth said I did as well. I was alive. What else had Seth's brother, Colin, shown me? Alex would become a Scottish fur trader, writer with a MacKenzie last name. So, futures changed. If I would have flipped alone, I would have surely died within five minutes. Seth crossed before me and I prayed my way to him. If I would have prayed my way to Alex and Tucker I'd been stuck in another battlefield. Now, they knew of the Battle of Falkirk, and I was sure that Colin wouldn't lead him back to the men. That was how I understood all of the impossible to be.

"There will be no battles fur him. If ye let him stay, I've already decided tae take' him tae th' New World."

I gasped. Would there be a new descriptor by Alexander's name, adventurer of the New World?

"But why would you leave Scotland? You love it here. You've made it your home all of these...years."

"Ye will no longer be here. Ye will be in th' New World before long. I'll wait fur ye there."

His hands were warm in mine, and I knew how easy it would be to forget where I belonged. But I couldn't do that tonight. Not here. Not with everyone watching. My voice was urgent, pleading.

"Where can we go?"

"Come on."

He pulled me up so fast that I lost my balance and fell into him. His face was against my hair and I heard him sigh against me.

He would be able to detect their movements, even in the dark with his military skill. Thank God for special forces. His arms came around me at once and I felt my body tremble and shake violently against him.

"Ye should go back tae th' fire. You'll catch a cold."

"I don't care about that. Just hold me. This is it, Colin, our last night."

He was my shelter. He was the warmth that I needed to endure this life ahead. He knew the answers. He could lead me to the truth, and not just about Christianity and my faith, but to who I could be.

When I was with him, I saw a version of myself I didn't know how to leave behind. And I knew the soul-light connection between us was real. But Seth was my life, my promise, my future. What I felt for Colin was urgent and impossible, strong and pure in its own way, but it belonged to another time. Another ache. Another road God had not asked me to walk.

"Tell me this, love. If I were a man, just a man, would ye choose me? Would ye be my wife?"

My mind let the images fill even the hidden places of me of what being his wife would mean. His woman. His love. For the rest of my life. Here. In this time. With Alex. I could choose him now and have Alex. A packaged deal.

My arms were around his neck and my fingers rested over his mother's ring. It would seem as if I should give it back to him. To slip it off and place it in his hands and tell him no. This could never be. Give your ring to someone else.

My voice shook with all of the love that we could never make. "Yes."

"Can ye imagine 'at I'm old? Can ye see me wearin' a white wig? I'll powder up myself an' be loch one ay those snooty barons. I'll act my real age."

Even though his words were light, I knew his heart was heavy as mine.

"You know that we can never be. Let's not talk anymore about this impossibility. In my mind, there's no choice to make. God has already chosen for us when He granted you the gift."

"Sing me one more song an' I'll hold ye until th' sun comes up."

His promise made me shiver again. Just being held by him was enough to make me want to fall apart and weep.

My mind was blank again. It was harder and harder for me to find my lyrics now and I knew that it was because he was going to be separated from me soon. And Alex didn't want to return. My reason for singing was gone.

"I don't think I can sing anymore."

He put his palm against my cheek. "Give me one last light from ye. Tae carry wi' me fur eternity. Just one more song. One 'at ye will sing fur only me."

And not Seth. He didn't have to say it. His name hung between us like a brilliant star.

I closed my eyes and my mental jukebox alphabetically scrolled for the perfect song in exchange for the promise worth more than currency, press E1, Evanescence, My Immortal.

Colin held me until the sun rose up our mountain. We made our way back to camp, and they were still snoring like hounds. I kicked at Tucker's foot and he jumped, knocking Alex off of him and coming up to his feet with one swift movement that surprised me. He was alert, eyes already focused on his surroundings.

"I didn't mean to scare you. The sun is up. Time to get Seth and go home."

Colin was already stepping up the pass, making distance between us again. For his own sanity and mine. For the feelings that we would have to hide. Tucker pulled the grumbling Alex along and I trailed behind my me. Alex started the conversation with me again as soon as we started over the summit, and back down again, but this time passable. Another prayer by Colin I saw fulfilled. What did he pray about me? Maybe nothing. Maybe that was the problem. He refused to bring me into his conversation with God in some sense of protecting me or thinking that was what I wanted? Was that why this was impossible? He hadn't believed enough in us?

Seth was waiting for us at the stone gate of the Brahan estate. I could see his tall figure in the distance. He'd probably seen our return and was our welcome party. My feet quickened the pace to him and I knew that if I wasn't careful, I would actually bypass Colin. But the more I looked in Seth's direction and knew he was the one waiting for me, I sprinted. Colin did not speed up to try to catch me, to pull me away from Seth and claim me as his own. Did I want that? I still thought like there was a choice to be made here. And all reason told me that there was no choice.

Seth did not run to me because of his leg, which I saw was still bandaged tightly with the makeshift board that Colin had fixed for him. His breath was shallow as I approached him, and his face was weary. Tired. Desperate. I'd never seen him so filled with remorse or regret or fear. It was hard to put the look into the proper place other than I knew that his heart was breaking and it was because of me. With his favorite uncle.

I was breathless and held on to my knees to catch my breath. No romantic swirls. I was in need of oxygen.

"I... I...found them."

His smile was there now, just at the sound of my voice. He laughed. "I see that."

"Seth, Alex wants to stay."

He frowned. His face was filled with the alarm I felt. "Stay? You mean here?"

"Please, please, Seth. Tell Jazzy to let me stay. She'll listen to you. Please, please, please."

"Wait one second, Alexander Dumas Chicand. I don't need to have this conversation with anybody but you."

"I love you, Jazzy. But I am meant to be here. I feel it. I think it's a God thing me being here."

My throat tightened. "Then if this is God, we aren't going to treat it like a child's adventure. You would be loved. Fed. Taught. Protected. Not used in war. Not sent into reckless danger or foolishness. Do you understand me? What if I say no."

Choices were so hard to make in this country. Why couldn't it have been what to wear to a Ceilidh or shortbread cookies versus Oreos or to have a walk near a lake or curl up with my Bible? Not love decisions, heart-wrenching, life-changing choices that affected more than just one person, a whole family, a whole slew of people.

Alex stood firm. "I'll find a way to come back. I'll run away every chance I get, and I'll keep finding Colin. I think I can do something with time, Jazzy. I don't think it's Tucker that got us here."

The certainty in his voice scared me more than the war ever could. He meant it. If I dragged him home by force, I might lose him to time again, and who knows what could happen then.

Tucker said, "I'm the one with the superpowers. Not you, Little Squirt. I always did wonder how we crossed back."

"I'll keep jumping, Jazzy. I will. I'll keep finding Colin."

Seth chuckled, my heart warming a little to the sound. "That sounds like somebody else I know."

"What if I say yes? What then?"

"I'll be good, and I'll love you forever. This is really what I want. Please, please, please say yes."

His hands were praying and his legs were crossed, too. I wondered if God had already answered his request. He must have been meant to be a New World explorer. Seth had told me once, who are we to mess with God's plans?

Colin's voice was low. "Say aye. I'll take him away from here. I'll feed him, teach him, protect him, and love him like my own son. He'll not be a soldier. Not while I draw breath."

I turned to Seth.

Seth shook his head. "Don't ask me what to do, Jazzline. This choice is yours to make, and yours alone. Make a choice you can live with."

"You can stay, but Colin is taking you to the New World. You won't be in this war-torn country for long. If you stay, you must follow Colin."

He started to scream up and down and flip on the ground like a karate ninja.

"Wait! If you promise me a few things."

He stopped kicking but jumped just the same. "What? Anything? Name it, Jazz."

"You promise to listen to Colin, stay by him. You study God's Word. You love the Lord and you do what is right. You learn how to pray for all the right things, and you be brave, and strong, and good. You find your light and you let it shine for good. I mean it, Alex! Promise me."

He put up those two fingers in a Scout's honor. "Aye, lass. I swear I'll do all those things and more. I'll make you proud you let me stay."

My tears flowed with what ended with an hour-long hugging, kissing, and fluffing of his hair. The way he had always needed me, and now he only needed me to let him go. Loving sometimes meant letting go.

Tucker was the first to break up my emotional uproar. "Can I please see Bree, now? Like right now! And I mean, can we just go home, now?"

"Now?"

Now meant goodbye to Colin. Right here in front of everyone. I could not hear his words against me. I just needed one more minute with him. Just to make sure he knew that I loved him. Just one more minute.

Seth pulled his hands through his hair and down his face. He was in such obvious physical pain, not to mention the tremendous emotional stress this whole threesome must have put on him as he sat back while I raced up some mountain. His eyes were hard as he looked at Colin. I had a feeling that he wouldn't have him as a favorite uncle on our return.

"It is best that we just leave now. A clean break is best."

"I have to say goodbye to...to...the MacKenzies."

My voice was a pleading whisper but flickering with Colin's light. Nothing to say to the MacKenzie's, only one.

"No. I've already told them goodbye for all of us. We have an urgent situation ahead of us with Bree. We must leave now. Call her name. She controls this, so call out to her."

Tucker frowned. "What's urgent about Bree? What is it? I knew how you kept avoiding me that something wasn't right. What is it, Seth? What didn't Jazzline tell me."

Seth searched me out. "You didn't tell him that he was going to have a baby? That Bree was pregnant?"

Tucker's mouth dropped. "What? What? Bree is having my baby? Jazzline, is this true?"

When I didn't answer him, he knew it. He threw Alex into the air shaking him around like a maraca. "Bree is having our child? Really? Oh, man! Oh, man!"

I couldn't find the words to explain the whole story to him. I figured I'd let Mr. MacKenzie at him first. But with the rampage of our soon-to-be-father circling around us, picking everyone up, including Seth in celebratory hugs, I had my chance to look at Colin one last time, and all the words unspoken passed between us like a bolt of lightning. I love you. I will always love you. All of me.

Seth must have sensed it, and I felt his arm come around my waist and I flinched. Crash. "We have to go about finding us a bridge or some dark prison cell, something."

"No. I know a way."

I grabbed Tucker and knelt down beside the still standing Seth. He could not kneel and I did not ask him to but held on to his left hand. The one that would soon wear our wedding band.

That reminded me. I let go of the ring on my finger. I did it so fast that the boys didn't notice. I passed it to Colin and squeezed his hand. I wanted to say, "Save it for me someday." But no words would come.

I turned to Alex who was now standing beside Colin and my voice was strong as I spoke to them one last time.

"I will always love you. For the rest of my life. You better take care of each other."

My words were for both of them. No one would have known. Except for Colin, and maybe Seth. But I had to say it. There was no way that I'd live my life with regrets knowing that I had my chance to say those words to him and let them pass me by.

"Listen to me. Pray to be with Bree before it is too late. Please pray with me. Take us to Bree, God. Please God, keep us safe together and secure in your travel to our time. I pray. In Jesus' name. Amen."

Black. Darkness, then light again. Prayer is truly a powerful gift that God gave to all of His people. If only they had the faith to use it.

# CHAPTER 19

# I Walk the Line

This time I did not faint. Only blink. I was here, not there. Just like Bree had described it to me when I had asked her before what it felt like to cross. My faith was stronger now. My belief in God was on solid ground. All because a man named Cornelius brought me closer to Jesus by his words and his light. I thanked God for giving Colin his gift because I'd been given a greater gift than my voice. His love and my salvation.

We were all there in a stark, sterilized, antiseptic-smelling, white room. My eyes registered on a massive framed picture of a mountain scene, magnificent. But the colors were all wrong. There was no snow covering this one, only a blanket of moss and purplish hues as the sky. Not the gray cloud that engulfed my whole being. And to think that I'd just traveled across one.

A man's brisk voice brought me to my senses. "Excuse me, what are all of you doing here? Or better yet, how did all of you get in here?"

I felt Seth's arm surround me protectively. "Dr. McRae, I'm Seth MacKenzie. My fiancé, Jazzline. And Tucker, the father."

"Oh, oh, right, I knew that." He knew that by the way he looked at Seth's face and noticed the scars peeking from around his hair as if to say, hello, recognize me, now?

"Sorry, sir. It's been a day."

A doctor calling him sir. Ridiculous. He didn't know the kind of day we were having.

He moved out of the way and two other nurses were in the room, busying themselves with routine tasks, holding a clipboard at a monitor that was connected to somebody that was blocked from my view. Cords attached, IV running. We were definitely in the twenty-first century. And when I heard the scream, I knew who the machines were attached to.

"Tucker! Tucker! I knew you were alive. I knew it. I hoped this whole time. Oh, God! Jazzline, you did it."

Her sobs were uncontrollable, and I watched as the monitor raced with the emotion. Beeps took over the room and the doctor waved his hand to motion us to stop the advancement. Soldier boy had other plans, however.

"I think you all should leave for a little bit so she can calm down. Your mother is right down the hallway. Please go and let her know that Brianna is in need of her."

Bree's voice came out in a threatening scowl. "You need to leave, now. Dr. McRae, this is my family. Leave me with them. I'm fine."

"Yes...yes...miss... I'll go check on some other patients and will be back shortly. Just calm your levels down before I leave."

She turned to the monitors as if to will them to her command. I had to stifle a laugh. This man knew Bree.

"The baby is fine. See. Now, let us be a few minutes, please."

Tucker was there the second the door closed and he pulled on Bree, up and out of the covers with her nightgown exposed and all. He kissed her full on the lips, the face, and her eyes. He was sobbing against her, his shoulders rocking back and forth. I went to the corner, held on to the wall, and let myself breathe. If I did faint or die, at least I was in a hospital.

Seth stood by her bedside, waiting for her to come up for air, tension clearly swimming across his already worn features. "Bree, are you okay? The baby?"

She grabbed Tucker's big hand and placed it over her belly. "Did you feel that? She's kicking! See!"

I could hear the bumps on the monitor of the baby's heartbeat.

"What month is it? Why are you here? Is everything okay with the baby? Are we too late?"

She laughed, that sing-song way that brought tears to my eyes. "It's April 2nd. My due date, silly. You practically missed the whole thing. Thinking about it, I'm glad you did. My emotions were getting the best of me at times. I might have taken it out on you without meaning to. Tucker, oh, baby." She grabbed his face between her tiny hands. "We're going to have a baby."

Tears were spilling out around her tiny fingers, dancing around on her hand in excitement.

"I see that! When did all this happen?"

"The minute God gave us this little miracle, I guess!"

She kissed him again and his hands were on her belly once more.

Seth said, "I don't think you should touch her, Tucker. In fact, I think you and Jazzline should best be waiting down the hall. We don't know what could happen? Why aren't you at Aunt Shea's?"

The beeps on the monitor rose with her excitement and the thud of the kicking was sounding on the extreme of violent.

"She's going to be a soccer star!"

I asked, "Is it a girl?"

"I couldn't find out the sex of the baby without Tucker. So, I've just been praying that he would be here to find out with me. Before...before...well, let's not go there. Oh, I felt that."

Her voice broke and she sobbed against him. Her nine months praying for a miracle, and here we were. In time for her to deliver the baby.

"What can I do? Do you need anything?"

He grabbed the water pitcher beside the bed and sloshed the water all over his pants.

Seth said, "Are any of you listening to me? Get out."

Bree laughed, "I'm not dangerous, Seth. It doesn't work that way. We've learned quite a lot since you've been gone through time."

She sighed happily. Her face flushed and gorgeous. The strawberry blonde swirling around her face in perfection.

"Speaking of time. Go on and get Dr. MacRae. It's time."

Tucker frowned. "Time for what?"

Seth said, "She means, it's time for the baby to arrive. We made it seriously in the nick of time."

Tucker fainted. Fell straight off the side of the bed, hit his head against the tray table on wheels and went rolling with it straight to the linoleum floor.

Seth pulled him up to his feet and laughed. "This is a first, huh? I'm usually catching Jazzline."

"Let me go get the doctor. Can you believe he would faint at a time like this? Men! I'm over all that now. I'm stronger now."

Bree screamed, "Get the doctor."

He pulled Tucker to the recliner rocker and plopped his big old frame down like a sack of potatoes. Then, he went to stand by Bree. I heard him ask was she truly okay, and she just smiled sweetly at him as I started to close the door.

She whispered, "I've never been happier in my life."

A sixteen-year-old girl delivering a baby for a guy who was still a senior in high school. April 2nd. We were in the middle of the spring semester of our senior year. We'd somehow skipped it. Not only skipping through time but crossing off birthdays and New Year's, and now senior year.

I couldn't worry about all of that now. It was only to find Dr. MacRae. I saw Mrs. MacKenzie first and when she looked towards me, her Mountain Dew can fell out of her hands and pooled around her feet. Her eyes turned to excitement, then to fear. And I knew it was because she did not see Seth with me.

I called to her down the hallway, not caring who I bothered. "Seth and Tucker are in there with Bree."

With that she came running to me, her pumps slipping on the soda but never missing a beat. She was carrying a bag of pork rinds and I smiled. Defiantly a pregnancy craving that she must have picked up from Tucker's side of the gene pool. What had I missed? Everything! And I would continue to miss so much with Alex and...

She hugged me and I reached into my hair to check the pin, and it was still in place. Thank God. She couldn't see my story play out in her head. If she did, though, she'd have the making of a tragedy that would definitely be a hit at the box office.

She cried against me. "I owe you my life. You saved my baby. You brought Seth back! Is he okay? Is he well?"

"Yes. We have to find Dr. MacRae. Bree says that it is time."

"Lord in Heaven. God help us." Her shrill scream brought the floor to a standstill, "Dr. MacRae, it's time."

He came around from the nurses' station. When I followed behind them, I ran my hand across the floor sign reading, MacKenzie Nursery. Of course, they owned a wing of a hospital. It would help to explain all of the lights that were about to be bouncing off the walls. The money would stop the story from being told. The story of a special family of powers carrying out God's light. Why couldn't this be told? It could bring more people to Jesus, I was sure. It brought me closer to Him.

Seth picked his mother up as soon as she entered the room, not giving her a chance to go over to Bree. His voice was hoarse. "I didn't know if I'd ever see you again. I love you, Momma."

She cried. "Oh, Seth. What is it? Oh, baby! I'm so sorry. Oh... Oh, God no!"

He didn't wear an abalone shell. None of his family did when they were together. They had no secrets between them. She hugged him in silence, and I watched the look cross his face of pain. Anguish. It wasn't all about me this time. There was something more. Something had happened those two days without me in those castle walls of Brahan that had changed him. I was too caught up in my own miserable existence of how my world was now crashed and laying in broken pieces against my feet.

One baby lost and one baby found in one day's time. God gives and takes away. I stood in the corner, away from the doctors and nurses and family. My place was holding up the wall. I heard the gentle encouragements of the pushing and soothing voice of Mrs. MacKenzie. Not one cry from Bree. Not one solitary awareness that she was in the slightest of pain. I'd heard a nurse say that in all of her life she'd never witnessed a birth as peaceful and painless for a mother, especially a young mother such as Bree who couldn't stop smiling, without medication or an epidural.

And my sun, Tucker, right there beside her holding her hand. Kissing her cheek. I wondered what was going through his mind as he watched his baby crowning its head in achievement. His eyes were brimmed with tears. He had a mixture of a sob and a laugh against his throat, and I couldn't help but close my eyes and imagine him as that young surfer boy, carrying Alex around on his shoulders. Playing football with Alex in our tiny backyards. Putting bandages on Alex's knees when he'd flipped off of Tucker's homemade skateboard ramp.

He would make an excellent father. As hard as it would be for him and her still in high school, I didn't doubt he'd do whatever it took to take care of Bree and the baby and dedicate their lives to being the best parents under God as they could be.

It was a baby boy. They'd all had a firstborn son and then daughter, in the entire line of MacKenzie's I'd met this time and in the past. Would I have Seth's son? And what would he be like? Would he have his full lips and liquid gold eyes? Would he be soft-spoken like me? What would his name be to give us the meaning of his light?

The baby was cooing. Only in that first instance did he cry until he saw the sun shining in his father's eyes and it dissipated as soon as Bree whispered to him in her arms. He immediately was placed on her breast. Seth stepped back, his eyes brimming with tears at his nephew. Would I have nieces and nephews one day from Alex?

Seth told me to make a decision that I could live with. I made it. I had made that choice alone, but either way, I knew I'd not be able to live with it, either way it went. If he would have come back with me, he would have been miserable, living out his whole life questioning how things could've been different for him, possibly resenting me for standing in what he called God's thing for his life. Something that I stole from him that could never be rectified. If he would have crossed, I could have held on to him for just a little longer, but then I had my own life to start. I would be married, moved away from our home, leaving Alex to a babysitting service. Not a real family. Not what Colin could have provided for him.

Tears fell as I saw the strawberry-blond curls of the baby and the lightly feathered freckles across the bridge of his nose. His mouth was now open, and the little coos escaped as Tucker's finger was tracing the line down his cheek.

Tucker turned to me and the look on his face was undeniably a man. He had grown up, right time he had. "I haven't even figured out what I will call him yet. We haven't had time to name him. What is his name, Bree?"

Bree kissed Tucker full on the lips. "We don't name him, baby. My grandfather names the children based on the light. We won't know until the seventh day during our dedication ceremony to God."

Seth came beside me then and I could see that he was exhausted. Circles rimmed his eyes. His hair was tangled. I sensed it from every pore of him that he was just not the same.

Sweat was now beading up on his forehead yet it was chilly in the room, reminding me of the morning in Scotland. He was flexing his arms back and forth and holding on to them as if he could squeeze it away. Seth wasn't right. Something wasn't right. Did Bree do something to him?

He moved to lean against the wall, and I could see his eyes changing. Right before me. The look on his face now was more than just pride for his nephew and love for his sister, who was also his best friend. It was almost like he saw this for us. A baby. A future. And even though my life had been ripped apart, for some crazy reason just being in the presence of this man, or the other, I felt the rise of hope within me. Hope for more.

I rested my head against his shoulder. "Can we go home now?"

"No. I think it is best if we stay here for the duration."

"What am I missing here?"

His hands went through his hair, he turned from me then and searched for the eyes of his mother who was crying uncontrollably by Bree's side. Her face was not one of a beloved grandmother excited for a birth. It was almost as if she had lost a son, not gained a grandson. But Seth was here.

"I need to be seen first. We are in Charleston. My parents flew Bree back to the states as soon as I crossed, and you followed. They needed to be here. Not just for Bree, but for me, too. They knew that."

"Why? What is it? What am I missing?" Something was wrong.

"They knew that I would be traveling back to the war. To death. To be there, with all of that...and now all of this time has passed... MacKenzie's...the hanging...the...the..."

He couldn't continue and Mrs. MacKenzie watched in horror as it was his turn to hit the floor. But he didn't fall so gracefully as Tucker with the rolling table as support. He crashed against the wall, leaving a mark where his head knocked against the sheetrock, then he slid down in a crooked heap right at my feet. The brace on his leg just ripped him sideways.

I saw the doctor turning from his congratulatory remarks and handshakes to Tucker, to a fit of alarm as the chaos started around me. Buttons were pushed, a stretcher was wheeled in with three male attendants. That was what it took to lift him up on the flat surface as he lay lifeless. This was not a faint. This was something more. I heard the doctor screaming for a nurse to contact Murphy stat.

He was out of the room, and I was running behind him. Tracking them through the corridor, down a separate hallway, I sprinted behind them, but they banged through a door that quickly closed, barricading me with a sign. My eyes scanned the unit sign, ICU and the palms of my hands covered it up as if to pray it away. Crash.

A woman was there, her uniform a pale lavender, and her eyes a soft brown. She had a slight scar under her right eye.

"Miss, you can't come through right now. I'm so sorry, but please understand. We have to take care of Seth now."

She knew his name. How dare she have the right to know my man. To call out his name like he'd been here before. What had Seth told me about Charleston? He'd come for visits every six months to be checked out. The words flooded my senses now. DLE.

I'd forgotten about his disease. How easy it was to forget the scars even though they were so visible on him. I saw none of them when I looked at him. Only the way he loved me. DLE. Not fatal yet. Internal organs. Checked every six months. It had been more than six months. In fact, I was sure a year must have gone by. What was it to be careful of? My mind hit the index of the book he had given me. The table of contents, page 231, stay away from sunlight as much as possible, stressful situations...stress. Stress. I had done this to him. I had caused this.

"Miss, are you okay? Do you need something?"

I stood in the middle of the hallway with my hands outstretched on the sign to block it from my view. ICU. I could feel the presence of others passing me, heard their idle chatter of a nurses' lunch break conversation, what was on television the night before. I saw the concern flash across her face for me but I could not speak.

Mrs. MacKenzie was by my side, turning my head like a doll, her hands grasping my chin. Her eyes revealing everything that I could not believe. But there was no disgust there, no blame. Only fear and hurt. Only pain at the prospect that maybe this would be the time when Seth would not cross back to us.

She had the cell phone in her hand and knew that she was talking to Mr. MacKenzie. My head swirled and I could feel a current rising in me that I could not describe. She just stood there in front of me, never letting go of my eyes as she spoke to him. She was still talking to him on the phone when he was beside us. He took the phone from her hands gently and placed it again in her palm.

His voice was gruff. He hadn't slept, apparently, or shaved, either. I wanted to reach out and touch his beard because he seemed to look so much like Seth.

"Is she alright?"

"No. Munroe, do something. Do something now."

But money couldn't open those key coded doors. Money couldn't buy us more time with Seth. Only prayer. She grabbed my arm and I somehow managed to pull my feet alongside of her but I was sure that she was practically dragging me down the hallway.

Her voice was urgent in my ear, "Pray, child. Pray for him. Sing. Do something."

A plain brown door opened to a small room, with red pews that could fit three people each. A stained-glass window was ahead of me, with a candle lit on a stool. She dragged me down the plush red carpet and pushed me down beside her. Her words were a fever of prayer, rushing across the room and around me in a whirlwind. She prayed for his recovery. She prayed for his strength. She prayed for his light. She prayed for his life. Words spilled from her in an unrecognizable tangle of Gaelic and English in manic fire against me.

And I sat there, motionless. I couldn't bring my hands together. I couldn't close my eyes. I could only stare ahead of me, my eyes losing focus on the hues of the reds and blues and greens of the stained-glass patterns of Jesus as the Shepherd, colors flickering in the candlelight.

Mr. MacKenzie was behind me. I felt his heaviness there. He sighed. "Maura, they said he asked for Aileanna."

Mr. MacKenzie's sister. The one who said she could bring peace to a family. Rest in peace. Seth knew he was dying. He told his mother he never thought he would see her again. The look on his face when I ran to him by the stone gate.

He continued. "I called her and the family. They will be here shortly." His voice gave way to his pain and he cried out. "I hope it will be in time. Time for what he needs. Look at her. Is she okay?"

Why did he keep asking that? Of course, I was not okay. I was far from okay. I'd just lost my brother. My brother who was a part of the air I breathed in that same day, just this morning, he died. He was dead to me in this time. I just lost a love, a painful ripping of my chest at the thought of it. And now, Seth. My one true constant. Seth, my life. My future. My north. My compass was spinning out of control, and I was lost at sea.

"Jazzline. Honey. The family is coming. Let's go tell Tucker and Alex."

She didn't know. In all of the birthing commotion, the story had no time to be told. She had not sought it out from anyone and she had not asked. Only assumed when she saw Tucker that Alex would be somewhere in tow.

I said, "Alex is dead. He died sometime in the 1700s. Colin can research and confirm the date for me. Now, Seth is dying."

The candle went out. Right then. I looked at it with terror. It just stopped burning. My mind screamed for it to burn again. That one single candle flame was the light. Frantically, I searched all around for a match, a lighter. Something, anything to start the flame. Only seconds had passed. I needed to light the candle. I screamed to Mr. MacKenzie to hurry up and get a flame but no words came out. It was only in my mind. Just my hands now shaking the candle as if I were trying to make the batteries connect.

I heard his voice by the door. The soft sound of him. Was I dreaming? I could not turn around to face him but my hand stopped in mid-air holding the candle like I was waving it at a ballad at an Air Supply concert.

"It doesn't work like 'at, love."

It was him. Invading my space, and all of my senses. Mr. MacKenzie spoke it again. This time, not to his wife, but to his brother. "Is she okay? What's wrong with her?"

"She thinks Seth is connected tae th' light of th' candle. She sees it as a sign."

Mrs. MacKenzie's soft hand found my shoulder and she pulled down my hand, trying to pry the candle from my grasp but it was no use. It was as if the wax had melted it there against my skin, refusing to let it go.

"Come on, dear. Let's go check in on some news. If he asked for Aileanna, then he is talking, dear. Please, come on. We're wasting time."

Seth had spoken. It wasn't too late. He wasn't dead. The family was already here. He was standing here.

"Go ahead, Munroe, Maura. I'll need a minute first wi' her. take care of Seth. Only a moment."

Mr. MacKenzie said, "We'll wait for you outside."

The door closed with a click. The candle dropped from my hand back to the altar, but I would not face him. He was there, right at my back. He was kneeling down and I felt his leg touch my shoe. And the shock of it was as if I had been hit by paddles against my chest, pumping the electricity through my body.

He whispered, "There she is. All of me. It's been a long time since I've seen ye, love. Turn around an' let me look at ye."

*All of me.* My song to him. Just sung the night before, but so many years for him had passed. He'd never forgotten. Nothing had changed. Everything was different. Heal Seth, I prayed.

I couldn't move. He crept around me and my eyes fell upon his face. Perfect. Beautiful. Soft liquid blue eyes the color of cotton candy and a blue-sky fair day. Hair, that brownish-blond highlight that lifted at just the right angle to make you want to reach up and smooth it down. The jaw was working again, straining. I closed my eyes. I refused to look at him any longer. He was the death of me.

"Jazzline, Seth is waking up. He's askin' fur ye, love. Yer place is wi' him right now but ye need not fear. Th' Lord is wi' him."

I pulled myself up, refusing to touch him for support. His eyes never left my face. He loved me still. Time had erased nothing between us. I had just been with him this morning. He had been with me only two centuries before. But I knew that it was like the morning to him. All of the suns that had risen and set on his life and he still loved me.

Seth needed me. All of me. He didn't need me walking on the line between the two of them. I closed the door but could see his head fall through the small window. He was praying now, his body rocking back and forth in a rhythm. His lips were moving but I could not hear through the door. I could not hear his prayer but I hoped that it was for Seth to live. God, please let Seth live.

# CHAPTER 20

# Signed, Sealed, Delivered I'm Yours

I saw them piled in a circle of awkward perfection in such a place as this. All of them with their knowledge of Seth's last wish and what that meant. Since Aileanna's gift was only used when those were of the time to cross from death to everlasting life or to let go of the death that lingered on, I took it as Seth's knowing he was about to pass on.

I counted them out. Colin was behind me in the chapel praying. Others were missing but I didn't have to search them out. I saw it on him anyway. The little clan was minus Sarah and the twins.

But the rest were there, all of the MacKenzie's that made up this special task force. What could the lights do for Seth? What name meant healing power? Restoration? Second chance? Mrs. MacKenzie held out an arm to me and I found my place beside her. She must have drawn strength from them all around her because her demeanor had changed drastically from the chapel to the entrance to the ICU.

The doors creaked open as if by magic, but then I saw the lady in lavender waving us all through. The door was cracked, his name was on a tiny slip of paper taped to the side of the wall. If I ripped it down, would it mean that he didn't truly exist in that room, and I could pray him out of there? Pray him to his bedroom under the stars. Separated from the world, from everyone. Not with all of this...this...situation.

Seth was sitting up in the tiny bed, overtaking it with his body. I caught a glimpse of him, and it made me stop my plans of tackling him. Monitors beeped, tubes inserted, eyes hollow. His grandfather and father walked in the room first, followed by his mother. I was behind them. I waited by the cracked door, holding on to the cold handle. I was next in line. I could hear him speak. He was alive.

"I'm so sorry, Momma."

He was apologizing for dying. He was the only one that would remember his manners at a time like this.

She cried. "Oh, baby. How long?"

That question was not directed at a doctor. They didn't need a prognosis, a date from someone other than their own seer. Would he tell it? Would he be able to love me? Would he have enough time to forgive me? Oh, God. Please give us time.

My ears strained to hear as Gillivary spoke through the crying now of his mother and father combined. "It's not th' time 'at matters. It's what ye decide tae do wi' it while ye still have left ay what God has granted ye."

"I want to marry Jazzline. That's what I've decided to do with the time. If she'll still have me."

Mrs. MacKenzie said, "She's here, baby. She's right outside the door."

"Can I be with her? Alone?"

Mr. MacKenzie spoke, "But you asked for the family? Aileanna? She's here waiting. Waiting to give you the touch to bring peace to you before you go."

"I asked for Aileanna for Jazzline. She lost her brother today."

Mr. Mackenzie asked, "What happened to Alex? Did he not cross with everyone?"

"All of you need Aileanna, so go and pray with her. I have peace over my death. But it won't be a second time today. Can I see Jazzline, if she wants to see me, that is?"

I didn't wait for them to step out, just pushed the door open the rest of the way and found my way to his bedside. My hand found his under the cover. I felt the surgical tape but squeezed his hand.

Gillivary sighed, and I could hear the tension in his voice hitting against my back. "I hear ye have claim tae 'er again. Th' marriage will be accepted. Best make it soon."

It was obvious he'd spoken with Colin. I was the reward, and Seth won the prize. Medieval. But in God's plan from the beginning. God appointed him mine, and I wouldn't let him go.

"That is, if she'll still have me?"

He might have won me, but he wasn't sure if he still had me. I didn't blame him. Honestly, my heart was still praying in that chapel or lost back in time having a New World adventure. What would I have left to give?

I asked, "What happened?"

He pulled his hand up and tried to rub it through his hair but I could tell that his movements were so painful to him, unnatural, even the simplest gesture that he had made so many times before. His eyes closed and his head hit the pillow, turning from me. His hair falling across his cheek and I couldn't help but pull it away from him. To memorize every line, every part of him.

"They said I had a heart attack."

"A heart attack? You're eighteen years old. Eighteen-year-olds don't have heart attacks."

"Yes, they do. More than just the Lupus. I see that now. I knew it but refused to see it. Jazzline. I'm so sorry that I have to die. That I have to leave you when we've just started our life together. If I were like him, just a little, if I had his gift, then I would not be here."

But you would not be mine, either. That was why I couldn't choose Colin. I could not love a man that lived forever and could only love a man for a little while. How could I love a man that was to die? How could I love either one of them knowing what I knew about them both? I would be alone. God was punishing me for being born. Born of parents as mine. My father always said it came out all wrong when I was born first, and it must have been a mistake.

"I caused all this, Seth. It's my fault."

Seth frowned. "What are you talking about? You didn't give me a heart attack. Jazzline, this is what will happen to me. This is beyond your control."

"I did this. The stress. The time. I made you cross. I did this. Oh, God, please forgive me."

"There is nothing to forgive. You did nothing."

"How long?"

"A few months. A year. It's not like I saw my own tombstone."

His hands were cold now. His body tightening. He could see it again. Even with me holding on to him in the present, his mind was racing towards death.

"What did you see?"

"I was dead today, Jazzline. I was already gone from you. And I didn't get to say goodbye."

"But what changed? What brought you back to me?"

God had granted us a second chance. A choice was made to spare his life.

"You. You and me. We... We are married...and...and... There is so much more to do, Jazzline. I get to do that with you."

His fingers entwined against my ring finger and there was nothing to twirl. I hadn't replaced his ring yet. It was still on the necklace. Colin's was returned that morning.

What did he want me to say? That I would marry him? I had already told him yes once, but I had told Colin the same. But that was only to keep Seth safe from crossing. Look at what good that situation had caused us. He was far from safe.

He started to sing and it startled me at first. I had forgotten how rich and deep his voice sounded, how it melted my soul. He sang a song that I remembered from a movie once, Hope Floats. Hope Springs Eternal. Hope Floats. All about hope. Both of them. My Seth. My Colin. It was a song by Garth Brooks, To Make You Feel My Love.

"I love you, Seth MacKenize. I'll marry you today. Let's not waste another minute. We don't need a castle, or to walk across a bridge. We don't need anything but each other. Just you, me, a beach. The stars. The Lord. I don't care. Let it be today."

His face broke out into that gorgeous smile that was just mine. For whatever time it would be. For whatever he knew. I didn't have to know it. From the moment I heard his voice call to me in that darkened room, and in that second that he touched my hand, I knew he was mine. And here he was. Mine, still. And he still wanted to marry me, even after my betrayal. My splitting apart at the seams. He wanted what I did have left, and he was already there.

His lips were on me again. Brushing across my cheeks and I sighed against him. "Well, then, let's go, baby."

He was serious. He pulled the covers back to reveal his hospital gown, his leg exposed, the new casts rising well above his knee. He started to rip out the monitor probes on his chest but I covered his hand before he could pull harder.

"Stop. I meant I would marry you when they release you from the hospital. Not today. Let them take care of you."

I couldn't help but laugh at him. He kissed me full on the lips as he pressed the call button.

His voice was husky and warm, making me want to just melt into him. "There's only way I want to be taken care of, and it will happen tonight."

A tired voice ready for the shift to be over blasted on the intercom. "Yes, Mr. MacKenzie?"

"Can you please send my family in? I'm ready to go home. Make the arrangements. Immediately." He kissed me again.

"Right away, sir. I'll get Dr. Murphy."

Mrs. MacKenzie was already protesting what she had heard over the nurses' station intercom. He held up his hand to silence the whole brood. Aunt Shea even had Bree there, pushed in the room in a wheelchair. Tucker was nowhere to be seen so I assumed he was fumbling around with a blanketed-up baby with soft strawberry hair somewhere down another hall.

"I'm ready to leave, Dad."

"No, son. Not yet. You need time."

"No. I don't have time. I don't have time to sit here with more tests and medication and doctors. Besides, Murphy can come to the house. I know my fate. I don't have time. Please, trust me on this. Bree, come here."

He motioned for her to get out of the wheelchair. She smiled through her tears.

Mrs. MacKenzie gasped. "Don't do it, Seth. Don't touch her, yet. It's only been a couple of hours, still."

Bree was already beside him. "I love you, brother. I will always love you."

He smiled at her, touching her hair, but not her skin. "Aye, lass. I love you, too."

Then, his hand touched her cheek and the monitors flashed and went out. There was nothing letting us know the status of things as if I could have deciphered all of the numbers and lines anyway.

But a shrill beeping noise came from one of the monitors, and a nurse appeared. "Who touched the screens? Who let all of you in here? Is it unplugged?"

She came over to the wall and saw that it was still connected. Bree short-circuited the wiring.

Seth's eyes were bright and his voice was as strong as it was when he was singing to me, "Dad, I'm ready now. I'm truly fine. Besides, I have a wedding to plan for. Jazzline said she would marry me today."

I could not look at his family because the shame took over me like a sudden summer storm. Wasn't it just a few days ago that we were having a Ceilidh engagement party announcing my marriage to Colin? I avoided his eyes but I could hear his pain from clear across the room. He made his presence known for the family's sake but cowered in a corner. Not like him, the man who thrived off of a front row seat pushing me around at every turn.

I whispered, "No parties, please."

Please, I beg you. If there is music, then that means dancing. And I was sure that Colin would somehow manage to be a partner for a dance, that meant holding me. I could not let him near me, ever again.

He laughed, "Who is ready for a wedding then?"

Bree clapped her hands, "I am! Momma, me, too?"

Mr. MacKenzie bellowed, "What? You and the baby will be out of here tomorrow. Not tonight."

"Seth, will you wait one more day? Please? I can't miss it. I'm the maid of honor. You owe me for locking me up."

She was still standing. The use of the wheelchair was just for hospital policy. This time, her feet were dancing from side to side. "Daddy, it would be the right thing to do...to marry Tucker. To give our baby a solid union before the ceremony. To bring our baby into our family the way God intended it to be, before we dedicate him to the Lord."

"You aren't old enough, dear."

"I am if you agree."

"This isn't the '50s. People will talk."

"They will talk anyway. We won't tell anyone. We will keep it a secret."

I looked to Colin. So many secrets. Between us.

Seth smiled. "She's right, Dad. Give her this. That is the right thing to do."

Gillivary added, "Aye, Munroe. I agree tae th' union. She is right young fur today's standards, but she has a bairn now. It is th' man's responsibility tae take care of his family God's way. Not th' way of th' world. I'll check into the legalities of it all."

Bree cried. "I asked God for forgiveness, and He has accepted my prayer. I made a mistake. But then again, I know this baby is no mistake. God has willed this baby into being. And Tucker has already asked me to marry him, just not now. Momma, please."

"I see her point, Munroe. We must forgive as well. It is what she does now that will make the difference. Let us give her that chance. God has already."

"I've already been dealt the biggest blow of my life. My son dying, a grandson born, my baby getting married, both babies..."

The same nurse had not left us. I was sure that she was not checking the machines any longer, only trying her best to keep up with the conversation. She threw up her hands then, "Keep your voice down, this is a hospital. Now, go ahead. I'm listening."

She threw her hand up across her mouth. Munroe's power for the truth worked on this nosy little nurse. She backed out of the room embarrassed thinking to herself why did she speak it aloud. She couldn't help herself. I knew the feeling.

Gillivary put his arm around Munroe. "Forgive. Ye can't serve th' light wi' hardness of heart an' unwillingness fur change. Ye must forgive tae be forgiven."

Bree stepped closer to her father, and he didn't refuse her. He grabbed her and held her in his arms and she let the tears come. The strong tower crumbling. Munroe held his ground with that powerful little spirit of a daughter and did not waver, almost seemed renewed by her strength that she was giving him.

Mrs. MacKenzie said, "Let's go ahead and take care of the paperwork for Seth. Bree, another day with the baby here, and we'll see to you."

She pushed the call button and asked for Dr. Murphy to be contacted. Within minutes he was in the room with release papers for Seth. He winked at me, then hugged Gillivary before leaving. A Scottish name maybe? Someone else carrying a light? A light of healing, perhaps?

The family began to filter out, one by one, informing Mrs. MacKenzie they would meet them back at the house later on. Where would they go? Fly on a magic carpet ride? I wanted to find out what we were to say to Tucker's mom. How would they have all of that figured out? My Mom. Alex. She thought him to be dead. Now, she was right.

Colin was not here either. Even though I did not look for him, I felt his presence gone. Seth was already pulling up the gown as his mother slipped over his shirt that he had crossed wearing. The one that he was almost hanged in. Now, the one he had a heart attack in. What a stink that shirt was. I would have it burned.

I turned away to give him privacy. Mrs. MacKenzie was speaking softly with Seth, using a motherly voice as if he were still a baby. Soothing and warm.

I whispered, barely enough for me to even hear. "Are you really dying?"

"We're all dying, Jazzline."

"Is this all true? Am I in a nightmare?"

Mrs. MacKenzie said, "We must love him while we have him, dear. I've been blessed with you these nineteen years, sweetheart. I'm sorry about Alex. Let's spend some time with Aileanna back home."

Mr. MacKenzie came back in the room, carrying Bree's bag. It was a pink Gucci overnight bag. Definitely not his. "Matthew 10:3 tells us that even the hair on our heads are numbered. I have learned in my life that we can't stop death. Only prepare for our eternal life in Heaven by fulfilling our purpose here on earth. By allowing God's love to shine within us."

Seth took my hand. "And my purpose is to love Jazzline. To take her as my wife before the end comes."

The end. Such a final stamp upon our life. How dare it be this way? I didn't choose it to happen this way? I didn't pray for this. He must have read my thoughts because he leaned into me and whispered and my body shivered with the sound of his voice.

"This was not your fault, baby. My course was decided upon at fifteen years old. It has been in motion since my birth. Do not blame yourself. Just love me."

"I do."

Tucker was there, standing beside Bree. His arm in the crook of a handle of an awkward blue gingham car seat.

"Wait? I thought ya'll were leaving tomorrow? What about the baby. I'm sure we are breaking protocols here."

The lavender dressed nurse was by their side. She was going along for the ride. Private care to the max. He didn't quite know how to walk steadily with it and I watched as the seat swayed with his walk. Now, Tucker had changed. He would step up to the plate. I prayed for him to hit a home run.

Maybe Colin would bow out gracefully. Not like him at all. He said he'd never stop until I was his. As we made it out into the sunlight that was still streaming against my cold face, I realized there was no snow. No ice. No rain or wind whipping me into a blizzard of emotion. Just the numb feeling was still there with the warmth of an April, Southern sun on my face. The numbness had settled over every part of me. None of this was real. It could not be real. This morning. Now here. My life.

The limousine was there waiting. There would be no quick flight home or a crossing. Just a long drive with a baby crying for nourishment. Bree singing a lullaby as I read the advertisement signs along Hwy 17. Seth held my hand the whole way home, rubbing my palm like he so often did which made me somehow want to be with him alone.

We pulled up to the gate and through the iron doors. M stood for marriage today. I never thought this day would come. And yet, here I was. Walking into the MacKenzie estate, with Seth's arm around me, up the stairs and into Bree's room, not my own that I shared with him so many nights under the stars.

Bree held the baby in one arm as she pulled the wedding dress out with the other and placed it in my arms. "You will wear this today. Not me. I can't fit into anything. I'll have to make war in momma's closet or call for something to be delivered. White or cream? I know it should be cream, but it will be white today."

I thought of that Billy Idol song, White Wedding. "Hey, little sister, what have you done?"

She laughed, "What is that?"

"Just a song you should know. Everyone should know Billy Idol. Am I really getting married today?"

"Appears so. We only have a few hours to get ready before the sun sets. That is what I always wanted, a wedding at Pawley's Island with the sun setting over the ocean the minute that I spoke the words, I do. You don't mind that we are having a double wedding? I just love it. I know Tucker does, too?"

Her voice drowned me even further and for the life of me I tried to focus on what she was saying but my hands were touching the dress. My dress. I do. To who?

There was a soft tapping at the door and it woke me from my dream. Mrs. MacKenzie was there with a sour look on her face, "Um... Bree... Jazzline. There will be no wedding today. Seth is upset. You might want to go speak with him."

"What's wrong now? Where is Tucker? What has he done now?"

Mrs. MacKenzie laughed. "No, dear. It's nothing like that. There is a twenty-four-hour waiting period before you can be married. Munroe and I were married in Scotland, we didn't know the rules. We have to all go down to the courthouse and fill out paperwork for a license. I've just spoken with Reverend Tims. He'll be ready tomorrow evening, dear. You must wait this one out another day."

Bree's smile returned, "Wonderful! That gives me another day for wardrobe and my veil. Oh, Momma. Do you think I could fit into your dress or could we have some quick alterations done? You've always wanted that for me, and I see that now. I want to wear it. I've given my dress to Jazzline."

Mrs. MacKenzie's eyes welled again and overflowed like a tidal wave. Her emotions had stayed in check for over three hours. Too much time to hold something in like births, deaths, and wedding announcements. We were a walking newspaper section.

She cried, "Go to Seth, dear. He needs you."

I placed the dress down on the bed and started walking through the closet. Mrs. MacKenzie laughed through her tears. "I should have known Seth would have found you when you stayed in here before."

"Come here."

Seth was lying in bed with the covers drawn up tight around him. He was attached to monitors, a makeshift hospital room right in his bedroom. Aileanna was sitting in the corner, quiet, with her hands drawn together in her lap.

"Are you upset? You don't seem to be."

"I'm only upset that I can't call you my wife tonight. I think I'm going to use that word in a sentence a lot. My wife went down to the store shopping. My wife decided we should go out tonight. My wife would like to know..."

"How in the can you can manage to stay so positive in light of the current circumstances?"

"I've had years to prepare for this, I guess. Jazzline, I'm not afraid about where I'm going. It's beautiful there."

"I'm so glad you came back to me."

"I want you to talk with Aileanna."

Aileanna rose from his desk chair and came over with her arms outstretched. I clasped my hands tight around my waist as if I were to hold myself together before coming unglued at the seams.

Her voice was soft and comforting. "I know what happened with Alex, and how he stayed behind. Think of him not gone but living in step with you, a parallel life in a different time. One that's playing out from this moment to eternity."

"He's gone."

"He's here. In many ways, he's still here."

I turned to Seth. "Has he visited you?"

"No. They don't always come back."

"How can I let him go."

Aileanna sighed. "You don't. You let him be. Not go. Let it be. When it's your time to see him again, you will. Heaven isn't far away from us. Only a blink. Hold my hand. You'll not let him go, but let him be."

I reached out to her, almost by a force not my own. It was like a hand was guiding mine to hers. When we touched, I felt a sensation, not cold and numbing but warm like the covering of a blanket over my very being. She squeezed my hand and prayed. I couldn't make out her words in Gaelic, but I knew she was praying for my peace.

A peace beyond my own understanding. One I couldn't comprehend. Only that Jesus could provide.

My voice broke, "I need to see Momma. I need to fix it with her."

Seth thanked Aileanna for her coming to visit. She kissed Seth on the forehead, and I thought she saw the light shine from his face. She told Seth to call her anytime. I prayed we wouldn't have to, only to check in, not to require her gifts of service.

I sat down beside Seth and held his hand. "I needed to wave a white flag before wearing a white dress. Momma will never understand why I disappeared all these months. Then, to come back like this. Insane. What will I say to her?

"I won't let you out of my sight." His voice was on the edge of anger. I could sense it rising in him and he sat up in the bed, the covers falling away, revealing his scarred chest, his broad shoulders, his muscles.

"Why? Is something wrong?"

"Aye, everything will be wrong until you are mine." He turned from me. His hair falling against him. "He is still here. I cannot risk you seeing him. I feel that if...if...you walk out of this room, I'll lose you."

"I chose you. Can't you see that?"

"I'll never understand why. He's...he's...he'll be able to love you forever, and I could only have a day...a month...a year." His voice hung on the word year a little too long and I knew what he was telling me.

"I would give my life to you fully for that year, just to be your wife. I love you, Seth." That was true. I would never lie to him again.

"But to take you like this, it's wrong, Jazzline. I should just let you love him and die alone."

"I can't deny what I feel for him. Don't ask me to say it. Don't. But I do know that I've loved you from the minute that I heard you in the dark. I loved you before him. You were made for me. You are my soul mate. God chose you for me, and I will stay by your side. My prayers will be enough for us. You'll see."

I knew the power of prayer. How it could change a circumstance. Mrs. MacKenzie wasn't the only one praying in that chapel. Colin was.

"I won't let him near you."

"I have to go see Momma and Luke. To try and explain this. Spring has come without us."

"You know you can't do that."

"I know I can't explain any of it, especially Alex. I meant getting married to you tomorrow. Just showing up like this after almost a year away. Missing school. Life. What am I going to say to her? And about Tucker, too." I had too much to worry about myself than to even begin to try and get a handle on the Tucker alibi.

"Come on, then. Let me get dressed. After we leave the courthouse, we'll go to Chica's."

"You can't be with me every second. I do have to take a shower."

"Come on, I'll go with you to snatch clothes from Bree." He was already dragging me through the closet doors. I felt like I would disappear through the wardrobe and never come back, become a princess of Narnia...but no, I was there in Bree's closet where he was yanking off jeans and a top from the clothes hangers. I was glad that Bree couldn't see.

"You can't see me tomorrow. It will be bad luck. What are you going to do then?"

He kissed me lightly on the lips. "I don't believe in luck. Only prayer. And I'm not taking my chances with you."

After Seth waited in the hallway while I showered and changed, we made our way down to his family who was already heading out the door, Bree screaming about the time and how we didn't need to miss the courthouse closing and make it another day to wait.

Gillivary nodded. "I know a judge down 'ere. No worries. It's set in motion."

We all were speeding down the driveway, one luxury car after another. I couldn't help but smile after I felt Seth's hand touch mine again.

"And just think. We got ourselves into this mess just because I wanted a stupid car."

"Mess? Stupid? Do you regret it? Any of it?"

My smile was gone. I could not be happy longer than a few minutes. Happy when the hot water streamed against my face. Sad when I realized Colin was hurting. Happy when I saw us all driving away, me a part of this family now. Destroyed when I knew that Alex would not climb into the backseat.

"You chose to let Alex stay just this morning. Seems like a lifetime ago."

His hand let go of mine and turned the station to my favorite, 80's station. I Can't Fight This Feeling by REO Speedwagon was playing and I quickly switched it off and found myself covering my ears as if I could still hear the music playing in my head. I could.

He didn't ask. He didn't have to. But at least he didn't know the rest of the lyrics. I was glad for once that he was not an 80's nut. I wondered if Alex died in the 1780s. He would have been in his fifties by then. Maybe that would explain my obsession with the music from that time. Just off a couple of hundred years, but close enough.

"What will I say to Momma?"

"What you feel. You can't live your life holding back, Jazzline. It won't do you or her any good. Just let her know that you're home now. Life has changed for all of us. For her, too, I suppose." His eyes were softer now.

"I don't know how I feel. I'm numb."

His eyebrow raised but he would not look at me. "About?"

"Everything."

This behavior from Seth did not seem normal. He was just released from a hospital bed, yet he had a smile on his face that lit up the day.

"God has given me the gift to take death for what it is. I know it's a part of life. I understand the passing, the crossing from Earth to Heaven to those who believe. And I believe. I have nothing to fear. God will be with me. Even in death." His eyes never wavered, his voice calm.

"But what about us? What about what we'll lose by you passing?"

"But we will share so much while we are here together. That will be enough."

"It will never be enough."

"Then, I'll love you a little more than I loved you yesterday. Tomorrow is not promised. We have to live every day as if it were our last. With God's love and faith, we will be able to endure anything. Life's trials, struggles, even death. Even possibly another soul mate."

I turned to stare at the passing vehicles as I watched the faces of all of the normal people on the route to baseball practice or errands. Normal stuff. Not us.

"I'm sorry, Seth."

"Don't be. You can't help this. Neither can I. I feel bad for him. After all this time."

"You feel bad for him?"

"I do. To love you for a lifetime, and still see you married to me. I feel so bad for him."

But he was smiling as he spoke his words. Meaning he probably only felt a tad bit bad.

We pulled up to Chica's. The old Volvo station wagon was parked where it always was. The line was the same, pilling out down the columns and out onto the steps. Luke would be waiting at the front, putting on his charm. Momma would be sweating it out with the oldies back in the kitchen. Should I have waited?

"Wait. I thought we were going to the courthouse first."

His family was gone through the maze of all of those normal people. I looked at my watch and it was surely getting close to closing and I knew how bad the traffic could get downtown.

"I thought that maybe your mother would like to ride with us." He clearly didn't know my mother.

"No, turn around. Now."

I wanted the actual license in my hands first. I wanted the sealed deal, the proof that it was to happen tomorrow before walking in to talk to her. Before she could do anything to me. Before something could stop this again.

"Are you sure?" His hand came to brush mine and I nodded. "If that's what you want."

And he pulled back onto HWY 17 without skipping a beat.

"I want this to..." I was about to say, be over...but no. I would not speak that. What did I want? How could I choose my words to mean really what I wanted to say? "I want to marry you, Seth MacKenzie."

He laughed. "Good. Because it will be tomorrow before you know it. Just wait until tomorrow night. I want to all you my wife and know we made it there by God's grace and favor alone."

I smiled, knowing. "Tomorrow feels possible now."

He whispered, "I love you, Jazzline."

I sighed against him, leaning into the man who still wanted me, even with the knowing. Knowing my past, my present, my future. He wanted me. And I wanted him. Even with my other half still walking the earth. Somewhere out there loving me.

I loved Seth fully. I loved Colin too, but it belonged to another time with another mystery I had to surrender. Seth was the life and love God had placed before me.

And I would give my heart to him. His fingers entwined with mine, and they were so warm against my skin. As we walked slowly up the steps of the courthouse, Seth figuring out how to control his crutch, step and kick, and hold me at the same time, with his family already in view, I heard the faint sound of a baby crying in the distance and smiled as I recognized the sound of my nephew. All was well with the world, just in this second. I could allow myself this little bit of happiness for this moment as Seth opened up the massive wooden doors for me to enter.

What the world would look like tomorrow, what obstacles, or challenges I would have to face, well - they would have their own time with me. I would deal with them as they came. Right now, I felt his arm come around me again as we approached the tiny window of the marriage license department and knew that my choice was what God had wanted for my life.

All of this. All of this was not by chance, by wishing, or by luck. I was in this place because of the will of God and by prayer. And that would have to be enough. Tomorrow would be a new day. A new start for us. And I kissed him on the cheek as we signed our names to a paper that symbolized with ink that the start was just around the sun setting and rising one more day. One more day with Seth MacKenzie. I sang Stevie Wonder's song, 'Signed, Sealed, Delivered I'm Yours' as all walked arm in arm down the courthouse steps. I didn't know how long I would have with him. But I knew that one more day was promised to us. He had seen us married, and it would be so. This I could count on. Or at least I prayed so anyway.

# Author Bio

JEN LOWRY lives outside of Raleigh, North Carolina and is a proud native of Robeson County. She is the author of a YA contemporary fiction novel, Sweet Potato Jones (2020 with Swoon Romance) and bestselling novels with Monarch Educational Services, L. L. C. Check out her thirteen published books and counting. You'll find her enjoying every second of life spent with her family (preferably in pajamas). If you ask her what she's reading it's probably more than one book. Learn more about Jen Lowry and her publishing company at www. monarcheducationalservices.com.

# Learn More About Lupus

If you would like to learn more about Lupus, please visit the Lupus Foundation of America site to understand more about the chronic autoimmune disease.

https://www.lupus.org/

You can become an advocate, join a Walk to End Lupus Now event or start your own!

Donate today at https://www.lupus.org/give/ways-togive

# *Author's Note*

If you, a friend, or a loved one needs help, please don't keep it inside.

There are family, guidance counselors, teachers, community and nationwide organizations that can offer help.

National Alliance on Mental Illness (NAMI): https://www.nami.org/

1-800-950-6264

TEXT NAMI to 741741

National Suicide Prevention Hotline:

https://suicidepreventionlifeline.org/

1-800-273-8255

TEXT HOME to 741741

Atrium Health Call Center

1-704-444-2400

Mental Health Resources http://www.mhresources.org

American Psychology Association http://www.psychiatry.org/mental-health/